DESIGNER GENES

Borgo Press Books by BRIAN STABLEFORD

DESIGNER GENES

TALES OF THE BIOTECH REVOLUTION

BRIAN STABLEFORD

THE BORGO PRESS

MMXIII

DESIGNER GENES

FIRST BORGO PRESS EDITION

Published by Wildside Press LLC

www.wildsidebooks.com

DEDICATION

For Gardner Dozois, without whose generous
participation the campaign would have expired
on the drawing-board.

CONTENTS

INTRODUCTION

All the stories in this book—and many others—were written as elements of an eccentric propaganda campaign that I have now been waging for nearly two decades. I was persuaded of the necessity of embarking upon this particular crusade by the arguments set out in J. B. S. Haldane's speculative essay *Daedalus; or, Science and the Future*, which was first presented as a lecture at Cambridge University on 4 February 1923 and then reprinted as a pamphlet by Kegan, Paul, Trench & Trübner (who followed it in the next seven years with more than a hundred other speculative essays, advertised as the "Today and Tomorrow" series).

In *Daedalus*, Haldane argued that the technologies that would remake human society in the second half of the twentieth century would mostly be "biological inventions," the most important of which would be new adventures in food science. He confidently stated that advances in the understanding of basic biological processes would produce many other technological applications of which the world already stood in dire need—but he also sounded a note of caution regarding the manner in which they were likely to be received by the general public. He wrote:

> "Of the biological inventions of the past, four were made before the dawn of history. I refer to the domestication of animals, the domestication of plants, the domestication of fungi for the production of alcohol, and to a fourth invention, which I believe was of

more ultimate and far-reaching importance than any of these, since it altered the path of sexual selection... In our own day, two more have been made, namely bactericide and the artificial control of contraception.

"The first point we may notice about these inventions is that they have all had a profound emotional and ethical effect. Of the four earlier, there is not one which has not formed the basis of a religion...

"The second point is perhaps harder to express. The chemical or physical inventor is always a Prometheus. There is no great invention, from fire to flying, which has not been hailed as an insult to some god. But if every physical and chemical invention is a blasphemy, every biological invention is a perversion. There is hardly one which, on first being brought to the notice of an observer from any nation which has not previously heard of their existence, would not appear to him as indecent and unnatural."

Haldane went on to expand this point, cleverly and wittily, eventually summarizing his conclusions thus:

"The biological invention then tends to begin as a perversion and end as a ritual supported by unquestioned beliefs and prejudices... With the above facts in your minds I would ask you to excuse what at first sight might appear improbable or indecent in any speculations which appear below."

The brief speculative future history included in the essay remains somewhat ahead of its time, although we are now beginning to catch up with it. In Haldane's speculative future history, food produced by synthetic algae causes a glut in the 1940s. The first ectogenetic child is born in 1951 and—in spite of a condemnatory Papal bull and a fatwa issued by the spiritual leader of Islam—artificial wombs are officially licensed for use in France in 1968, becoming universal in the early twenty-first century.

Haldane deserves the attention and congratulation of all modern writers of speculative fiction, not so much for his extrapolation of the potentialities of biotechnology—which should have been obvious to any thinking person in 1923 and are entirely beyond dispute today—but for his anticipation of the kind of reactionary response that such innovations as cloning and the genetic engineering of food crops would generate. He was the first person to recognize and call attention to the great irony of biotechnological progress—an irony that has comprehensively blighted all but a few examples of speculative fiction dealing with such innovations.

One might quarrel with the details of Haldane's catalogue of great biological inventions, omitting as it does the most fundamental and most crucial of all—cooking and clothing, which between them necessitated the domestication of fire and the development of all the tools whose use perfected the association of hand, eye, and brain—but the gist of his argument is unchallengeable. Everything that we now think of as "human nature"—and, indeed, almost everything we now think of as "nature"—is in fact the product of biotechnological intervention. Everything that we think of as good, every worthwhile human achievement, and every Utopian dream of the past that has ever come to fruition owes its existence to biotechnology. That is the simple truth—and yet, paradoxical as it might seem, one of the corollaries of the grateful awe with which we cling to the produce of the biotechnological discoveries of the past is that we are bound to regard with the deepest suspicion the biotechnological discoveries of our own day, and all those yet to be made.

Haldane's chief rival as a scientific essayist in the early 1920s was his close friend Julian Huxley, who extrapolated the ideas contained in *Daedalus* in a brief satirical parable, "The Tissue-Culture King" (1926). In this story a Western biotechnologist places his skill at the service of a tribal king in central

Africa, developing a whole series of production lines. Within the Factory of Kingship—also known as the Wellspring of Ancestral Immortality—the scientist grows tissue cultures of the tribal king and his favored subjects, which are revered by the tribe, whose religious beliefs assign considerable virtue to the principle of symbolic renewal. In the Factory of the Ministers to the Shrines, research into endocrine secretions has enabled the production of giants for the king's bodyguard and many monstrosities that have also become objects of considerable reverence within the tribal religion.

Animal monstrosities are mass-produced in the third part of the complex, the Home of the Living Fetishes, three-headed snakes and two-headed toads being the items in greatest demand among the tribesmen.

The question raised by Huxley's tale is whether the application of such new biotechnologies in the developed nations would be any less perverted by fetishes and taboos than they would be in the dark heart of Africa—but the author was content to leave it to his younger brother, Aldous, to develop that line of thought further in *Brave New World* (1932). The most eloquent testimony to the accuracy and force of Haldane's argument is that for the next fifty years this magnificently cynical and brutally sarcastic comedy was never supplemented, let alone surpassed, by any similarly-comprehensive account of a biotechnologically sophisticated society. There seems to have been a tacit admission by the writers of the next two generations that this cleverly extended and calculatedly sick joke had said all that needed to be said on the subject. Its substance has permeated modern consciousness to such an extent that it is one of those rare books that seems perfectly familiar even to that vast majority of readers who have never bothered to open it.

Everything that has happened in the field of biotechnology since 1982, however—up to and including the current controversies regarding cloning and genetically modified food—provides conclusive evidence that Haldane was a far better prophet than he could possibly have wished. The vast majority of civilized human beings, who are in every respect the products of biotechnology and who consider the biotechnologies of the past to be entirely and definitively natural, seemingly cannot contemplate the biotechnologies of the present—let alone those of the future—without a suffering the same reflexive tidal-wave of neurotic anxiety and unreasoning antipathy that led Aldous Huxley to write *Brave New World*. This has always seemed to me to be a ludicrous imbalance direly in need of correction.

It is for this reason that I have spent a great deal of time during the last twenty years in the production of essays and stories that attempt to construct hypothetical societies in which biotechnologies are boldly and promiscuously deployed to the benefit and betterment of human individuals and human societies. I recently completed a series of six novels mapping out a future history in which the (mostly) wise application of biotechnology eventually leads our post-human descendants to a Utopia of sorts—though not without meeting and overcoming numerous technical and social problems along the way. The novels in question, in the order in which they were designed to be read, are: *The Cassandra Complex* (2001), *Inherit the Earth* (1998), *Dark Ararat* (2002), *Architects of Emortality* (1999), *The Fountains of Youth* (2000), and *The Omega Expedition* (2002).

The stories in this collection, like those in my earlier collection, *Sexual Chemistry: Sardonic Tales of the Genetic Revolution* (1991), are exercises in the same spirit, some of them being spin-offs from the series and others investigating alternative biotechnologies not featured in the series. They are mostly comedies, comedy being the best fictional medium for presenting serious ideas, and the only medium suitable for the imagination of future technologies in the arena in which they will make the most profound and progressive difference to our lives: the home. I suppose that it would be wildly optimistic to hope that they might be capable of changing the way that anyone might think about the potential of biotechnology—but what kind of a world would we be living in if it did not have room for a few wild optimists alongside the legions of pessimists who are steadfastly convinced that discovery can have no product but disaster?

ACKNOWLEDGMENTS

"What Can Chloe Want?" was first published in *Isaac Asimov's Science Fiction Magazine*, March 1994.

"The Invisible Worm" was first published in *The Magazine of Fantasy & Science Fiction*, September 1991.

"The Age of Innocence" was first published in *Isaac Asimov's Science Fiction Magazine*, June 1995.

"Snowball in Hell" was first published in *Analog*, December 2000.

"The Last Supper" was first published in *Science Fiction Age*, March 2000.

"The Facts of Life" was first published in *Isaac Asimov's Science Fiction Magazine*, September 1993.

"Hot Blood" was first published in *Isaac Asimov's Science Fiction Magazine*, September 2002.

"The House of Mourning" was first published in *Off Limits*, edited by Ellen Datlow, St. Martin's Press, 1996.

"Another Branch of the Family Tree" was first published in *Isaac Asimov's Science Fiction Magazine*, July 1999.

"The Milk of Human Kindness" was first published in *Analog*, March 2001.

"The Pipes of Pan" was first published in *The Magazine of Fantasy & Science Fiction*, June 1997.

WHAT CAN CHLOE WANT?

While her parents argued in their usual niggling fashion, Chloe watched the piglets sucking at the sow's teats. She didn't quite understand what the argument was about. She rarely did. Mostly she tried to shut out the sound, by concentrating hard on something else. For the moment, there was only the sow and its piglets, and so she concentrated on those. The pigs and piglets she had seen in her picture-books were pink, but these weren't; their skin was much the same color as Daddy's: a very pale brown.

The sow was huge. If it had been able to stand on its hind legs it would have been two feet taller than Daddy, who was not a small man, but it couldn't stand on its hind legs. In fact, it couldn't stand at all. It was too fat. It had to be fed through a tube.

What must it be like, Chloe wondered, to have to lie down all the time, having food pumped into you? It must be like being a baby all over again. Although it was feeding its own babies now, the sow's life had come full circle; it had started out as a tiny helpless bundle of flesh, and had ended up as a giant helpless bundle of flesh.

Someday, Chloe knew, the sow would just be meat: bacon, ham, and sausages. Even the eyes and the bones could be ground up to make sausages, or so one of the boys at school had told her. He might have been lying. Anyhow, some of that huge mass of flesh would become human flesh by being eaten. Some of it might even become her own flesh. It was an intriguing, if slightly unpleasant, thought.

The argument faded away, for the moment. Mummy was tight-lipped and silent. Daddy had turned away to talk to the red-faced man who had brought them into the shed. "Can you bring it out?" he asked. "I'd like her to touch it—to hold it—if that's okay."

"Sure," said the red-faced man. "Why not?" He climbed over the bars and went to pick up one of the piglets. It squealed when he took it away from the teat. He brought it back, and knelt down so that Chloe could reach out to it.

Chloe wasn't sure that she wanted to touch the piglet, but Daddy obviously wanted her to. She ran a tentative finger along its side and twitched its ear. It was warm, and its skin was soft and smooth. The sensation was nicer than she had anticipated.

"She doesn't *want* to, Mike," her mother said. "You can *see* that."

"She's just nervous," Daddy said, taking the piglet from the man and cradling it in his big hands. "Go on darling, it's okay. Stroke her."

Chloe stroked the piglet. She was a good girl. She always did what she was told.

"This isn't *necessary*," Mummy said. "It really isn't."

"She ought to have the opportunity to understand," her father replied, stubbornly.

"*Understand!* She's seven years old, Mike. How can she even *begin* to understand?"

"She won't always be seven. Do you want to hold her, Lovely? Go on—take her."

Chloe's hands weren't big enough to cradle the piglet the way her father had. She had to clutch the tiny creature in her arms, as though it were one of her dolls—except that it resisted her, and she had to clutch it tightly to stop it wriggling out of her grasp. She tried to hug it, the way Mummy hugged her, but the piglet didn't want to be hugged. The piglet wanted to get back to its mother's teat.

"Be careful of her coat, Mike," Mummy complained. "She'll

get dirty. Please take it away—they're neither of them enjoying it."

Chloe was wearing her sky-blue raincoat with the belt. She'd got it dirty before, and Mummy hadn't seemed to mind overmuch. Even so, when the red-faced man reached out to take the piglet back, Chloe wasn't sorry to be rid of it.

"That's the piglet that's going to save your life," her father said, as she released it. "The one you just held in your hands."

"Mike!" wailed Mummy, in her most exasperated voice. "Do you have to?"

"Yes," said Daddy, firmly. "It's important. She ought to understand what's happening, as best she can." But he didn't try to explain it to her—not then.

* * * * * * *

The next time Chloe's father brought her to visit the piglet, Mummy stayed at home. That was better, because it meant that Daddy wasn't always talking over her head; except for what he said to the men in white coats, everything he said was meant for her. She preferred that.

The piglet was no longer in the pen with the sow. It had its own pen now, not in the shed any more but in the big house, in a place where there were all kinds of machines and everything was clean. The piglet was running back and forth now, and taking notice of things, and it didn't squeal at all. When Chloe and her father knelt down outside the pen it came towards them, looking at them from its pretty dark eyes. Chloe wondered if it recognized her.

"Is it safe to reach through?" Daddy asked the man in the white coat, and when the man in the white coat said that it was, Daddy took her little hand in his and put it between the bars. The piglet didn't mind being stroked this time, and Chloe didn't mind stroking it.

"They're looking after her very carefully," Daddy said, "because she's a very special piglet. All the piglets in here are special. They all have human hearts."

"Why?" Chloe asked—not because she particularly wanted to know, but because Daddy was wearing an expression that told her that he expected to be asked.

"They're growing hearts for people whose hearts don't work very well. Your heart doesn't work very well—that's why you're ill so often, and not as strong as other children at school. You need a new heart, but hearts aren't easy to come by. Sometimes, the doctors can take a heart out of a little boy or girl who's been killed in an accident, but not all hearts are alike. Sometimes, when a boy or a girl gets someone else's heart, their body reacts against it. They can take medicine that stops the reaction, but that makes the body much more vulnerable to all sorts of illnesses. The best replacement heart for someone like you is a heart made by your own genes—genes are the things inside you that make you *you* and not somebody else—and the only way to make one of those is to put some of your genes into a baby pig, long before it's born. Then the pig grows a heart exactly like *your* heart, only healthy. This is the piglet that has your heart, Chloe."

Chloe took her hand away, and looked at the piglet that had her heart. The piglet looked back. She knew that Daddy wanted her to ask another question, so that he could tell her more, but she didn't know what to ask. This was the piglet that had her heart. What more was there to say? But there *was* more, and Daddy obviously wanted to make certain that she heard it all.

"The piglet has to take medicine to make it grow very quickly," Daddy said, patiently. "All piglets take that sort of medicine anyway, because farmers want them to grow as quickly as possible so as to produce more meat, but *your* piglet has to take extra-special medicine, because it has your heart, and it has to be a strong heart. In not much more than a year the piglet has to grow a heart as big and strong as the hearts that boys and girls take eight or nine years to grow. It's clever of the scientists to be able to do that—though not as clever as being able to make a pig with a human heart."

"When will they do the operation?" Chloe asked. She hoped it would be a long time in the future. She didn't like being in hospital.

"Next year," Daddy told her. Chloe was relieved. Next year was a long way away.

"Will they put *my* heart into the piglet?" Chloe asked. She knew that the answer was no, but she asked anyway, anxious to reassure her father that she was taking an interest. He liked her to ask questions, even dumb ones—especially dumb ones, it sometimes seemed.

Daddy put a protective arm around her shoulder. "That wouldn't be any use, Lovely," he said. "They have to let the piglet die. But that's what happens to pigs anyway; they're killed for their meat as soon as they're big enough. I want you to understand that, Chloe."

She did understand. Pigs were meat or providers of human hearts; one way or another, some of their flesh became human flesh. What she didn't understand was why Mummy got so tight-lipped about Daddy bringing her to see the piglet that had her heart—or, for that matter, everything else she got tight-lipped about. There was no point asking; it was the sort of question that simply wasn't dumb enough to get an answer.

* * * * * * *

Chloe told her best friend Alice about visiting the piglet that had her heart, and within a matter of hours it was all around the school. At home time some of the children chanted, "Chloe has a pig's heart! Chloe has a pig's heart!" It wasn't that they didn't understand which way round things were, it was just that they didn't care enough about accuracy to let it spoil a good chant. A teacher who heard them got annoyed, the way teachers always did when the other children were nasty to Chloe, and reported the matter to her mother, who blamed it on her father.

"The next thing you know," Mummy complained, "we'll have animal rights nuts slashing the car tires."

"I want her to understand," her father said, obstinately. "I want her to know what's happened to her. This won't be the last time she has to face that kind of stupid knee-jerk reaction. I want her to be able to confront other people's superstitious fears and idiotic jokes without getting upset. I want her to be secure in her own mind."

"I know all about what *you* want," Mummy retorted. "What does Chloe want? That's what I care about."

The one thing Chloe wanted, at that particular moment, was not to be asked what she wanted. She hated it when one or other of her parents asked her what she wanted when she knew that one of them wanted her to say one thing and the other wanted her to say something else. She hated to be forced into picking one of them and disappointing the other. Mostly, she kept quiet, even if that meant they got mad at her instead.

"She's an intelligent girl," Daddy said. "She's capable of taking it all aboard. She needs to know what's going on."

"She doesn't need to visit the damn piglet once a fortnight. She doesn't need to be dragged along and forced to look it in the eye. She doesn't have to be taken on tours of factory farms and *abattoirs* to understand where her dinner comes from, so why does she have to be taken to that horrible lab to watch the damn piglet doing its exercises?"

The damn piglet really did do exercises. Daddy had explained to her that it wasn't like the sows out in the shed, which would have heart attacks if they over-exerted themselves. *Her* piglet had to keep fit. *Her* piglet had to be in tip-top condition, because it had her heart, and had to look after it for her, to make sure that it was a strong and healthy heart when they transplanted it.

"She's interested," Daddy insisted. "Aren't you, darling? You like going to see the piglet, don't you?"

"Like hell she does," said Mummy. "You'd rather stay home, wouldn't you? You'd far rather play with your Nintendo, wouldn't you?"

Chloe didn't answer. She concentrated hard on the TV screen, which was displaying a Tom and Jerry cartoon. Tom had just been squashed flat by a steamroller and was struggling to regain his shape.

"You see, Lovely," Daddy said, putting his hand on her shoulder and trying to turn her away from the TV, "you're part of something very important. A lot of people are like those silly kids at school—they let their gut-reactions get the better of them, and they think there's something *creepy* about transgenic animals. You're going to be a kind of walking advertisement for the scientists who are saving your life, and it's important that you know what's at stake."

"What the hell are you telling her *that* for?" her mother demanded. "You think she doesn't feel bad enough having a bad heart without having to be a walking ad for the wonders of modern science? She's a seven-year-old girl, for Christ's sake! *You* can talk to all the effing reporters when the time comes. *She* doesn't have to do it."

"It's better if she doesn't have to be hidden away," Daddy said. "It's better if she can speak for herself. If she understands what's going on, she'll be able to cope with all the questions, and the prejudices of idiots won't upset her."

It wasn't easy to figure out who won the argument, but at least they didn't force her to take sides. By the time they all had to sit down to eat dinner, the row had dwindled away into a frosty silence. Chloe didn't mind frosty silences; they were generally less taxing than polite conversations. The next day, though, Daddy took her to see the piglet yet again, while Mummy fretted and fumed at home.

* * * * * * *

The last time Chloe saw the pig that had her heart it certainly wasn't a damn piglet any more. It was bigger and heavier than she was, although that was partly because she was even thinner than usual just then. She hadn't been well, and had missed a whole week of school. Christmas had come and gone and "next year" had become "this year," which wasn't a distant prospect at all.

The pig that had her heart was lean and lively; it didn't look at all like the chubby pigs in her picture-books. Its hide was far rougher now, and its once-soft ears were now so bristly that Chloe had begun to understand why people sometimes said that you couldn't make a silk purse out of a sow's ear. The pig looked as if it ought to have been out of doors, rooting around in a field, but it was still kept indoors, and not in the shed either. It had a run in a windowless basement lit by harsh striplights, where everything was just as clean as it had been in the old lab.

Chloe wasn't allowed to touch the pig this time; she just stood at one end of the run and watched it from behind the bars. It galloped up to see her, and she could tell that it really did recognize her. It knew that it had seen her before, that she had visited it regularly since it was very tiny. It didn't know, of course, that it had her heart, but it knew that there was *something* between the two of them, that they weren't just strangers.

"You don't have to worry about her, Chloe" the man in the white coat said to her, gently. "She won't feel a thing. She'll just go to sleep and never wake up. She's had a better life than most living creatures—better than most people. You mustn't be sad for her."

If I'm made of all the things I've eaten, Chloe thought, as she looked at the mashed cereals and mixed vegetables that were just then being poured into the pig's trough, *then even the bits of me that aren't made directly from vegetables are made from second-hand vegetables. But what are vegetables made of? Soil and water? I'm mud, really, and my heart's mud too. All mud, eaten once or eaten twice.*

"It won't do any harm for her to be a little bit sentimental," Daddy said to the scientist. "It's only right that she should know what'll happen—that her life will only be saved by virtue of the sacrifice of another living creature. Her mother wants to hide it all from her, but I want her to understand, and that's what Chloe wants too. Every seven-year-old wants to understand everything. I did. I still do."

"I don't want to go into hospital," Chloe said, although she knew full well that it wouldn't do any good.

"I know you don't, Beauty," Daddy said. "Nobody ever does. But the doctors have to make you better. The doctors have to put your new heart inside your body, before the old one gives up altogether. We all want you to get better, don't we?"

The pig was already tucking into the food that had been put into its trough. It ate greedily, just like a pig was supposed to. Chloe was glad to see that it had a good appetite. After all, it was her heart that was filling the pig with such energy, such enthusiasm. When she got her new heart, that would become *her* energy, *her* enthusiasm.

"I want to play football," she said contemplatively, "for Queen's Park Rangers."

Daddy and the scientist laughed. "That's what comes of moving down south for the sake of work," her father said.

"It could be worse," the man in the white coat observed. "She might want to play for Millwall."

* * * * * * *

After the operation she was in hospital for weeks on end. She missed a whole half-term of school, which was good. She knew that when she went back the other kids would be ready and waiting, avid to chant: "Chloe has a pig's heart! Chloe has a pig's heart" now that it was true. Except, of course, that it wasn't really true. She had her own heart, lovingly designed by her own genes, without the flaw that had spoiled the one she had been born with.

"Soon," Mummy told her, as the day of her release finally approached, "you'll be able to go anywhere you like. "You'll be able to run fast, and climb, and do anything you want."

"Except play for Queen's Park Rangers," Daddy put in, because he liked private jokes.

"This is a new beginning," Mummy said, making a big show out of ignoring him. "This is the *real* beginning of your whole life."

"And you owe it all to science," Daddy said, "and to the other Chloe."

"I do wish you'd forget all that, Mike," Mummy said, petulantly. "And I do wish you wouldn't keeping calling the damn pig *the other Chloe*. What are you trying to do, give the poor kid a complex?"

"It's you who's trying to give her a complex," Daddy retorted. Chloe hoped that they weren't going to ask her to decide which one of them was giving her a complex, because she really didn't know.

"She's just a little girl, Mike," Mummy said. "I'm her mother, for Christ's sake!"

"She's not *just* a little girl," Daddy insisted. "She's *our* little girl—not to mention a miracle of modern science, and a heroine of the genetic revolution."

"I don't *want* her to be a scientific miracle and a heroine of the genetic revolution," Mummy said. "I want her to be a little girl like any other little girl, who doesn't get made fun of by her schoolmates, and who doesn't get doorstepped by tabloid journalists, and who doesn't have to have her head full of morbid fantasies about *pigs*."

"You can't always get what you want," Daddy pointed out, "and there's no way we can armor her against the curiosity of the world—but we *can* make sure that she doesn't have any morbid fantasies, and the way we can do that is to make sure she understands exactly what's happened to her, and how, and why."

"The nurse said she had a nightmare only the other day," Mummy reported, resentfully.

"*All* kids have nightmares," Daddy said, flatly. "*Did* you have a nightmare, darling? What was it about?"

"I don't remember," Chloe said, truthfully, fearing that the truth might not suffice.

"It's okay, Lovely," Mummy said, putting a reassuring arm around her shoulder. "You'll be home soon, and everything will be all right, won't it?"

"Yes it will," said Daddy. "*Everything.*"

Later, when they had gone off in the car—not fighting exactly, but not really speaking to one another either—Chloe thought about the pig. She knew that Daddy wanted her to think about the pig and Mummy didn't, but she didn't feel that she was taking sides because she couldn't *not think* about the pig without thinking about it. Anyway, she couldn't help but wonder what had happened to the rest of the pig now that they'd taken out her heart.

Presumably, it would all be bacon and sausages by now, and if they'd left a little bit of her behind when they'd cut out the heart, that would be sausages too—and through being sausages, might eventually end up being a little bit of someone else's heart. There probably wasn't anyone in London, except vegetarians and girls who wore headscarves and weren't allowed to show their knees, who couldn't look at a pig—any pig—and think: *there might be a little bit of me in that pig.*

What would happen, she wondered, if one of the girls in the headscarves who weren't allowed to eat any kind of pig-meat got born with a bad heart? They'd probably have to grow her heart inside a lamb—which was a pity, in a way, given that lambs were so cute. Pigs were more human: smarter, less woolly, not in nursery rhymes.

Chloe was a little pig, she thought. *It had a human heart.* But when she ran through the readily-available rhymes for "heart" it seemed better not to carry on.

Do I really want to be a miracle of modern science? she wondered, and answered, *Why the hell not, for Christ's sake?* She liked swearing, although she never did it aloud. She was a good girl, even if she did have a pig's heart.

She wondered if Mummy and Daddy were going to get divorced, and if so who would get custody of her. She decided, eventually, that she didn't really mind, as long as they didn't make her decide.

Afterwards, she threw her doll out of the bed, because she was too old for dolls now that she had a new heart. Then she decided that it might be better to play for Millwall than Queen's Park Rangers, if it would make men in white coats sit up and take notice. Then she thought about the pig again: the other Chloe; the creature who had died for her sake, like some kind of hero in a TV show; the animal who had grown up far too quickly so that it could make her a new heart.

When I grow up, she thought, before she went to sleep, *I'm going to be a genetic engineer. I'll keep headless chickens and grow potatoes the size of bungalows, and I'll have trees that grow hearts and brains instead of apples and pears, and I'll make my husband have the children and I'll never never never ask them what they want, unless I want to know.*

THE INVISIBLE WORM

Rick first noticed the sick rose when he went to lift Steven for his morning feed, but he didn't pay any particular attention to it because his mind was on other things—mainly Steven's voice. For one so young, Steven had a lusty pair of lungs, and when he exercised them Rick wasted no time in responding. The sound went through him like a knife.

Rick sometimes wondered whether everyone might have some built-in, unique and secret sensory key, which, when turned, would plunge him into a private Hell of unparalleled excruciation. If so, he thought, some horribly unkind whim of chance had surely given Steven the uncanny knack of hitting it spot on.

The silence that fell once he had established the baby in the feeding-nook was a blessed relief, but the relief was—as usual—tinged with guilt. Now, when Rick looked down at the baby, sucking vigorously away at the teat, he was able to feel conventionally loving. It was only when Steven cried....

He had not expected that having a baby in the house would be so disturbing, so frequently painful. He knew perfectly well how lucky and how privileged the household was—he and his five co-parents had waited nearly ten years to come through the waiting-list after first submitting their application for a license—and he was sure that he loved Steven as much as any co-father could, but he had never imagined that being carer-of-the-week could be so stressful, so exhausting, and so nerve-wracking.

The problem, he supposed, was that he had never been around babies much. Nobody had, these days. Even as a baby you didn't get to be around babies much, no matter how much effort your co-parents put into the awkward business of arranging play-times.

Rick did not dare to admit the extent of his confusion and difficulty to his five co-parents—not because they would not understand, but rather because they would *insist* on under-standing, at great and wearisome length. They would schedule a fortnight of evening meetings so that they could all discuss the psychological roots of existential unease and the hazards of bonding failure, and spend hours lamenting the fact that the emotional underside of human nature had been shaped in the long-gone days when it was usual for people to be biologi-cally related to the children they reared. He preferred to suffer their unthinking impatience; one could only take so much five-handed moral support.

It was in order to subvert his vague annoyance with himself that Rick went back to inspect the imperfect rose. He had to make an effort to pull himself together before he could examine it properly. He couldn't remember which of his co-parents had pressed so hard for pink decor in the nursery, but it certainly hadn't been him; he didn't like wallflowers and he thought that pink roses were terminally cute.

The rose didn't look well at all; its pink petals were exten-sively mottled with ochreous yellow. Rick was tempted to pluck the flower immediately and hurl it into the cloaca to which all the rest of the nursery's wastes were consigned. Another would grow to take its place, in time. He reached out to do it, but then he hesitated. He realized belatedly that the sickening of the rose might conceivably be a symptom of something serious. The nursery was supposed to be free of all non-functional biota, even kinds that were harmless to everything except wallflowers.

Rick studied the petals again, more carefully. Then he scanned the neighboring corollas. They too were beginning to show early signs of discoloration.

"Oh *pollution*," he murmured. "Why me?" Carer-of-the-week was nominally in charge of the house as well as the baby, but that was usually a sinecure because nothing ever went wrong with the house.

There was a screen set into the rosewood half a meter to the left of the yellowing rose, and Rick punched in the code for the house's cellular troubleshooting program. He entered the location codes, and watched the screen, hoping fervently that no human action would be necessary in facilitating treatment of the trouble-spot.

But the screen flashed up: ALL CLEAR.

"How can it be *all clear*, moron?" he asked, out loud. "It's supposed to be an eternal bloom, immortal unless picked."

Unfortunately, the cellular troubleshooter was a low-grade system. As artificial intelligences went, it really was a moron. Rick pressed RETRY, but he knew it wouldn't get him anywhere. The message stubbornly held its centre-screen ground.

Across the room, Steven let go of the teat and began to exercise his lungs again. He was a light but frequent feeder, and he tended to mop up a lot of air when he ate. The feeding-nook was a clever piece of design, but it wasn't versatile enough to take care of *every* need.

Rick hurried over to pick Steven up, and hoisted the naked baby high on to his left shoulder. Then he began walking round and round the cradle, rubbing Steven's back gently and rhythmically. Inevitably, Steven could not be content with a delicate burp. He brought a few milliliters of milk back with the air, and dribbled it down the back of Rick's shirt. Rick stripped off the shirt and dropped it into the laundry-port, trying hard not to curse the child.

The next item on Steven's schedule was his morning bath. He was, of course, clean already—the cradle was fully-equipped for waste-disposal—but the co-parents knew from their assiduous studies how vital it was to maintain a child's water-familiarity. The household soviet had designed the carer's routines with that in mind. The baby-bath, like the cradle, was an outgrowth of the nursery wallwood, but it normally stood empty for hygiene's sake. Rick activated the tear-ducts, and stood cuddling Steven while he waited for it to fill up. Steven was no longer wailing, and there was nothing to distract Rick's attention from the gentle trickle of water.

Because the bath was dark brown, Rick did not immediately observe that anything was amiss. It wasn't until there were eight or ten centimeters of liquid in the shallow bowl that he realized that the water was discolored. He dipped his hand in and brought out a little of the liquid, cupped in the palm. It was faintly straw-colored, and it had an odd feel.

He knew then that the problem was serious. A sickly wallflower was one thing, but an unidentified substance in the baby-bath was something else: it was a naked threat to the well-being of the household's most precious member.

The household had no in-living biotechnician. Three of the co-parents worked in construction and deconstruction, and therefore knew something about house-systems, but Don and Nicola were away on-site somewhere in South America and Dieter was strictly a mud-and-sand gantzer who couldn't tell left-handed wood from right. Not only was there no expert help on hand, but there was no one in the house who could reasonably be interrupted at work in order to commiserate with him. Rosa—who was in Ed and Ents, like Rick himself—was busy tutoring. Chloe was plugged into a robominer way down in the mid-Atlantic trench. Dieter had a DO NOT DISTURB sign posted.

Rick went back to the screen, activated the camera, and called a doctor.

The doctor was a little slow coming on screen, but at least she didn't put Rick on hold. The ID code on the screen told him that her name was Maura Jauregy. She looked overdue for a rejuve, but Rick found that slightly comforting. Wrinkles—provided that they were subtly understated—still seemed to him to be somehow emblematic of wisdom.

"I'm Richard Reece," said Rick, though he knew that

the doctor's screen would already be displaying his name and address. "I think our house has a problem, but the lar keeps flashing an ALL CLEAR signal. The symptoms aren't extreme—a few wallflowers that look as if they're sick, and discolored bathwater—but they're in the nursery, and we can't take any chances with the baby."

Dr. Jauregy could see the baby, because Rick was holding him up to the camera, and she nodded to indicate that she understood.

"I'm activating my diagnostic AI now, Mr. Reece," she said. "Can you lower the drawbridge to let it in?"

Rick punched out the codes that would open the house's systems to interrogation and investigation by the doctor's specialist software. He watched her face while she studied a datascreen to the left of camera. She had an old-fashioned professional frown, which was really quite charming.

"Mmm...," she said, speculatively. Then she looked straight at camera again. "Could you help me out, Mr. Reece? Can you remove a few petals from the affected flower, and a cupful of water from the bath? Place them in two separate sections of the dispenser-unit. No need to activate any analysis-programs; I'll use my own."

He did as he had been asked, and then politely placed himself in front of the camera again, so that he and the doctor could look at one another. Her professional frown gradually deepened, until it seemed to Rick to be positively funereal.

"Very odd," she said, after a while. "Very odd indeed."

"The nursery systems were only installed a couple of months ago," said Rick, knowing that his input was probably unnecessary but feeling that he ought to make an effort to help out. "We didn't have our own womb put in; we collected Steven after delivery. The wood and the wallflowers are dextro-rotatory—they're supposed to be non-metabolizable by all feral organisms and fully immune to all natural pathogens."

"Of course, of course," said Dr. Jauregy, contemplatively. "The trouble is that so much progress has been made recently in dextro-rotatory organics that there's an awful lot of dr-DNA floating around. It might be something that got into it at the manufacturer's and lay dormant. On the other hand, it might be something else. Exactly *what* though...."

"You don't know what it is, then?" said Rick, feebly.

"Not *yet*," agreed the doctor, obviously choosing her words very carefully. "There's a slim possibility that the root of the trouble isn't organic at all. It might be a fault in your electronics, at the silicon/biochip interface. If something in the software were interfering with the nutritional upkeep of your organics, that would account for the fact that your lar won't recognize that anything's amiss. You've definitely got bugs of *some* kind rattling around in the walls, but it might not be easy to figure out exactly what they are. Are any members of your household professionally involved in cutting-edge biotech?"

"No," said Rick. "We're just ordinary people. No intellectuals here."

"It's probably something very minor," the doctor said. "But it will need investigating. I'll have to come over."

"In person?" said Rick, in astonishment. He had never known a doctor to make a house call before—although he supposed, on reflection, that doctors who specialized in the diseases of houses probably had to do it fairly frequently.

"It makes it easier to prod and poke about," said Dr. Jauregy, "and although it might well be something utterly trivial, it's got my AI thoroughly confused. I'll pick up a robocab and be with you in two hours or so. I'll leave my systems hooked up, if you don't mind—feel free to call the cabscreen if anything else comes up."

"No problem," said Rick.

"I don't suppose...," the doctor began, and then paused.

"What?" asked Rick.

"Have any of you any *enemies*?" she asked, trying to imply by her manner that she naturally assumed that the answer would be "no," but that she felt obliged to check it out just in case.

"You think someone might be doing this *deliberately*?" said

Rick, utterly horrified by the thought. "You think someone might be trying to *poison our house?*"

"I doubt it," she said with a slight sigh, perhaps also doubting her own wisdom in having asked the question. "As I said, it's probably something utterly trivial. Two hours, then." And then, having deftly planted the seed of an awful anxiety, she switched off.

* * * * * * *

Chloe was still mentally lost in the ocean-depths, even though her body was peacefully slumped into an armchair in her cubby-hole. Dieter, though he probably wasn't working at all, still had his systems programd to post DO NOT DISTURB messages in response to all inquiries. As soon as Rosa had finished her tutorial, though, she responded to Rick's appeal for someone to talk to.

"Of course we don't have any enemies," she said, when he'd recounted the whole of his conversation with the doctor. "Who could possibly want to hurt our house—our *nursery*? It's probably an innate fault in the system, which is only just beginning to show up. Have you checked the rest of the house?"

"All except the cellar," said Rick. "But I wouldn't know what to look for, would I?"

The house's systems were arranged in the conventional fashion. The inorganic parts of its brain were in the attic-space under the roof; the pump controlling its various circulatory systems was in the cupboard under the stairs. Rick had opened both cubby-holes to look in, but there had been nothing visibly amiss. He hadn't gone down into the cellar mainly because he didn't much like the cellar, which was cramped and crowded. All the waste-recycling systems were down there; so were the knotted roots whose growing-points extended deep into the ungantzed substratum on which the foundations were built, scavenging for minerals and water. The lighting down there was minimal; it was the only part of the house that was actually *gloomy.*

"It has to be the new systems," said Rosa, as though trying to convince herself. "It's not right, though—it's not as if we cut any corners cost-wise. Those nursery-fittings were the best we could afford. It's not right."

"It might be *because* they're state-of-the-art that all the bugs haven't been ironed out yet," Rick suggested. "New technologies always have teething problems—just like babies."

She didn't seem to be listening. "You don't suppose Dieter brought something back on his boots when he came back from Africa, do you?" she said. "He was carer last week, wasn't he?"

"He was in the middle of the Kalahari desert," said Rick. "That's the last place in the world where you might pick up a bug capable of metabolizing dextro-rotatory proteins."

"He came back on a plane," she countered, combatively. "Planes these days are full of dr stuff."

Rick couldn't help thinking that Rosa wasn't being as supportive as she might have been, and he felt let down. It was strictly taboo to love one of one's co-spouses significantly more than the others, lest one be thought guilty of singling, but Rick always felt particularly vulnerable with Rosa. She wasn't as good-looking as Chloe or Nicola, but there was something about her that always made his heart feel as if it might melt, and he didn't like it when she was annoyed with him.

For once, he was grateful when Steven began to whimper; having someone to talk to didn't seem to be helping much.

"I'd better feed him again," said Rick.

"He can't be hungry already," Rosa complained. "It's not time."

"He didn't have much last time," Rick answered, apologetically, "and he burped some of that back again." He realized even as he spoke that there just might be a sinister implication in what he was saying. "Oh pollution," he said, softly. "I can't just put him back in the nook, can I? Not if the nursery's sick. What can I do, Rosie?"

"Take him to the dining-room," said Rosa. "The main system

can mix baby-milk just as well as the nursery-nook."

"But it hasn't got a teat!" Rick protested. "I can't feed him with a spoon, can I?"

"Get the dispenser to mould one out of soft plastic," she said. "There must be a program for it *somewhere* in the library. One that fits on to a bottle. It's a bit twenty-first century, but it's bound to work."

"He won't like it," said Rick, mournfully.

"It's not good for him to get bogged down in a routine of comforts," said Rosa, sternly. Because she did so much work in primary ed she considered herself the household expert on child-rearing, although she was very particular about not doing more than her fair share of caring. "He needs a bit of innovation and improvisation occasionally—especially at the elementary level.

Steven had by now begun to amplify his whimpers, and was getting set for a full-scale bawl. Rick hurried away with him, hoping that he could find the requisite program, and that the dispenser could deliver the goods in time to save his ears from too much torture.

* * * * * * *

"There have been some developments, I'm afraid," said the doctor mournfully, when she arrived at the house. "The lab has completed the scan of the rose's dr-DNA and the extraneous matter in the bathwater. It all looks a bit iffy. I've had to call in some help, but you mustn't worry. We've caught the problem early, and it's just a matter of backtracking to figure out how it started. When the other people arrive, we're going to have to seal off the nursery for a while and usurp control of the house's main systems. You'll have to wind down any work you're doing, and you might experience some localized control problems, but everything will be all right and with luck we'll be out of here in a matter of hours. *Don't worry.*"

The last piece of advice was difficult to follow, and it became even more difficult when the first of Dr. Jauregy's "other people" arrived. His name was Ituro Morusaki and his ID declared him to be an officer of the International Bureau of Investigation. "I'm sure there's nothing to worry about," he said, breezily. "But we have to take precautions, whenever there's a possibility that a crime might have been committed."

"What crime?" asked Rick.

"Any crime," answered the IBI man, unhelpfully.

"You mean software sabotage, don't you?" said Rosa, with a keen edge of anxiety in her voice. "You think we're the victim of a terrorist attack! But why us? What have we ever done to anyone?"

Officer Morusaki put up his hands defensively. "No, no!" he said. "We mustn't jump to any conclusions. We simply don't know what we're dealing with, and it could be *anything*. Please don't worry."

He didn't hang around to be questioned any further. He disappeared into the nursery, to confer with Dr. Jauregy.

By this time Dieter and Chloe had been alerted to the fact that something was seriously amiss, and they had joined Rick and Rosa in the main common-room.

"Well," said Chloe, "*I'm* squeaky clean, greenwise. What did you get up to in Africa, Dieter?"

"Helping to reclaim the Kalahari desert is hardly an eco-crime," Dieter countered, testily. "The Gaians can't possibly have anything against *me*. What are Don and Nicola doing down in Amazonia? That's the Gaians' number one area of concern, isn't it? Maybe *they*'ve done something to piss off Mother Earth's Avengers."

"Don't be ridiculous," Rosa told them both. "They're only techs, not planners. Gaians don't send electronic mail-bombs to the likes of *us*."

Steven wasn't at all happy with the bottle that Rick was trying—inexpertly—to force into his mouth. There was something about the teat that he didn't like, in spite of the fact that he was hungry. His face was red and his eyes were screwed up tight and he was mewling pitifully. It wasn't a full-blown tantrum yet, but it was going on that way. Rick gritted his teeth and tried to be patient, yet firm.

"Do it *gently*," Chloe advised. "You're upsetting him. We all have to keep calm, for *his* sake."

"I heard about some practical joker who used a random-number generator to send copies of a spoiler virus through the net," said Dieter. "Maybe that's what happened—maybe our number just got thrown up at random."

"Don't be silly," said Rosa. "This isn't something that flashes silly messages on our screens—it's something that's sabotaging our *nursery*. What kind of joker would do a thing like that?"

Steven, clearly despairing of half-measures, began to yell. He hadn't yet begun to strike the secret note, but Rick could tell that the gathering crescendo was heading in that direction

"Oh, come *on*, Rick!" Dieter complained. "Can't you at least keep him quiet, so we can *think* about this. This is important!"

Rick abandoned the bottle and tried to jolly Steven out of the crying fit by bouncing him around a bit. He knew that it wasn't going to work, but at least it demonstrated to the others that he was *trying*. Silently, he willed the baby to be quiet, but the power of positive thinking that he was trying to exercise kept getting interrupted by silent pleas and curses.

"Wrap him up," said Rosa. "He's not in the nursery now and the ambient temperature's too low for him—find him some-thing soft and warm and comforting, then try the bottle again."

The torrent of advice did nothing to soothe Rick's temper; it only made him more aggrieved. But the one thing he couldn't do was to hand Steven over to someone else and say, "*You* take care of the little brat." That would really call down the wrath of Heaven upon him.

The lar informed them that someone else was at the door, and Rosa went to let in the second of Dr. Jauregy's expected helpers. His name was Lionel Murgatroyd, and his ID informed them that he was with the Ministry of Defense.

"The Ministry of Defense!" said Dieter, incredulously. "What is this—World War Five?"

"No, no, no," Mr. Murgatroyd assured them. "It's nothing to worry about—nothing at all. A routine notification under the rather-be-safe policy. Please don't let your imagination run away with you. It's just that where novel DNA is concerned, especially when it seems to be a bit on the nasty side, we have to be extremely careful."

They didn't have time to ask Mr. Murgatroyd any more questions, because he was seized by Officer Morusaki and hauled into the nursery.

"We have to seal everything up now," said Morusaki cheerfully, as he prepared to close the door behind him. "We're taking control of all the house's systems except for the fundamental subroutines, so you won't be able to phone out or call up data from the net. You might experience some slight problems while we're running tests, but please be patient."

The nursery door closed behind him, and the four householders exchanged helpless looks. Nobody wanted to start asking accusative questions about who might or might not have got the house a front-line posting in the next Plague War. The thought was too preposterous to entertain.

Steven was still bawling, despite the fact that Rick—following Rosa's suggestion—had managed to summon up a warm and soft ultrawoolly shawl. Rick tried unsuccessfully to persuade the baby to accept the makeshift teat, but Steven obviously wanted the nursery nook and wasn't prepared to accept any second-rate substitutes—not, at least, without making his protest first. Rick had retreated to the corner of the room furthest away from his co-parents in the hope of reducing the nuisance level slightly, but it was a futile gesture.

"I know one thing," said Dieter, raising his voice above the din. "Whatever it is and however it got into our systems, this thing is dangerous. It has weapon-potential. They want to tame it before they stop it—that's why they're beavering away in there under the protection of a full-scale security shield."

"Don't be ridiculous," said Chloe. "If it's organic, it must be dextro-rotatory. It can't hurt anything living—not *really* living. It can only affect right-handed proteins."

"Chloe, darling," said Dieter, with uncharacteristically bitter sarcasm. "Half the world lives in houses made from dr-wood, and dresses in dr-clothes. There are dr-components in virtually every machine our factories produce. A virus that could eat its way through dr-materials would be the ideal humane weapon. It could wreck a nation's property without actually killing anyone."

"You're being silly," said Rosa, shortly. "There aren't any lr-viruses that destroy all laevo-rotatory materials, even after three billion years of lr-evolution. Why should a universally-destructive dr-virus suddenly turn up out of the blue? And if it did, why on earth would it make its first appearance in our nursery? Rick, can't you keep the poor little mite quiet for a while."

Rick interrupted the murmurous stream of soothing noises that he was emitting into Steven's ear in order to say "No." Then he added, "Oh, *pollution!*" as he realized to his discomfort that the ultrawoolly had suffered a sudden attack of stinking stickiness.

He moved rapidly to the disposal chute, hitting the control-button with his elbow because his hands were over-full with the bottle and the wrapped-up baby. The lid failed to respond to his signal. He jabbed it again, and then again, but nothing happened.

He turned round to complain but saw that Rosa was now busy giving Dieter an extended, if inexpert, lecture on the elements of dextro-rotatory organic chemistry. Dieter, obviously resentful of being treated as if he were one of her primary ed counseling cases, was busy going red in the face. Rick knew that if he called their attention to what had happened, they would merely point out with some asperity that the chute's systems must have fallen prey to the side-effects of the probings being carried out by the investigators in the nursery.

The door to the staircase that led down to the cellar was only a couple of feet away, and Rick kicked the control panel, probably a little bit harder than was necessary. He sighed with relief when it opened, and he went swiftly through it. He glanced back as the door slid shut behind him, but only Chloe was taking any notice, and her expression showed profound relief that the crying baby was being taken away.

Rick figured that it would probably be possible to dispose of the polluted ultrawoolly into the cellar chute, and that, even if it turned out not to be possible, he could at least abandon the horrid thing, sluice Steven down, and then have another go at persuading him to take the bottle without having to suffer the censorious glares of his co-parents. He took the six steps two at a time, and made his way along the narrow corridor between the massed root-ridges to the portal set in the basal trunk.

The portal opened readily enough, and he sighed with relief. He had thrown the ultra-woolly in before he realized that all was not well within the chute.

Instead of falling away through empty space to the reclamation-chamber, the soiled garment landed in a pool of turbid water whose surface was only a couple of centimeters below the opening. Because of the odiferous nature of the stain on the shawl, Rick did not at first notice that the water was also rather noisome, but when he leaned over to take a closer look, the fact became abundantly clear.

He also noticed that the level of the water was slowly rising. The house was evidently experiencing difficulties in the water-works.

Rick's first supposition was that the three investigators in the nursery must already know about this problem, given that they had taken over all the house's systems, but then he remembered that the lar had stubbornly insisted that nothing was wrong in the nursery. Perhaps, given Mr. Murgatroyd's declared allegiance to the philosophy of better-be-safe, they should be told.

Rick climbed back up to the cellar door, which had closed automatically behind him, and brought his knee up to tap the control panel.

The door didn't open.

Rick cursed. He hung the loudly-squalling Steven over his shoulder, switched the feeding-bottle from his left hand to his right, and tapped the panel again with his fingers.

The door still failed to respond.

Rick turned to the screen beside the door and poked the keyboard beneath it. The screen remained dead, as he had expected. The men in the nursery had presumably switched off the circuitry for some arcane purpose of their own.

He turned around to look back at the waste-chute. The portal was still open, and the water level had now reached its rim. Water began to spill over. While Rick watched, the floating ultrawoolly was carried over the lip of the precipice, and fell soggily to the floor, where it sat lumpenly in a rapidly-spreading pool of discolored liquid.

"*Pollution*!" said Rick, with feeling. "Pollution, corrosion and *copulating corruption*!" The obscenities seemed oddly ineffective, given their incipient literality.

He knew that there was no point at all in shouting for help. The house was well-designed, and the walls and ceiling were far too efficient at damping out sounds.

He realized that he was trapped.

* * * * * * *

Even though he knew there was no point, Rick yelled for help; there seemed no harm in trying. In the meantime, he struggled to think of something more likely to get results.

Steven responded to the unexpected competition with a moment's startled silence, but then began to compete with a will, increasing his own efforts to be heard. Within seconds he began to hit *that* note. The din was too appalling to be tolerated, and Rick shut up.

Steven didn't. Rick gritted his teeth and tried to shut out the sound, but the screams went deep into the core of his brain.

Rick went to the top of the cellar steps and kicked the door, very hard. Nothing happened, and he kicked it again, even harder. Then, holding Steven carefully at arm's length, he rammed it with his shoulder.

The door absorbed the brutal mistreatment with dignified ease, swallowing the sound of the impacts. The blows had discharged a little of Rick's frustration, but he wasn't sufficiently masochistic to keep going until he did himself an injury.

"Shut up, you little bastard," he said to Steven, with asperity. He had never before dared speak aloud to the baby in such hostile terms, but he felt that he might as well take what meager advantage he could of the fact that no one could hear him. He didn't mean it, of course—not *really*.

He looked down at the floor, which was now covered by a thin scum of something horrible. The scum was slowly being elevated by the water on which it floated. He watched it for a minute or so, watching the meniscus climb the knobbly walls of the root-complex. He estimated that the level was now rising by about a centimeter per minute, and noted that the flow seemed to be increasing. His feet were less than a meter above the surface, and he knew that he wasn't much more than a meter-and-a-half tall. His mental arithmetic could do the simple averaging well enough, but he didn't know how to figure in the possible effects of the accelerating flow.

"Shut up!" he said to Steven, in a low but fierce tone. "This is *serious*. If we aren't out of here soon...."

At a centimeter a minute, he knew, they would have four hours. Four hours, looked at dispassionately, was a long time, but Rick already knew that it was the highest possible figure. The faster the rate of flow was increasing, the quicker that four hours would become three, and then two...and all the while, it was also being eroded by actual elapsed time. Rick looked about him at the cellar, whose narrow passages and dim lighting had always made him feel slightly claustrophobic. His mental arithmetic wasn't up to calculating the actual cubic capacity of the room, but the looming root-processes and the thick central trunk of the house had never seemed more massive.

Steven also seemed utterly convinced that something was badly wrong. He was certainly yelling as if he believed that his life was in danger.

"*Please* shut up," complained Rick, changing tactics. "For Gaia's sake, let me think!"

After all, he told himself, he was bound to be missed. Chloe, Rosa, and Dieter might already have noticed that he was gone, and might have begun to get worried...except, of course, that they couldn't know that the cellar was being flooded. They would undoubtedly discover as soon as they tried it that the door was stuck, and they would undoubtedly figure out that it was a side-effect of whatever Dr. Jauregy's troubleshooting crew was doing, but they wouldn't necessarily feel any sense of urgency about getting him out. In fact, they might be profoundly glad that they no longer had to listen to Steven's crying, and in no hurry at all to expose themselves to it again. They might be sitting upstairs right now, joking about his bad luck and his parental incompetence.

It was, he decided, definitely time to get worried.

Rick sat down on the top step, biting his lip anxiously, and began to rock Steven in his arms. Steven continued to cry, but not quite so loudly. The crying seemed slightly less appalling now—indeed, it suddenly seemed to be entirely appropriate, given the situation. It was no longer so excruciating.

"Okay son," said Rick, looking down into the baby's screwed-up eyes and making every possible effort to be civil, "we've got to think about this logically. The odds are that we'll be out of here long before that tide of filth is up to the soles of my sneakers, but just in case...*just in case*, mind you...we ought to figure out some way of attracting attention to our predicament. The three wise men might have got the house's nerve-net into a terrible tangle, but they can't have anaesthetized it entirely. We have to wake it up. It's fighting sabotage with sabotage, but it's the only way." He was trying to sound calm, for his own sake rather than for Steven's, but he couldn't fool himself. He was scared—really scared.

For a moment he consoled himself with the inspiration that the house's central supply-tank and reclamation unit couldn't possibly contain enough water to fill the cellar completely, but no sooner had the elation of this thought buoyed him up than he noticed a distinct whiff of sterilizing fluid in the air.

"Oh *pollution*!" he said, as his heart skipped a beat. "It's the water from the pool, too...we really are in trouble."

Steven just went on bawling, but Rick took that as an indication of agreement. He stood up and descended to the third step, then turned around to lay the baby down on the top one. He wiped his fingers on his shirt, and looked around for something that he could use to hurt the house—not much, but just enough to make sure that the act would not go unnoticed.

Unfortunately, the tool cabinet that was set in the wall beside the staircase wouldn't open, and all the tools that might have sufficed to pry it open were inside. His anxiety grew, and the nausea induced by the vilely mixed odors of the dirty water made it feel even worse.

"Corruption," he said, unsteadily. It wasn't so much the thought that he was going to have to use his bare hands to attack the root-processes as the thought that he was going to have to stand calf-deep in the rising tide of filthy water while he did it. He knew that he would have to snap one of the slimmer rootlets, and the thinnest ones were all close to ground-level.

He looked down at Steven, who was lying on his back like a stranded beetle, kicking his legs and screaming as if he were about to burst.

"All right," he said. "I'm going."

He stepped down into the murky water, feeling it ooze unpleasantly into his soft-soled shoes. Two squelching strides took him to what looked like a suitably fragile bundle of root-fibers, and he managed to get his forefinger around a single filament that was no thicker than Steven's smallest digit.

He pulled at it. Then he heaved upwards with all his strength, bracing himself with his feet. He fully expected the rootlet to break, but his expectation was not based in experience—he had never before had any occasion to try the experiment. The root was far tougher than it looked, and more elastic. It stretched a little, but it didn't snap.

Rick didn't bother to swear. He simply forced a second finger around the rootlet, and gathered all his strength, making sure that he would exert the maximum leverage of which he was capable.

He heaved.

The pain in his fingers was indescribable, but he did not relax until he was convinced that it would take less force to tear them off than it would to snap the rootlet. He extracted the two digits with difficulty, and nursed them tenderly while he looked down, furiously, at the stubborn filament. While he watched, there was a sudden surge in the flow of turbid water, and a wave swamped the rootlet.

He realized that he was knee-deep, and that the flow was fast becoming a flood. Four hours had been a hopelessly optimistic estimate even at the time. Now, though he did not pause to measure and calculate, he figured that he had less than forty minutes.

We're going to drown! he thought, wildly. *We're really going to drown!*

Rick was fifty-three years old; nine-tenths of his life still lay before him. Steven was less than six months old…but in spite of the fact that he really did love the child, Rick could not help thinking that his own tragedy was the greater. Steven had hardly begun to be aware of the world, and had no sense whatsoever of the magnitude of his possible loss. To Steven, the present situation was no worse than being offered a bottle with an unfamiliar teat, but to Rick….

Rick had never been in mortal danger before. He had never *felt* that he was in mortal danger before. The fact that he was in his own home, and that the only baby he was likely to be licensed to look after for at least two hundred years was with him, depending on him, made the feeling ten times worse than it could have been had he been somewhere out in the wild and still-slightly-dangerous world.

He looked around desperately, cursing the strength and economy of modern design and the careful tidiness of his co-parents. There was not a single object lying around loose, and everything built into the house's systems was built to last, resistant to any and all attempts at vandalism. He couldn't see anything that might be used as a lever or a club.

Steven howled and kicked on the top step. Again he struck that horrible, hellish note.

Don't panic! Rick told himself, knowing that it was already too late; he was in no condition to take such advice.

It had to be something dead, Rick instructed himself, trying against the odds to be reasonable. The problem with the rootlet was that it was part of the living structure of the house, as was everything wooden—even the stairs. On the other hand, all the house's inorganics were buried deep inside the living tissues, except....

He struggled back to the foot of the stairway, and up it. His eyes were fixed on the mute and useless screen beside the door. His breathing was ragged and his heart was racing.

He didn't know how strong the plastic screen might be, but he had seen people hurl objects through offending screens on half a hundred vid-shows, so he knew that it could be done, and that it produced shards with sharp edges.

He also knew that he had nothing to hit it with but his fist, and that those sharp edges were going to do nasty things to his knuckles, but he wasn't about to wait around hoping that it wouldn't be necessary.

Rick came back to the second step and braced himself again, laying his left palm flat against the unopenable door. He balled his fist up as tight as he could, ignoring the pain in his two damaged fingers, and psyched himself up for the punch, telling himself sternly that he must follow through, hitting with all his might.

Steven's howling seemed to grow even louder as Rick focused his attention and let fly.

His fist rebounded.

The shock of the reaction sent a wave of pain through his hand into his wrist and all the way up his arm and he howled in agony. He cursed volubly, not bothering with the customary euphemisms. He felt that he was about to burst into tears, although he could not tell whether it was pain or terror that had brought him to that pitch of anguish.

As soon as the pain began to die down, though, he started thinking again, madly and furiously. He knew that his shoes were too soft, and that there was no way he could contort himself into such a position that he would be able to lash out at the screen with his bare heel. If he was to hit the screen again he would have to use either his fist—the left, this time—or his head.

Rick had no idea how hard his head was, or how much force he could get into a butt, but he knew that it would give him a terrible headache if the screen didn't break. He cursed the wonderful resilience of modern materials, and the marvelous ingenuity of modern technics. He inspected the keyboard beneath the screen, wondering if there might be a weak spot anywhere there. He tried inserting his fingernails into all the cracks and crevices, but he was too well-manicured to have much effect. He thumped the keys a few times, not too heavily, just in case the keys might respond to the extra pressure, but nothing happened.

He conceded that he was going to have to hit the screen again. He tossed up, mentally, between head and hand. Hand won.

He moved right to the edge of the step, shoving Steven a little closer to the wall. Again he braced himself; again he psyched himself up. Then, perversely, he looked down at the rising tide of filth, which was now only one step down. He could see that if the screen didn't break this time, he was going to have to pick Steven up and hold him, to keep him out of harm's way.

He turned back towards the screen, and stared at it as though it were something utterly loathsome, which had to be destroyed. He felt that his entire nervous system was screaming—resonating with that dreadful note that only Steven could produce, and which only he in all the world could properly appreciate.

He launched his left fist at the screen, with every last vestige of his strength, howling aloud in fury.

The screen imploded, bursting into fifty or a hundred shards, some of which peppered his face before falling. Only a handful hit Steven, and none did him any damage.

Oddly enough—or so it seemed—the successful blow did not hurt Rick's hand nearly as much as the unsuccessful one had, but the shards did indeed cut him in a dozen different places, and blood began to ooze out everywhere. The biggest, sharpest triangular shard was still stuck to the rim of the casing, but Rick pulled it out easily. Then he began poking at the machinery inside the screen. There were bare wires on display now, and circuit-boards—lots of complicated and vulnerable assemblies. He cut, slashed and scraped with gay abandon...but nothing happened. The machinery was quite dead and disconnected.

Rick was alarmed to find himself trembling. He bent down swiftly to pick Steven up, snatching him away from the turbid floodwater just before it reached the edge of the trailing shawl. Then he looked around desperately. All the thinner root-filaments were under the surface now, but there was still plenty of bare wood visible—wood that was scratchable and cuttable. But where was he to cut? Where was he to scratch?

He felt that he could no longer think, no longer plan.

Steven was still screaming, and his tiny hand grappled with Rick's ear. The baby sounded truly desperate, as though he had somehow sensed that things were going from bad to worse, and his anxiety fed Rick's, redoubling it yet again.

Rick held the triangular shard high in the air, with one point outwards, desperate to find some target to aim at. Carelessly, he leapt down into the foul-smelling fluid. His feet were on the floor but he was waist deep. He held Steven over one shoulder, and reached out to hack at the root-bundles near the steadily-climbing surface.

The jagged edge made a scratch, but did not cut deeply. Rick ran it back and forth as fast as he could, trying to make the cut deeper. Steven yelled in his ear, and the sound was so frightfully loud and urgent that it filled his head and brought forth tears of frustration in astonishing profusion.

He chopped and sawed and cursed for three full minutes before he suddenly realized that the surface of the flood had not swallowed up the spot he was attacking, and was no nearer to doing so than when he had started.

The flow had stopped, and the water-level had stabilized.

Rick was astonished by the wave of relief that flooded over him—a sudden realization that they might not be going to die. He did not realize how convinced he had been that he was doomed until the fear was suddenly swept away.

He threw the blunted plastic shard away, and took hold of Steven in both hands, pulling the baby around to cradle him against his chest.

"It's all right, son!" he said, as his tears of frustration became tears of amazement. "We're going to be all right!"

Steven's wild yelling abated, as though the message had got through. By slow degrees, as Rick hugged the baby to him, rocking gently from side to side, silence fell. The water level did not begin to fall, but it did not begin to rise again either. There was stability; there was peace.

Steven was no longer crying and Rick was no longer weeping.

Rick stood where he was, not moving an inch, for several minutes more. Steven put his face into the hollow of Rick's shoulder, and went to sleep, quite oblivious to the fact that the hand with that Rick was supporting his tiny bald head was still leaking blood from a dozen ragged cuts.

Then the door above them slid suddenly aside, and Rosa's voice, utterly aghast, said: "Corruption and corrosion, Rick! What are you *doing* to that poor child!"

* * * * * * *

Dr. Jauregy wasn't licensed to practice medicine on humans

but she cleaned up his cuts and bandaged his hand. She had sufficient sense and sensibility not to start telling him what a fool he'd been, and he was glad of that. He'd heard enough from Rosa, Dieter, and Chloe about what he ought to have known (that he wasn't really in danger), ought to have thought (that the sensible thing to do was wait), and ought to have done (nothing).

At first he had been astounded by their attitude, deeply wounded by their accusative tones. It had taken him some little while to realize that they had not the least understanding of what he had been through. He had done his best to point out that hindsight gave them calculative advantages that he had sadly lacked, but they had refused to listen, and even seemed intent on blaming him for the fact that the cellar was flooded, simply because he had been down there when it happened.

Rick was still seething with frustration and annoyance. He found it quite appalling that no one seemed to have the least idea of what he had been through, but he now realized how absurd his appearance and his conduct must have seemed to anyone who had not shared his experience. He dared not try to explain how terrified he had been, because he knew that it would only make him seem ridiculous. It was bad enough to have panicked, when—a things had turned out—panic had been quite unnecessary, but trying to explain how and why he had panicked, and attempting to justify his panicking, could now only make things worse.

Now that hindsight had delivered its verdict—that he had not drowned, and therefore had never been in real danger of drowning—all that he had suffered had been for nothing.

It was all horribly unfair, but there was nothing he could say or do to defend himself.

Mr. Murgatroyd was the only one who thought of offering any kind of apology, and even that was far from satisfactory. "Altogether unforeseen," he assured them, peering solemnly at Chloe, as though she and not Rick had been the one who had been hurt. "That's the trouble with unprecedented situations, I'm afraid. New bugs, new symptoms. Sorry we couldn't cope any better."

"Do that mean you now know what it is?" asked Rick, sourly. "Or is it still a big mystery?"

Mr. Murgatroyd opened his mouth to reply, but paused because Officer Morusaki had just re-emerged from the cellar. "It's okay," said the IBI man. "The water level's going down. The house can take care of it all—give it six hours and the pool will be full again. The wood will mop up all the pollutants and redirect them all back to the reclamation tank. The rootlets are fine—he didn't do any real damage there. You'll need a new screen, of course, and a new set of circuit-boards—by the time they're installed, it will all be as good as new."

Rick felt the pressure of disapproving stares, but was determined not to feel guilty. "What about the nursery?" he said to the man from the Ministry.

"We've identified the culprit," said Murgatroyd, cheerfully. "As we said, there's nothing to worry about—nothing at all. Within forty-eight hours, everything will be back to normal."

"In the meantime," Dr. Jauregy put in, "just as a precaution, don't use the nursery systems—the main system is perfectly safe."

Morusaki nodded in agreement, smiling as he did so. There was something extraordinarily infuriating about the way they all looked. It wasn't just that they were carefully refusing to say exactly what it was they had found—each of them seemed to be possessed by a glow of private pleasure, which suggested that they were extremely pleased about their discovery. Rick glanced at Rosa, who was reluctantly holding the baby, and at Dieter; he could see that they were aware of it too.

"I think we're entitled to an explanation," he said, testily, to the doctor. "Don't you?"

Dr. Jauregy looked at Officer Morusaki, who looked at Mr. Murgatroyd, who looked dubious.

"If we really were the target of some new Gaian terror-weapon," said Rick, combatively, "I think we should be told—even if it wasn't aimed specifically at us."

"It's nothing like that," said Mr. Murgatroyd, swiftly. "I told you—my being called in was purely a matter of routine. It's nothing like that at all—but we're living in such interesting times, you see. The defense of the realm has become something of a nightmare, with so many viruses around, organic and inorganic. We have to be very careful. Plague wars aren't like the old heavy metal wars, you know; nobody bothers to declare them, and the weapons are very difficult to spot."

"But this isn't a new plague war, is it?" said Rosa, flatly.

"No," Mr. Murgatroyd confirmed, evidently quite glad about the fact. "It isn't. It's something very different. Not war, not terrorism...more like *creation*, really. The birth of a new kind of nature. Heaven only knows what the Gaians will make of it."

"Are you sure...?" Morusaki began, but Murgatroyd silenced him with a gesture.

"It won't hurt to explain," he said, although he let loose a slight sigh, which signified that he would probably rather not have been asked to do so. "You see, there have already been a number of reports of newly-evolved dr-DNA viruses. Perhaps newly-*de*volved dr-DNA viruses would be a better way of putting it, because we think they emerge by the mutation of chromosomal fragments displaced from the nuclei of dr-cells. There have also been suggestions that one or two of our very own laevo-rotatory nuisance-organisms are taking aboard dextro-rotatory biochemical apparatus so as to become facultative hybrids. A whole new phase of evolution is starting up... our artificial biotechnologies are beginning to spawn their own mutational progeny. I think that's very exciting, don't you?"

"But the whole point of making artifacts from dr-DNA is that they're immune to disease and decay," objected Rosa, stubbornly. "If they've started giving birth to their own diseases, that's *terrible*."

"I said it had to have weapon potential," said Dieter, in a tone of profound satisfaction. "What you're saying is that our house—*our house*—has accidentally spawned a mutant virus that's capable of messing up half the world's property. That's why you're so smug, isn't it? The next Plague War might not have begun today, but you think you've just got one step ahead in the arms race, don't you?"

"Of course not," said Mr. Murgatroyd. "What we've found is certainly a dr-virus, and it certainly seems to have arisen by spontaneous mutation, but it's not the doomsday weapon. Seen from one point of view, it's just the first of many minor nuisances that will soon be cropping up here, there, and everywhere. There's so much dextro-rotatory structural material around nowadays that it was only a matter of time before new bugs evolved to feed on it. It's been a wide-open ecological niche just begging to be colonized."

"The Gaians aren't going to like it," said Rick, vindictively trying to puncture Mr. Murgatroyd's good-humor. "It adds a whole new dimension of meaning to the idea of technology running wild."

"On the contrary," said Dr. Jauregy, who had now finished attending to his battle-scars. "They'll probably see it as Mother Nature hitting back, defying us in our quest for perfect order. Your brand-new dr-virus might become a hero of the Counter-Revolution...or do I mean the Counter-*Evolution*." She grinned at her joke, though it seemed feeble enough to Rick, and nobody else laughed.

"Hey," said Dieter. "Is there anything in this for us? I mean, this is our house—we ought to have patent rights, or something!"

"I'm afraid not," said Officer Morusaki, smoothly. "There can be no patent rights in a spontaneous product of mutation unless the mutagenic process is deliberately induced."

"What about rights of discovery, then?" said Dieter. "We discovered it, didn't we?"

I was the one who discovered it, thought Rick. *There's no "we" about it.*

"You observed a sick rose," said Mr. Murgatroyd. "You could hardly be said to have discovered the invisible worm that sickened it. That honor, I fear, belongs to Dr. Jauregy, Officer

Morusaki, and myself. But if it makes you feel any better, there is no way in which any of us can profit personally from the discovery, because we are all here in our official capacities. Your house will share with our names the credit of a dozen footnotes in scientific journals and reference books, but none of us will make a penny."

"Except for me," Dr. Jauregy said, with polite regret. "I'm afraid I'll still have to bill you for the consultation and the treatment—and for the replacement of the screen downstairs, if you want me to see to that too."

Dieter's resentful stare switched from Mr. Murgatroyd to Rick, who simply looked away, pointedly refusing any comment.

"You mustn't be distressed," said Murgatroyd, amiably. "It really is best to look at it my way. This is a significant moment in the history of life on earth—the beginning of a new evolutionary sequence—and it began in your nursery.

"It's a kind of miracle, in a way: a happy gift of providence. Who knows what dextro-rotatory DNA might eventually produce, in the fullness of time, now that it has taken its first small step towards independence from the shaping hand of man? Let's try to rise above mere matters of commerce, and fix our minds on that. Your nursery had a bad turn, and your cellar got flooded...but that wasn't what really happened here today. What really happened is that something new revealed itself to the world...something *really new*, and *alive*."

Rick was still mad at everyone, and his hands still hurt like hell, but he suddenly saw what Murgatroyd was getting at, and he saw that Murgatroyd was right. At the molecular level, something significant had happened...something far more important than a cut hand, or a fit of panic that might or might not have been too stupid for words.

A miracle. A happy gift of providence.

"Where is it now?" he asked, soberly. "If you're going to cure the house, how are you going to preserve the virus?"

Mr. Murgatroyd opened his case, and took out a plastic bag—probably one of several that he had in there. The sealed bag contained a single rose plucked from the nursery wall. As yet, it didn't look sick.

They all stared at it for a few seconds: all seven of them.

Then Mr. Murgatroyd put the rose back in his case, fastened it up, and headed for the door. It opened for him with what seemed to Rick to be craven servility. The doctor and the IBI man followed.

* * * * * * *

When they had gone, Rosa came over to Rick, and dumped Steven into his lap.

"Well," she said. "That's that. I've got a counseling session in five minutes."

"Oh corruption," said Chloe. "I should have been hooked into that robominer twenty minutes ago."

Dieter had already disappeared, as though by magic.

Rick didn't feel too bad about being left alone. They had not even begun to understand what he had gone through, and that devalued the reassurance of their presence. Although he still felt in need of someone to listen, someone to sympathize, he knew that none of them could fulfill that role.

Steven opened his eyes, met Rick's eyes momentarily, and began to wail.

Rick looked down at the child, and his heart sank. *Forty-eight hours*, he thought, remembering what the visitors had said. It would be forty-eight hours before the nursery nook was safe for normal use. Until then....

He got up and went into the kitchen, to salvage the bottle and the teat. It was a bit twenty-first century, but he figured that with luck it ought to work, now that Steven was hungry enough.

It did. After spitting it out once, Steven compromised and started sucking. Silence fell.

Rick stroked the baby's head with the hand that the doctor had dressed and sealed with syntho-flesh. It felt very odd.

"We really were in trouble down there, you know," said

Rick, levelly. "Not that anybody gives a damn one way or the other, now it's all come out okay. I was trying to save our lives, because I had every reason to think they needed saving."

Steven didn't even spare him a glance, but that didn't matter.

"You understand, don't you?" Rick continued. "You were there, and you were yelling even louder than I was. You knew what we were going through. You know what I did, and why. It's our secret, kid—just yours and mine. *We understand.*"

He had started saying it simply in order to have something to say, but as he spoke the words aloud he realized that they were true—or, at any rate, nearly true.

He had not been alone in the cellar; he had not panicked entirely on his own behalf. He had been scared for Steven too. He had been right to be scared for Steven, to panic for Steven, to go to the limit...for Steven. Whatever his co-parents thought of him, he'd done what he had to do, and he didn't have to apologize to anyone.

Steven spat out the teat, and gathered himself for a whimper, which would inevitably turn to a whine, which would turn to a....

Rick stood up, and took the baby and the bottle into the nursery, hoping that the sight of familiar surroundings would help to set Steven's mind at rest. A dozen roses had been picked and taken away, but there were hundreds left; not one of them looked sick.

"Look," Rick murmured into the baby's ear. "Look at all the beautiful roses. Everything's okay."

He tried to push the teat back into the baby's mouth, but Steven resisted. The baby was crying now—building up yet again towards that frightful note.

"At the end of the day," Rick went on, stubbornly, "Murgatroyd was right, wasn't he? We just have to stop thinking about it as a disaster, and start thinking about it as a beginning, don't we? A miracle happened here today, and you and I were here to see it. We should be grateful for that. We *are* grateful for that, aren't we?"

Again, he had said it just to have something to say, but again he realized that it was true. As Steven began to yell, and the pitch of his yelling cut through to the very heart of him, Rick suddenly realized that it would not and could not affect him the way it did unless there was some special bond between them, some indefinable but unique harmony. If one only looked at it sensibly it was not, after all, some malevolent worm gnawing at his soul, but an affirmation of the fact that they meant something to one another...that they had an understanding.

Rick pressed the makeshift teat into the baby's mouth, gently but insistently fighting the baby's refusal to make it welcome.

"Take your time, son," said Rick, soothingly. "Take your time. There's no hurry at all. We have all the time in the world, if we need it...all the time in the world."

And he looked around, at all the beautiful roses—all the bright pink roses, which, with tender loving care and a little luck, would live for centuries.

THE AGE OF INNOCENCE

Sybil and her best friend Gwenan got their first real sex education when they were eleven years old, watching their great-
great-great-great-grandparents playing in the park.

The park had several dense clumps of bushes whose principal *raison d'etre* was to provide cover for frolicking ancients.
Most of the carers who took ancients out to play were adults,
who almost invariably made a big show of staying out of the
bushes while their charges got on with it, but Sybil and Gwenan
were curious enough to take the first reasonable opportunity to
slip into the bushes unobserved and find out what went on there.

They were not entirely surprised, but the visible reality of
sexual intercourse seemed much more absurd than the theory
had implied.

"Surely our *parents* don't do things like that?" said Gwenan,
in hushed tones, the first time they saw it happen.

"Not *now*," Sybil informed her, airily, taking her customary
pride in the narrow margin of her greater wisdom. "People lose
the urge when they get to be a hundred or so. That's why the
second century is supposed to be the prime of life—all their
creativity can be concentrated in *useful* channels. It only comes
back again when the higher brain functions begin to disappear,
and by the time they get to three hundred or three-fifty they're
slaves to it. I heard Mother say so, when she was talking on the
phone to Aunt Genista."

Gwenan became embarrassed then, and turned away, but
Sybil didn't. It wasn't that she didn't feel awkward spying on

them, just that her curiosity was stronger than her guilty unease. All sorts of questions ran through her head. Were ancients capable of loving one another, after their fashion, or did love vanish along with self-consciousness—and if it did, could they even be said to love their descendants? Would ancients have sex with *anybody*—anybody, that is, who was small enough—or did they prefer particular partners? *Why* did ancients like sex so much, given that they were quite incapable of procreation? *Did* they actually like it, or was it just a kind of compulsion?

She studied the grimaces on the great-great-great-great-grandparents' little faces, trying to fathom the meaning of the expressions. Her mother had often warned her not to read too much into great-great-great-great-grandmother's expressions, but Sybil couldn't help trying to figure them out. Great-great-great-great-grandmother was still human, after all, still capable of joy and sadness, irritation and contentment, if not of actual thought.

When it was all over, Gwenan's great-great-great-great-grandfather rolled away, looking contented but not particularly joyful. His tiny eyes were dark and bird-bright, and he was whispering to himself rapidly and incoherently. Sybil's great-great-great-great-grandmother, on the other hand, looked joyful without being particularly contented. Her blue eyes were misty, and she was gravely silent. Sybil's great-great-great-great-grandmother was a very quiet ancient, as ancients went. Mother said it was because she hadn't been overfond of talking even in the days when she had an active mind.

Sybil thought that her great-great-great-great-grandmother was still rather pretty, after her own ancient fashion. If she had been filmed against a miniaturized background of some kind, Sybil thought, it wouldn't have been immediately obvious that she *was* an ancient. She still hadn't lost the last lingering echoes of adult presence and adult poise, in spite of the fact that every time she came to the park she made straight for the bushes.

* * * * * * *

By the time they had watched the ancients indulging their sexual appetites three or four more times, even Gwenan became appropriately blasé about it. That didn't stop her becoming fearfully embarrassed about watching if there were any other people around, but the event itself no longer caused her to blush crimson—and it was usually possible to slip in and out of the bushes without being observed. For Sybil, the fundamental mystery of it persisted. It somehow seemed to be the key to what being an ancient was all about—and she couldn't help wondering, crazy as it might seem, whether ancienthood rather than adulthood might somehow be what being human was all about. Even though adulthood generally lasted at least twice as long as ancienthood, ancienthood was where everyone ended up: it was life's culmination, life's denouement.

As it happened, the day of the accident was one of the days that Sybil and Gwenan watched, perhaps more closely than they ever had before, studying the details of the process and—in Sybil's case—wondering what refinements and nuances had to be added in order to transform it into *adult* sex, and hence into authentic love-making. It was the seventh occasion on which she had been able to give such matters patient and serious consideration; she had not the slightest reason to suspect that it might be the last.

"I don't understand where the urge could possibly come from in the first place," Gwenan said, as she peeped out of the bushes to make sure there were no adults around before emerging into the warm sunlight. "All things considered, I think I'd rather do without."

"You won't have the option," Sybil told her, with a world-weary sigh. "We change according to an inbuilt cycle. Innocence, childhood, adulthood, second childhood, and back to innocence again. It's called the wheel of existence. It carries you round whether you like it or not. The urges come when their time is due, and go when their time is done."

"You got that from a holovid tape," Gwenan said, accusatively.

"Of course I did," Sybil said, meticulously dusting herself down. "How else are we supposed to learn what's what—or understand what's what when we see it?"

"Well I think it's disgusting," Gwenan countered, defiantly. "It's not right. People their age ought to have more...more dignity."

"Dignity doesn't come into it," Sybil reminded her. "They outgrew that long ago. Anyhow, it's natural, so it doesn't matter whether you like it or not—it's just the way things are."

Gwenan could be so slow that it was sometimes hard to believe that Sybil was only five months the elder of the pair, especially in view of the fact that Gwenan looked older. Sybil realized, though, that these things were relative. Five months might be hardly anything in the context of an entire human lifespan, but it was a yawning gap between two eleven-year-olds.

When her own great-great-great-great-grandmother had been eleven, Sybil calculated, Gwenan's great-great-great-great-grandfather must have been thirty-one, possessed of a vastly different wealth of experience—but now they were both pushing four hundred, twenty years didn't mean a thing. They didn't have an atom of self-consciousness between them, and the patterns of ingrained habit that were the legacy of their separate lifetimes were virtually identical.

"Do you realize," said Gwenan, slowly, while the temporarily-sated great-great-great-great-grandparents were dressing them-selves again, "that we'll be like that one day?" It was as if the thought had only just occurred to her, although Sybil couldn't imagine that anyone might be capable of avoiding conscious-ness of that particular fact even for half an hour.

"It'll be okay," Sybil assured her. "We've already had prac-tice being tiny and mindless—we'll be able to do it again easily enough when the time comes."

The two ancients had stretched themselves out in the sun, tiredly, but Sybil knew that it wouldn't be long before they were raring to go again. Their energy came in short bursts, but they always made the most of their time outdoors. They really weren't very much like babies, in appearance or behavior. The proportions of their bodies were quite different, retaining adult ratios in spite of the loss of mass, and their behavior was equally distinct. In spite of what holovid pomposity termed the wheel of existence, there was a world of difference between progressive innocence and decadent innocence.

"It's not the same," Gwenan insisted, revealing that even she understood that much, in her own rough and ready fashion. After a pause she went on: "I don't think it's fair that we should have to do this, you know. Why should *we* be the ones who have to take the family ancients out for their walks, and chop up their food for them, and clean out their attics? That's not natural. In most families, adults look after the ancients. *That's* normal."

Looking after the family ancients was the first serious responsibility that Sybil and Gwenan had ever had to undertake. At first they had agreed that it was a vile imposition and an awful nuisance having all the work of cleaning and food-preparation to do, but it hadn't taken long for Sybil to figure out what their parents meant when they said that kids could learn a lot from their great-great-great-great-grandparents. Ancients might have grown out of self-consciousness, but the habits they retained had a lot of fascinating humanity in them. Looking after an ancient was supposed to be good for a child—an invaluable part of preparation for adult life. Sybil no longer thought that she had adequate grounds to disagree with that—but she couldn't help thinking that Gwenan did have a point. Children had so much to learn while they grew, and so little time, whereas adults were already *finished*, and had all the time in the world to be what they were and do whatever they had to do.

"Most families don't have children," Sybil pointed out, pensively. "Adults have to do most of the work of caring for ancients—that's just simple arithmetic. Ancients are ancient for a hundred years but children are only children for a little while." She had only just begun to carry out calculations like that, and found such matters of proportion oddly but endlessly fascinating.

When the great-great-great-great-grandparents were up and ready again, Sybil and Gwenan took their respective charges by the hand and led them over the brow of the hill and down to the lake. Sybil liked the lake far better than the bushes at this time of year because the water lilies were in full bloom and the water-birds had downy chicks trailing after them in tight formation.

The ancients agitated for permission to take their clothes off all over again and go swimming. Sybil and Gwenan were only too glad to let them get on with it.

If there was one thing ancients liked better than sex it was swimming—and that, to Sybil, was a far less understandable urge. But swimming was a much more satisfactory activity from her point of view, because it lasted much longer and exhausted the ancients more fully, and gave Gwenan and herself the chance to have a really good chat about things that actually mattered, like clothes and holovid shows and all the horrid iniquities of programd schoolwork and parental control.

By the time they both had to go to their separate homes, Gwenan was in a thoroughly good mood, and Sybil felt positively happy. They fixed a time to meet on the next day before they parted at the park gates.

Unfortunately, while Sybil and her great-great-great-great-grandmother were making their way along the main road to the pedestrian crossing, the ancient suddenly spotted something bright lying on the central reservation, and took it into her stupid, empty little head to run to get it.

* * * * * * *

"It wasn't my fault!" Sybil wailed, hysterically. "It really wasn't. There wasn't anything I could do."

"I know, darling," her mother said, hugging Sybil to her bosom and patting the back of her head. "Even the robotruck couldn't do anything, and artificial reflexes are much faster than yours. You really mustn't blame yourself."

"She never did anything like it before!" Sybil continued, protesting at the injustice of it all. "I'd have held her hand if I thought she might. How was I to know that her road-safety habits had worn off?"

"You couldn't, darling," her mother assured her. "It's not so bad. She was very old, you know, and she can't have felt a thing. When the time comes to die, it's best to go like that—like switching off a light. She had a good life...a *very* good life. It's a miracle she survived so long, considering the times she lived through when she was my age. I always find it hard to believe that the world has so many more ancients in it than children, when I remember how many of great-great-great-great-grandma's generation didn't make it to a hundred. All lives have to end eventually, though—it was just bad luck that it had to happen so soon after you started looking after her."

Sybil wasn't so young that she couldn't see a certain irony in the fact that her great-great-great-great-grandmother had survived the third and fourth plague wars *and* the second nuclear war, had travelled extensively in the sub-Saharan swamps of Africa and the rugged hills of Antarctica, and had flown to the moon and back twice, only to be run down by a robotruck two hundred metres from her front door. Nor was she unable to extrapolate that pattern of irony to an appreciation of the fact that great-great-great-great-grandma had survived being looked after for thirty years and more by her own parents, well over two hundred years of looking after herself, and eighty-some years of being looked after by various other descendants before a mere six weeks of Sybil's tender care had seen the end of her.

"I'm *so sorry*," Sybil said, packing all the meaning she could into the simple phrase. "It wasn't that I didn't want to look after her. It really wasn't. I didn't mind. I would have looked after her till I was sixty or seventy if I'd had to, *honestly*."

"Hush now, darling," her mother said. "There's no need for you to be so upset. It was just an accident. It would have happened just the same if I'd been with her, or anyone else.

She wouldn't want you to be upset. It's just one of those things. People do die, darling. In the end, everybody dies. It's perfectly natural. It doesn't matter whether they die in their sleep, or in an accident, or just drop dead...it happens. People get old, and when they get old they forget things. Given time, they forget *everything*, even the things they need to do to stay alive. That's just the way things are, darling."

Sybil had run out of sobs and painful declarations, so silence fell for a minute or two. All she could think of, though, was the way her tiny, pretty great-great-great-great-grandmother had looked while she lay on the road, shattered and bleeding, while the life just ebbed out of her. Her blue eyes had been wide open, frightened and uncomprehending. Although Sybil understood only too well how deceptive the expressions of ancients could be, she couldn't help reading far too much into that last desperate stare: a sense of utter loss, not of life as such but of life's happiness, life's color, life's stubbornness.

Sybil didn't doubt for a moment that everything her mother had said about the goodness of great-great-great-great-grandmother's life was perfectly true, but that didn't mean that there was any vestige of goodness about her death. It didn't matter how ancient an ancient might be, death was still a tragedy, a travesty, and a trauma. And all the stuff about the inexorable turning of the wheel of existence was just a bad joke, or an ineffectual attempt to hide from the awful reality.

When Sybil's mother finally spoke again, her tone was very different. "Mind you," she said, with a deep sigh, "it's going to be hell on earth arranging the funeral."

* * * * * * *

"Arranging funerals," Sybil told Gwenan, while they sat beside the lake watching Gwenan's great-great-great-great-grandfather swim, "is hell on earth."

"Do you think he misses her?" Gwenan asked, staring at he tiny head bobbing in the water. "He doesn't seem to."

"Plenty of other pebbles on the beach," Sybil observed, indulging her new-found delight in cynicism. "According to psychologists, they don't form any personal attachments once they're past three hundred, and they're pretty fickle even before that, when adulthood is decaying into second childhood. According to the best estimates, even the most intense adult bonds rarely last more than twenty or twenty-five years. We're only human, after all—not like swans, which mate for life."

"*I'm* not fickle," Gwenan said.

Only because you haven't got the urge yet, Sybil, thought—but there were more important things than that to talk about. "Hell on earth," she repeated, insistently.

"Why?" Gwenan asked, obligingly. "You only have to dig a hole in the garden and put the casket in. It's easy."

"*That*'s easy enough," Sybil said, carefully duplicating one of her mother's finest sighs. "The problems start with figuring out how to notify all the interested parties, and getting some response, and finding somewhere for them all to stay...it's a matter of simple arithmetic, you see."

"No, I don't," Gwenan said.

Gwenan's great-great-great-great-grandfather attempted to climb up on a lily-pad that couldn't possibly support his weight, and splashed back into the water in a most ungainly fashion, giggling all the while.

"Look at it this way," Sybil said, glad that all her scrupulous calculations weren't going to go to waste. Everybody has two parents, even if they only live with one. Every parent has two parents, and every grandparent has two, and so on. That means, when you work it back, that everybody has *sixty-four* great-great-great-great-grandparents."

"Sixty-four's not so many," Gwenan objected. "Anyway, most of yours will be dead already, and whoever's looking after the rest probably won't even know that they're distantly related to your great-great-great-great-grandmother."

"That's not the point," said Sybil, with a sigh. "The point is that it works the other way around too. Nowadays, of course, hardly anybody has more than one child, but back in great-great-great-great-grandmother's day no one knew how overcrowded the world would eventually become, because it was much more common for people to die at a hundred or a hundred and fifty, even leaving wars and such out of account. People sometimes had four or five children, and two was utterly commonplace. The problem, you see, isn't counting up my great-great-great-great-grandparents—it's counting up great-great-great-great-grandmother's six generations of descendants. Not easy. Then you have to try to find them all. Some of them are on the far side of the world, some on Mars, some in the Lagrange colonies."

"That's no problem," said Gwenan, scornfully. "They're hardly likely to take an interplanetary trip just to go to a funeral."

"But they all have to be *told*," Sybil said, impatiently. "And they all want to be there in electronic spirit if not in the flesh. It's a difficult and time-consuming, believe me."

"*You* don't have to do it," Gwenan pointed out, determined not to pander to Sybil's imaginary martyrdom.

"We all have to pull together at a time like this," Sybil said, darkly, quoting her mother word for word. "Everybody has to do their bit."

Gwenan's great-great-great-great-grandpa was now trying to pluck one of the huge golden water-lilies, and failing miserably. He flopped and floundered amid the floating vegetation, scaring the moorhens, gabbling on and on whenever he could get his head above water. When he was an adult, Sybil thought, he must have been exceedingly fond of the sound of his own voice.

Gwenan changed tack. "I suppose," she said, ruminatively, "that you could get another one. If you have sixty-four great-great-great-great-grandparents, and even more great-great-great-grandparents, you could take in one of the others instead. You've got the attic all fixed up, haven't you? Everything ready and waiting."

"*Get another one!*" Sybil echoed, distastefully. "We're not talking about pets you know. Ancients are people. Our attic was great-great-great-great-grandma's *home*."

"I bet whoever's got the others would be only too pleased to let you have one," Gwenan said, sarcastically. "My Mum's always trying to get rid of *him*, but everyone who might be able to take him keeps right on telling her how good it is for a little girl my age to have an ancient for company. *Company!* I'd rather have my great-great-great-grandma from Birmingham—at least she can still talk a *bit* of sense, even if she doesn't say much—and at least she's three-quarters my size. I'm twice as tall as *he* is, and he never says anything meaningful, even though he hardly ever shuts up for more than five minutes at a time."

"Size isn't important," Sybil said, mechanically. "Anyway, he won't get any smaller now."

"He might," Gwenan objected.

"No, he won't," Sybil insisted. "People can't keep on shrinking forever. After a certain point the organs won't work any more because they don't have enough cells to do all the different jobs that cells have to do to keep the organs working." Sybil felt that she might have phrased this explanation a little better, but she hadn't quite understood the educational holovid from which she'd plucked the pearl of wisdom. She figured, though, that Gwenan—who was at least three stages behind in her school-work, because she got bored too easily when she was alone with a keyboard and screen—wouldn't be able to challenge her.

"He might not get any smaller," Gwenan said, "but I'm still getting bigger. Either way, we grow apart. What they say about second childhood and the last age of innocence is all rubbish. Children don't have *anything* in common with ancients—not really. It's all just an excuse, to make us look after them."

Gwenan's great-great-great-great-grandfather was climbing out of the water now, rubbing himself dry before putting his clothes back on. He looked completely done in.

It's a wonder more of them don't drown, Sybil thought. "I suppose you'd rather be living in the bad old days," she said aloud, in a mock-adult tone, "when nobody lived past a hundred and everybody got *diseases* and *cancers* and things."

"Yes I would," said Gwenan, unequivocally. "What's the

point of living to be four hundred if you end up like *that?*"

Gwenan's great-great-great-great-grandpa was having trouble putting his pants on. Although he remembered well enough what he had to do, his fingers had lost so much of their dexterity that it wasn't easy for him to go through the motions, especially when he was cold and tired.

"There's no point complaining about it," Sybil told her friend, dutifully suppressing the pang of sympathy she felt, out of respect for great-great-great-great-grandmother's memory. "It's just the way things are. No matter how clever the doctors are at clearing cells that don't work out of the body, so they don't get in the way, they can't put a stop to *all* the ways in which we get older. It's something to do with the stuff in our genes having to be copied over and over again. No matter what the doctors do, mistakes still happen and always will. I read somewhere that we begin to die before we're even born, and that there's no way round it, even though the genetic engineers have finally stretched the length of our lives to the true limit."

"That's silly," Gwenan complained. "You must have got it wrong. It's no use pretending to be so clever. You might have a good memory, but you don't have a clue what most of it means."

"I'm beginning to understand," Sybil countered, defensively.

She realized, as she said it, that it was true. She *was* beginning to understand the mysteries of life and death. The tragedy of great-great-great-great-grandma's death had served to hasten the onset of that understanding.

While Gwenan went to help her great-great-great-great-grandfather finish dressing, and to do what she could to soothe his irritable frustration, Sybil murmured, "Hell on earth" yet again—but she didn't really mean it.

* * * * * * *

In the event, the funeral went very smoothly. It was so interesting that Sybil would have said that she'd enjoyed it, except that funerals weren't the kind of thing you were supposed to enjoy.

With a little help from Sybil, her mother had managed to locate sixty-five of the seventy-two living descendants her great-great-great-great-grandmother had turned out to have. Seventeen were ancients themselves, too old to make any kind of response on their own account, and six were children—but five of the ancients and two of the children were brought to the funeral by their guardians. Twenty-one of the other forty-nine were off-planet and a further thirteen thought that it was too far to come, so there were only fifteen *real* family guests, plus seven extras. A dozen neighbors, plus assorted ancients and Gwenan, made up the company.

Aunt Genista was a great help with the organization of the meal, where almost everybody ate too much, and accepted all the credit fulsomely, but Sybil knew that her mother had done all the really difficult work, doggedly and methodically. It wasn't just that she had pulled a representative sample of great-great-great-great-grandmother's descendants together for the day, but that she had taken the trouble to make sure that *all* her family knew what had happened. It was only at times like these, Sybil realized, that the widely-scattered individuals descended from a particular ancient could have any sense of connection, of relatedness, and of the true working of the great mechanical wheel of existence.

One of the children was a boy in his twenties who thought of himself as an almost-adult and was far too grand to talk to an eleven-year-old like Sybil, but the other was a nine-year-old boy named Jacob who thought it quite pleasant to have a distant cousin. Sybil knew that she and Jacob would probably never meet again as children, and might be entirely different people by the time another funeral brought them together, but she also knew that they would remember one another then, and in the meantime would be in some small sense part of one another.

While the messages of condolence from non-attenders were being played on the holovid, Sybil, Gwenan, and Jacob huddled together in a corner so that they could exchange unobtrusive whispers.

"When I'm thirty," Jacob told them, "I'm going to join the space service. I'm going out to the moons of Saturn."

"Why Saturn?" Gwenan asked.

"Because it's got better rings," he explained. "There aren't any ancients out there, you know. It's an *adult*'s world."

"Actually," Sybil told him, "it's an AI's world. People are a tiny minority—even fabers. You'll have to be somatically modified, you know, if you want to be a real spaceman. You need four arms to work in low gravity."

"Titan's got gravity," Jacob informed her. "It's okay to have legs on Titan. What are you going to be?"

"Lots of things," Sybil told him, loftily. "Lots of *different* things. To start with, though, I want to be an engineer. A human engineer, I think."

"Making fabers?" Jacob asked, exposing the limitations of his imagination.

"Making *new* people," Sybil replied, haughtily. "Better people."

"I don't know what I want to do," Gwenan confessed. "It's difficult to think that far ahead, when there's so much to learn. But I don't want to work at a screen. I want to use my arms and legs as well as my eyes and fingers."

When the messages had all been displayed, everybody went out into the garden, to the side of the grave. There were no other graves in the garden; Sybil's mother hadn't been living in the house very long before Sybil was born, and great-great-great-great-grandmother was the only ancient who'd ever lived in it.

Sybil's mother made quite a long speech, going through the various phases of great-great-great-great-grandmother's life— all the things she'd done and places she'd been—but the task of saying the final few words had been delegated to Sybil. Sybil had worked hard on her speech, knowing that it was an unparalleled opportunity to impress a whole company of adults with her intelligence and maturity. She knew that she could be the star of the ceremony if she were clever enough, and that she might thus be able to erase the lurking suspicion that it had been *her fault* that great-great-great-great-grandmother had been killed.

"I'm sorry that great-great-great-great-grandmother died while I'm only eleven," she said, doing her level best to sound sincere. "It would have been nice to look after her for a little bit longer. I'll miss her, because she was such a happy person. I know people say it's easy to be happy when you're an ancient, because people shed their worries along with their defective cells, but I don't think it's as simple as that. I think being happy is a habit like all the other habits that keep people going when they're very old, and I think it's difficult to be happy, even if you're an ancient, if you didn't get the habit while you were an adult. I don't know for sure, but I think maybe it's not so easy to be happy when you're an adult, if you haven't been able to learn it when you're a child, and maybe it's not so easy to learn it when you're a child, if you don't have a happy ancient to show you how. I'm glad I had a happy ancient to show me how, just for a little while."

Everyone applauded. Sybil knew that the applause was a ritual, just like her speech—she had said what she was supposed to say, the way the turning wheel of life demanded; it was all performance, all programming—but that didn't mean that the applause was fake, or that what she'd said wasn't true. She thought that she'd done a good job, and given great-great-great-great-grandma a proper send-off, and that was only right, given that she had been looking after great-great-great-great-grandma when the robotruck killed her.

* * * * * * *

Afterwards, when she thought everyone else had gone inside, Sybil went back to the grave, and looked down at the little mound of earth.

"Three hundred and seventy-six years," she whispered to herself. *"Three hundred and seventy-six years."* It was a lot. The day before, she had counted all the way from one, just so that she'd really know how many it was. "It's a big wheel that takes so long to turn."

She turned around abruptly as she heard a noise behind her, wondering if she'd been overheard, but it was all right. It was only Gwenan's great-great-great-great-grandfather, all by himself for once. He barely glanced at Sybil as he walked past her, and went to stand at the edge of the grave, looking down. The expression on his tiny face—far tinier than a baby's—was quite unreadable, but he wasn't muttering away the way he usually did, and his silence seemed appropriately solemn.

Sybil knew that the old man couldn't possibly understand what had happened. He couldn't even *begin* to understand the idea of death, and probably had no memory at all of her great-great-great-great-grandmother—but something had brought him here anyway, and something made him pause where he was, uncertainly staring infinity in the face.

Within the slowly-dying pattern of his habits, Sybil thought, the vestiges of a fuller and better humanity must still be lurking. Was the sadness of his unaccustomed silence the ghost of love, or grief, or just that particular and peculiar helplessness in the face of the inevitable that people never quite overcame?

After a minute had passed, Sybil reached out and took him by the hand. He didn't resist.

"Come on," she said, solicitously. "We'd better go back inside, before you catch a chill."

SNOWBALL IN HELL

From the very beginning I had a niggling feeling that the operation was going to go wrong, but I put it down to nerves. Scientific advisors to the Home Office rarely get a chance to take part in Special Branch operations, and I always knew that it would be my first and last opportunity to be part of a real *Boy's Own Adventure*.

I calmed my anxieties by telling myself that the police must know what they were doing. The plan looked so neat and tidy when it was laid out on the map with colored dots: blue for the lower ranks, red for the Armed Response Unit, green for the likes of yours truly, and black for the senior Special Branch officers who were supervising and coordinating the whole thing. We deeply resented the fact that the reports from the surveillance team had been carefully censored, according to the sacred principle of NEED TO KNOW, but there seemed to be no obvious reason to suppose that the raid itself wouldn't go like clockwork.

"But what are they actually supposed to have *done*, exactly?" one of my juniors was reckless enough to ask.

"If we knew *exactly*," came the inevitable withering reply, "we wouldn't need to include you in the operation, would we?"

I could tell from the reports we had been allowed to see that the so-called investigation into the experiments at Hollinghurst Manor had been a committee product, and that no one had ever had a clear idea exactly what was going on. Warrants for surveillance had been obtained on the grounds that the Branch's

GE-Crime Unit had "compelling reasons" to suspect that Doctors Hemans, Rawlingford, and Bradby were using "human genetic material" in the creation of "transgenic animals," but it was mostly speculation. What they really had to go on was gossip and rumor, and the rumors in question seemed to me to be suspiciously akin to the urban legends that had sprung up everywhere since the tabloids' yuck factor campaign had finally forced the government to pass stringent laws controlling the uses of genetic engineering and to set up the GE-Crime Unit to enforce them. Once it existed, the Unit had to do something to justify its budget, and its senior staff obviously reckoned that whatever was going on at Hollinghurst Manor had to be yucky enough to allow them to get that invaluable first goal on the great score sheet.

It seemed to me that the whole affair had always had a faint air of surreal absurdity about it. The illegal experiments that Hemans and his fellows were alleged by rumor to be conducting were unfortunately conducive to silly jokes, ranging from lame references to flying pigs to covert references to the raid as the Boar War. Even the Home Office joined in the jokey name game; it was some idiot under-secretary who decided to code-name the "target" Animal Farm, borrowing the most popular of the derisory nicknames it had accumulated during the surveillance. It was, alas, my own people who took some delight in explaining to anyone who would listen why the people inside had allegedly taken to calling the project "Commoner's Isle." (It was because the place where the ambitious scientist had conducted his unsuccessful experiment in H. G. Wells' *The Island of Doctor Moreau* had been called Noble's Isle.) When the inspector in charge of the Armed Response Unit assured us at the final briefing that the people in the manor didn't have a snowball's chance in hell of getting past his men he couldn't understand why the men from the ministry snickered. (In *Animal Farm*, Snowball is the idealist who gets purged by the ruthless Napoleon.)

In a sense, the inspector was right. When the Animal Farmers found out that they were being raided and ran like hell they *didn't* have a snowball's chance in hell of getting past his men. Unfortunately, that didn't make them stop running and give up.

The part of the plan that included me involved uniformed policemen smashing their way through the main door and making as many arrests as possible while my people went for the computers and any paper files that were still around. We didn't expect to get all the records out—we'd been told at the briefing that Hemans, Rawlingford, and Bradby would probably start crunching diskettes and reformatting hard disks as soon as they were roused from sleep—but we figured that there'd be more than enough left to salvage. They were scientists, after all; keeping back-up files ought to have been second nature to them.

Unfortunately, it wasn't that simple. The Animal Farmers didn't bother with shredding and reformatting; they just torched the place. Nobody had thought to give us gas-masks, and the fumes that met us in the corridors of the manor were so foul and instantly dizzying that we should have know that they were toxic and turned back immediately. Actually, that was what most of my colleagues did. I was the only thoroughly stupid one. I kept on going, determined to get to the office that was my designated objective. It was hopeless—but it was my one and only *Boy's Own Adventure* and I hadn't been trained to an adequate sense of self-preservation. I was just on the point of blacking out when I heard shots fired in the woods, and realized just how badly awry the operation had gone.

* * * * * * *

I would certainly have died if I hadn't been pulled out of the fume-filled corridor—and by the time my own team got around to noticing that I was missing it was far too late for *them* to do anything constructive. It was the Animal Farmers who saved me—not the scientists who had actually set up the illegal experiments, but a handful of lesser beings who'd turned back when the shooting started in the hope of finding a safer way out on the other side of the house.

I woke up with a terrible headache and stinging eyes, coughing weakly. It felt for a minute or two as though my lungs had been so badly scorched that I could no longer draw sufficient oxygen from the warm and musty air that I drew into them—but that, mercifully, was an illusion born of distress.

I managed to crack open my weeping eyes just long enough to perceive that it was too dark to see what was happening, then shut them tight and hoped that the pain would go away.

Somebody lifted my head and pressed a cup of water to my lips. I managed to take a few sips, and decided not to protest when a female voice said, "He's okay."

While I lay there collecting myself, a different female voice said, "It's no good. There's no way out up there. As the fire draws air upwards, our supply's being renewed via the tunnel to the old ice-house, but there's no way through the grilles. They haven't been opened in half a century and the locks are rusted solid. Hemans should have taken care of them years ago. He should have known that this would happen one day."

"There's a hacksaw in the tool-box," a male voice put in. "If we get to work right away...."

"They were *shooting*, Ed," the second female told him. "They're trying to wipe us out, just like Bradby always said they would. They don't even want to ask the questions, let alone hear the answers. They just want us dead. Even if we could get to the lakeside, they're probably waiting for us. We wouldn't stand a chance."

"What chance have we got if we wait here, Ali?" Ed replied. "Even if the fire burns all day tomorrow, they'll come to pick over the ruins as soon as they can. If they're still in the woods by then, they'll certainly be all around what's left of the house. The tunnel's our only chance. If we can just get to Brighton, to a crowd. Then London...we can pass, Ali. I know we can. We can hide."

I wanted to tell them that nobody wanted to shoot them, that they'd be fine if they sat tight until it was safe to go upstairs and then surrendered, but I knew that they wouldn't believe me.

What on earth had made them so paranoid? And why had the ARU men opened fire?

"Ed's right," said the female who'd given me the water to drink. "If they have the ice-house covered, we're dead—but all the exits upstairs will still be useless when the fire dies down. We have to start work on the grilles. Somebody ought to watch this one, though—he's not badly hurt. If he doesn't come at us, he'll give us away."

"We should have left him where he was," Ed opined, bitterly. "He's not going to be any use as a hostage, is he?"

"He wouldn't be any use as a corpse," the unnamed female retorted. "He'd just be an excuse for branding us as murderers, justifying the ethnic cleansing."

Ethnic cleaning! What on earth had Bradby been telling them? And who the hell were they, anyway? I couldn't help jumping to the obvious conclusion, but I refused to entertain it. I was supposed to be a scientist, not some sucker who'd swallow any urban legend that happened along.

"We don't know that the others who came in with him all got out," Ali pointed out.

"No, we don't," the other female admitted, "but we did know that he hadn't. If we'd left him where he went down, it *would* have been murder."

"It would have been suicide," said Ed, "But Kath's right, Ali. They'd have *called* it murder. They'll have to justify the shooting somehow."

I coughed again, partly because I needed to and partly because I wanted to remind them that I had a voice too, even if I hadn't yet obtained sufficient control of it to formulate meaningful utterances.

"You'd better stay with him, Ali," the male voice said. "If he gets aggressive, hit him with this."

At that stage, I could only guess what "this" might be— some time passed before I was able to make out that it was an axe—but I wasn't about to make any trouble. I was still trying to convince myself that I hadn't breathed in enough poison to be mortally hurt, and that I hadn't done sufficient damage to my lungs to prejudice my long-term ability to breathe. I heard two sets of feet moving away across a stone floor, and I forced myself to relax, collecting myself together by slow degrees.

Eventually, I felt well enough to begin to feel angry. I stopped being grateful for being alive and started resenting the fact that I had come so close to dying. Setting the fire had been an act of pure spite on the part of the mad scientists. People like me—law-abiding geneticists, that is—had collaborated with the Home Office in drawing up the careful legislation that presumably defined whatever the Animal Farmers were doing as unacceptable, but they had simply been too arrogant to comply with the law. On top of that, it seemed, they had taken the view that if we wouldn't countenance the research, then we couldn't have the results. They had obviously decided that if they had to go to jail, they'd take all their hard-won understanding with them— and woe betide anyone who got in their way.

Once I began to get angry, I didn't stop. If Hemans and Co. really had been transplanting human genes into the embryos of pigs in order to turn out simulacra of human beings, it was unforgivable, and the murderous fire was piling injury on insult. I'd never been convinced that the Animal Farmers *had* done what Special Branch said they'd done—I'd gone through the doors of Commoner's Isle still wondering whether it was all going to turn out to be a big mistake, exaggerated out of all proportion—but the fact that the place had been torched with such alacrity suggested that they must have done *something* that they were desperate to conceal.

Unless, of course, that was what we were supposed to think. There was still a possibility that we were all being taken for a ride—that it was all a game, intended to discredit the GE-Crime Unit and the Home Office advisors before they began to get their act together.

While I lay there being angry, it occurred to me that I might be in a uniquely good position to find out exactly what the Animal Farmers were really up to.

* * * * * * *

When I was finally confident that I could hold a conversation, I had already formulated my plan of campaign.

"Is Ali short for Alison?" I asked. I was able to open my eyes by then, and they had accustomed themselves to the near-darkness sufficiently to let me see that the person standing guard over me was a blonde teenager, perhaps fourteen or fifteen years of age. She was too young to be a lab assistant, so I seized upon the hypothesis that she was probably someone's daughter. We had been warned that some of the live-in staff at the manor had children, but we hadn't expected them to be abandoned when the shit hit the fan.

"Alice," she informed me, stiffly.

"As in Wonderland?" I quipped, hoping to help her relax.

"As in *Through the Looking Glass*," she retorted. It didn't seem to be worthwhile asking her what the difference was.

"I'm Stephen Hitchens," I told her. "I'm not a policeman—I'm a geneticist, currently employed as an advisor to the Home Office."

"Bully for you," she said, dryly. I wondered whether she might be older than she looked—maybe sixteen or seventeen—but I concluded in the end that natural insolence, like puberty, probably arrived ahead of its time nowadays.

"Why did the scientists set fire to the house, Alice?" I asked.

"Why did armed police surround it?" she countered.

"None of this is your fault, or mine," I assured her. "I was just trying to recover the records of the experiments the scientists had done. They should have made sure that you were safe before they started the fire. They're not your friends, Alice. Did your parents work for Dr. Hemans?"

"In a manner of speaking," she told me, as if relishing a hidden irony.

"What manner of speaking?" I demanded, although I could hardly help seeing the obvious implication. If she wasn't the child of someone on the staff, she had to be one of the experimental subjects—or, I reminded myself, someone *pretending* to be one of the experimental subjects.

"The kind of work you do in a sty," she replied, casually confirming the inference she must have known I'd take. "The kind of work where your pay arrives in a trough."

If it was true, then she certainly had come from Wonderland— but was it true? Wasn't it far more likely to be a lie, a carefully constructed bluff? Was it to hear this, I wondered, that I had been hauled out of the corridor and brought down here into near-darkness? Could the Animal Farmers be using me, trying to convince me that they had achieved far, far more than they had? If so, what should my policy be? Should I run with the bluff and let her make her pitch, or challenge her and refuse to believe that she was anything but what she appeared to be?

"You're telling me that you're not human?" I said, just to make sure that she wasn't just making a joke. I knew as soon as I'd said it that I'd framed the rhetorical question wrongly. What she'd actually told me was that her parents weren't human.

"Like hell I am," she said.

Like Snowball in hell, I couldn't help thinking. *Play along*, I told myself. *Find out what she has to say.*

"So you think you're human," I conceded. "You can certainly pass for it, probably in a far brighter light than this—but if your parents really were pigs, you must understand that other people might not see things the same way." As I said *that* I realized that her creators—or drama-coaches—must already have put it in much stronger terms. That was why Ed and Kath had been so paranoid about the possibility of being shot down—that and the fact that the ARU really had opened fire.

"I know what I see when I look in a mirror," Alice told me, perhaps to make sure that I'd understood how clever her reference to *Through the Looking Glass* was. "It's not the image itself that's important, of course—it's the fact that there's an I to see it. A human I—and I don't mean an e-y-e."

Cogito, ergo sum, she might have said, if she—or whoever had written her script—hadn't been so anxious about the need to stay viewer-friendly. I hadn't enough anger left to prevent me from wondering whether Special Branch might always have known exactly how human the Animal Farmers' experimental subjects looked, and whether their senior officers might have taken it upon themselves to decide that the ministry didn't need to know until the shooting was well and truly over. If they had, and my captors knew it—or even if they hadn't and my captors merely believed it—I might be in deeper trouble than I thought.

"What about Ed and Kath?" I asked. "Are they like you?"

"They're human," Alice assured me, in a tone that left little doubt as to what kind of human she was talking about. She was telling me, in her own perverse way, that they were the kind of humans who were made as well as born: the kind that started off as a fertilized ovum in a sow's belly before the genetic engineers got to work.

Dr. Moreau had remade beasts in his own image by means of surgery, but modern scientists had much cleverer means at their disposal—and the degree of success they might be expected to achieve was far greater. I had to remind myself again that all of this could be a bluff run by a thoroughly human child, and that I was only playing along to see how the story would go.

Alice had relaxed a little since she first started talking, but the way she held her shadowed head and the way she gripped the axe she'd been ordered to hit me with if I got out of line suggested that she wasn't about to get careless. Now that she'd made her first impression, she was busy reminding herself that she was stuck in a cellar beneath a burning building with a man who might be dangerous. All in all, philosophical discussion seemed the safest way to build a modicum of trust.

"You think you're human because you have a human mind: because you're self-aware?" I said, earnestly—trying with all my might to sound like the dull and harmless scientist I actually was (and am).

"All animals are self-aware," Alice replied, calmly. "I'm aware that I'm human. I love and respect my fellow men, no matter what the circumstances of their birth might have been."

"How do you feel about pigs?" I asked.

"I love and respect them too," she replied. "Even the ones that aren't human. I don't eat pork—or any other meat, come to that. How do you feel about pigs, Dr. Hitchens?"

I eat pork. I also eat bacon, and all kinds of other meat, but it didn't seem diplomatic to talk about that. "I don't think pigs are human, Alice," I told her. "I don't think they can become human, even with the aid of transplanted genes."

Her answer to that certainly wasn't the kind of answer I'd have expected from an ordinary teenager, or even an extraordinary one. "How did humans become humans, Dr. Hitchens?" she asked me. "A handful of extra genes, obligingly delivered up by mutation, do you suppose? Perhaps—but perhaps not. Just because a human and a chimpanzee only share ninety-nine per cent of their genes, it doesn't necessarily follow that the variant one per cent is solely responsible for the differences. Even if it is, it's not a matter of different protein-making stocks. It's a matter of *control*. The one per cent is almost entirely homeotic." She might have been parroting something Hemans or one of his co-workers had said, but I didn't think so. She seemed confident that she was making sense, and that she understood the import of her argument—but she hesitated, just in case I didn't.

"Go on," I said, interestedly. The invitation was enough to set her off with the bit between her pearly, neatly-aligned teeth.

"Most of what it took to turn apes into men," she told me, as if it were a matter of absolute certainty, "was a handful of modifications to the ways in which genes were switched on and off as the cells of the developing embryo became specialized. You don't need dozens of extra genes to grow a bigger brain. All you need is for a few more unspecialized cells to become brain cells. You don't need dozens of extra genes to make a clever hand or stand upright, either. What you need is for the cells that differentiate into bone and muscle to distribute themselves in slightly different ways within the developing embryo. Becoming human isn't so very difficult, once you get the hang of it. Cows could do it. Sheep too. Lions and tigers, horses and elephants, dolphins and seals. Dogs, probably; cats, maybe; rats, perhaps; birds, probably not. You have to get right down to snakes and sharks before you can say that there's no chance at all. We all start out as eggs, Dr. Hitchens, and every egg that can make a pig or a donkey or a goat can probably make a human, if it only invests enough effort in shaping the brain and the hand and the back-bone. That might be an unsettling thought, but it's true."

It *was* an unsettling thought. I had already thought it, and it had already unsettled me—but the fact that Alice was prepared to confront me with it—perhaps on behalf of Hemans, Rawlingford, and Bradby, but more probably on her own initia-tive—was even more unsettling.

I reminded myself again that it might be a lie, a careful hoax intended to persuade me, falsely, that the men from Commoner's Isle had mastered godlike powers—but if it was, it was begin-ning to work.

* * * * * * *

"Would you like to live as other humans do, Alice?" I asked, ostentatiously leading with my chin. "Would you like to go to school, to university, to get a job, to get married one day and have children of your own?"

"I do live as other humans do," she replied, blandly refusing to see what I was getting at. "I've been to school. I expect that I'll do all the other things when the time comes." Her tone said that she didn't expect any such thing—that she expected to be pursued and captured, shot at worst and imprisoned at best. Her tone told me that she expected to have to fight for her life, let alone her entitlements as a human being, and that she wasn't about to take any bullshit from me while she had an axe in her hands.

"I'm not sure that you'll be allowed to do anything that other teenagers routinely do, Alice," I admitted, figuring that it was best to pose as the honest man I really am. "The scien-tists who shaped your brain, hand, and backbone were breaking the law. That's not your fault, of course, but the fact remains that you're the product of illegal genetic engineering. The law doesn't consider you to be a human being—and nor do the vast majority of human beings. All the things you hope you'll be able to do depend on the willingness of human society to admit you as a member, and that willingness simply isn't there. There's a sense, you see, in which it isn't enough just to define yourself as human—it's for human society as a whole to decide who belongs to it and who doesn't."

"No it isn't," she replied, promptly. "White people once refused to define black people as human, and German gentiles once refused to define Jews as human, but that didn't make the black people or the Jews any less human than they were. The only people who became less human because of those refusals were the people who tried to deny humanity to others. They were the ones who were refusing to love and respect their fellow men, the ones who weren't acting morally."

She was carrying the argument better than any fourteen-year-old should have been able to, and she wasn't trying to conceal the fact. I couldn't help wondering whether that might be a mistake, if she ever got the chance to plead her case before a wider audience. Nobody loves a smartarse, especially if the smartarse is a jumped-up pig. If you want to pass for human, you can't afford to be too good at it—and, as Alice had stubbornly insisted on pointing out, real humans frequently aren't very good at it at all.

"Do you think the scientists who made you were acting morally?" I asked. "They knew what kind of a world they were bringing you into. They knew what would happen—to you as well as to them—when they were found out, and they must have known that they'd eventually be found out."

"I could understand a slave who was reluctant to bear children who would also be slaves," Alice replied, "but I can also understand those who didn't refuse. They knew that they were human, and that their children were human too, and they had to hope that the fact would one day be recognized. To have refused to bear children would have been giving in to evil, consenting to its effects."

"Why do you think the men who made you destroyed their records, Alice?" I asked. "Why do you think they were so eager to burn them that they endangered your life—not to mention mine?" *Because they didn't want anyone to now the true extent of their success*, I told myself. *Because they wanted to be able to run this bluff.*

"Because they wanted to be able to use their knowledge as a bargaining chip," Alice said. "For our benefit as well as their own. If you'd got the records, you'd have put a stop to everything. Because you didn't, we still have something up our sleeves." She seemed to think that it was a reasonably good argument— which implied that in spite of all her hard-won sophistication she really was the mere child she appeared to be.

Theoretically, I thought, an animal embryo modified to replicate human form ought to develop as neotenously as a human embryo, and an animal brain modified to accommodate all that a human brain could accommodate ought not to be educated any more rapidly. If so, Alice shouldn't be any cleverer than a fully human child reared in similarly exceptional circumstances— but without access to her school records, I knew that it would be dangerous to take too much for granted, or too little.

"No one will bargain with them, Alice," I lied. "They broke the law, and they'll be punished. Perhaps it's best if their discoveries are lost. That way, no one will be able to repeat their error."

"That's silly, Dr. Hitchens," Alice said, calmly. "If it's a mystery, that will just make more people interested in solving it. And if it's not so very difficult to solve...."

She left it there, as if it were some kind of threat. She was still trying to convince me, in her own subtle fashion, that my world had just ended and that another had just begun, and that if she and all her fugitive kind were slaughtered by the ARU's guns they would be martyrs to a great and unstoppable cause

"Have you read *The Island of Dr. Moreau*, Alice?" I asked.

"Yes," she said.

"What do you think of it?"

"It's a parable. It tells us that it takes more than a little cosmetic surgery and a few memorized laws to make people—*any* people—human. That's true. Whether humans are born or made, the test of their humanity is their behavior, their love and respect for their fellow humans."

"How many naturally-born humans would pass that test, do you think?" I asked.

"I have no idea," she replied. "Lots, I hope."

"Would I pass it?" I asked.

"I have to hope so," she said, casually, "Don't I, Dr. Hitchens? But I don't actually know. What do you think?"

"There wasn't supposed to be any shooting," I told her. "The police were supposed to put everyone under arrest. If your makers hadn't set fire to the house and told everyone to scatter and run, no one would have been hurt. Then, the matter of your humanity could have been decided in a proper and reasonable manner." I hoped that I was telling the truth, but I had a niggling feeling that the plan to which I'd been admitted wasn't the whole one. The GE-Crime Unit *had* called up the Armed Response Unit.

"Well," said Alice, "that isn't the way things worked out, is it? It seems to me that the matter of our humanity, as you put it, has already been decided. You'll never be sure, of course, that you've got us all. Even if Ed and Kath can't get to the old ice-house, and even if they run into the police when they do, you'll never be sure how many of us got out under the noses of your surveillance unit before they figured out that the apparently obvious wasn't necessarily true."

She was definitely feeding me a line there, but I couldn't tell whether she was feeding it to me because it was false, or because it was true. I thought the time had come for me to make a grab for the axe and take control of the situation. I was probably right—or would have been, if I'd actually succeeded.

I suppose, on reflection, that I was lucky she only swiped me with the flat of the blade. If she'd hit me that hard with the edge, she could easily have fractured my skull.

* * * * * * *

When I woke up again I was in a hospital bed. My head wasn't aching any more and my eyes weren't stinging, but I felt spaced-out and bleary. It took a few minutes for me to remember where I might have been, if things had worked out differently.

I learned, in due course, that the fire brigade had found me while searching the cellars for survivors and had handed me over to the paramedics before midnight. Unfortunately, the medication they'd fed me ensured that I didn't wake up again until thirty-six hours later, so I'd missed all of the official post-mortems as well as the remainder of the action—but the urgency with which the Unit moved to debrief me reassured me that the adventure still had a long way to run.

"There were three of them," I told Inspector Headley. "I only saw one of them, and it was too dark to see her features clearly. She had blonde hair, cut to shoulder length, and very even teeth that caught what little light there was when she smiled. I couldn't swear that I'd be able to recognize her again, dead or alive. Her name was Alice. She called the others Ed and Kath. They were trying to reach an old ice-house on the edge of the lake, but the tunnel had been blocked off. Did you get them?"

"What else did they tell you?" Inspector Headley countered, Jesuitically.

That wasn't a game I intended to play. "Did you get them?" I repeated.

"No," he conceded, reluctantly. "But the tunnel was still blocked off—had been for the best part of a century. Nobody got out that way."

"But you didn't pick up three stragglers in the house?"

"No," he admitted, "but if you'll pardon my pointing it out, Dr. Hitchens, I'm the one who's supposed to be debriefing you. Yes, they *could* have been piglets—and no, we wouldn't have believed that if we hadn't had the autopsy reports your colleagues carried out on the ones we shot. Personally, I'd have passed every one of the corpses as human, and I wasn't the only one who wouldn't believe otherwise until your colleagues came back to us with the results of the DNA tests—but we didn't capture any of the piglets alive. Now, would you mind telling me exactly what happened to you?"

"Not at all," I said. "But there's one thing I need to know. Was the shooting always part of the plan? Did you always intend to kill the children?"

He seemed genuinely shocked. "Of course not." he said. "They wouldn't stop. They just kept on running. They *were* warned."

The problem was, I knew, that they'd already been warned. They'd had far too many warnings for their own good.

I recited the whole story, in as much detail as I could remember, into Headley's tape-recorder. I watched his expression becoming more troubled as I spoke, and I gathered that Special Branch was just as confused as I was as to what might be real and what might be bluff.

"This has turned into a real can of worms," he told me, when he'd switched the recorder off. "We don't know how many of the piglets might be missing. We've been waist-deep in lawyers ever since we got Hemans and his friends under lock and key, including lawyers claiming to represent your fugitive friend and her alleged litter-mates."

"How many died?" I asked.

"Only seven," he said, so weakly that it was obvious that seven was either far too many or far too few. "Three of them were real humans. Unfortunate, but it *was* their own fault. I think they wanted us to shoot, to put us in the wrong. I think Hemans told those kids to keep running no matter what, because he *knew* that some of them would be killed. Cynical bastard."

I had already told him that Bradby had warned his experimental subjects that an attempt might be made to wipe them out, but I wasn't convinced that the warning had been cynical. It seemed to me that he might have been honestly concerned, and rightly so. If Alice and the others *had* got away....

"We might not find it easy to prove in court that the other four *weren't* real humans," I told Headley, although that news must already have been broken to him. "Did the DNA tests throw up any evidence that they were transgenics?"

Headley shook his head. He seemed to understand the implications of the question. Transplanting human genes into animals was clearly and manifestly illegal, but if Alice had told me the truth, that wasn't what had been done to her. If Alice really was a pig through and through, genetically speaking, then there was a slim possibility that Hemans' lawyers could argue that what he and his colleagues had done wasn't illegal at all. And if Alice was as human as she seemed to be in every respect except genetically, her lawyers might have a field day trying to establish exactly what the law might and ought to mean by "human"—assuming that the Unit ever caught up with her.

Whatever had been intended, it was obvious that the raid had been a colossal cock-up. It would be up to the minister to pull everyone's irons out of the fire, and to look at the broader implications of what we now knew. Men like me were the minister's eyes and brains, so it would be up to us to figure out what the real implications of the Animal Farm fiasco might be. Governments had been brought down by matters of a far more trivial nature and it was too late to hope that the situation could be contained. The cat was already out of the bag—or the pig from the poke.

Headley admitted, when I questioned him further, that without the records that had gone up in smoke, there was no way to know for sure how many experimental "piglets" there had been. They had always been kept inside, away from the prying eyes of the surveillance team, who wouldn't have recognized them for what they were if and when they'd caught glimpses of them. Their creators and the piglets themselves knew the real number, but no one would ever know whether any figure they might offer was to be trusted. Now that we knew for sure that the piglets could pass for human, at least while they were still alive and kicking, we had to consider the possibility that some of them already were passing, in Brighton or in London, or anywhere at all.

If my evidence could be taken at face value, at least three piglets had escaped. Headley told me that other debriefings had produced evidence that at least two more, both female, might have evaded their pursuers in the woods behind the manor house. He was enough of an intellectual to understand my observation that it added up to a better breeding population than God had placed in Eden or Lot had led from Sodom.

As a scientist, of course, I wasn't at all sure of that—engineered organisms hardly ever breed true, and it was perfectly possible that even if the ersatz girls could produce offspring, the offspring in question might have snouts and tails—but we had to consider the worst possible case. Bringing human-seeming babies out of a sow's womb might sound no more likely than making silk purses out of sow's ears, but we had moved into unknown territory, scientifically speaking. What did I know, given that I had never dabbled in illicit experimentation? What did any of us know, unless and until Hemans, Rawlingford, and Bradby condescended to enlighten us?

I suppose that I was lucky to be kept on the project, given that I'd ended up in hospital, but I was needed. I'd been brought in to analyze data, not to conduct interrogations, but the changed circumstances necessitated my taking a new role. My conversation with Alice had put me one up on my colleagues, so I was hustled out of the hospital with a bagful of pills as soon as the doctors could be persuaded to let me go.

"We haven't charged them yet," Headley explained to me, while I was being taken to the police station where Hemans, Rawlingford, and Bradby were to be questioned. "At the moment, they're supposed to be cooperating voluntarily with our enquiries. We're keeping in mind the possibility of charging them with arson, kidnapping, and child molesting, but we want to see how they and their lawyers are going to play it before we go in hard. If they're prepared to come clean and tell us where their backed-up data is—assuming they do have backups somewhere—we might still be able to tidy up the mess."

It seemed like a reasonable assumption to me, although I wasn't sure how reasonable our mad scientists would prove to be.

* * * * * * *

I went into the interview with Hemans thinking that I was the only one on our side who'd actually thought the matter through, and the only one to have grasped the full complexity of the issue. I thought that I might be approaching the high-point of my career—a taller peak than I had ever dreamed of scaling—if only I could keep my wits about me.

The interview was being video-taped, of course, but the tape wouldn't be admissible in court.

I couldn't measure the exact combination of emotions that mingled in Hemans' expression as he looked at me, but there was at least a little contempt and at least a little distaste. I couldn't understand that. When I'd first met Hemans, way back in '06, he'd been working in the public sector himself, helping to tidy up the loose ends of the Human Genome Project—but even before the HGP had delivered its treasure, its workers were being sucked into private enterprise. Comparative genomics was supposed to be the next big thing. I didn't hold it against Hemans that he had jumped ship, and I couldn't see any reason why he'd hold it against me that I hadn't.

It was obvious by '06 that the attempts that had been made to patent human gene sequences and develop diagnostic kits based on HGP sequencing data wouldn't bear much commercial fruit in the immediate future, because they'd be tied up in the courts for years. The precedents for patenting animal genes had, however, been established by the Harvard oncomouse and all the disease-models that had followed in its wake. Given that all mammals had homologues for at least ninety-five per cent of human genes, the obvious thing for ambitious biotech companies to do was to steer around the moral minefield by concentrating their immediate efforts on what could be done with animals. Pigs were already contributing organs for xeno-transplantation, so they were a natural target for sequencing and potential exploitation, and there was nothing surprising in the fact that Hemans and his co-workers had decided to concentrate their efforts in that direction. What was surprising, though—and disturbing—was that they'd decided to cross the line that the European Court had drawn regarding the uses to which human genes could be put. What was even more surprising, to me—and even more disturbing—was that the way Hemans looked at me when I sat down to question him showed not the slightest trace of guilt or shame. That made me wary, and wari-ness made me even more punctilious than usual.

"First of all, Dr. Hemans" I said, carefully, "I've been asked to apologize on behalf of His Majesty's Government for the unfortunate deaths that occurred during the course of the police raid on Hollinghurst Manor. The police had reason to believe that a serious breach of the law had taken place, and they were proceeding in full accordance with the law, but they deeply regret the fact that so many of those fleeing the building refused to stop when challenged, forcing the Armed Response Unit to open fire."

"Never mind the bullshit, Hitchens," he countered, curling his lip disdainfully. "Are they going to charge us, and if so, what with?"

"Okay," I said, easing my tone according to plan, in order to imply—falsely, and perhaps not very convincingly—that there would be no more bullshit. "They haven't decided yet whether to charge you, or with what. There are several different schools of thought. As soon as they catch up with one of the escapers—and they will—the hawks will want to move. You have until then to make your offer, if you have one to make."

"Aren't you the one who's supposed to be making offers?" Hemans countered.

"No," I said. "I'm not. You're the one who knows whether the experiments being carried out at Hollinghurst Manor were illegal, and to what extent. You're the one who knows the identities of the children who were living in the house, and the extent of the irregularities surrounding the registration of their births, their schooling, and whatever else might come up. If you want to offer explanations and excuses before the police draw their own conclusions, you'd best do it quickly."

He didn't laugh, but he didn't seem to be intimidated either. "You must have determined the identities of the ones you killed," he said.

"On the contrary," I replied, carefully. "The police haven't been able to match the bodies with any public records or any missing persons. That is, in itself, cause for concern. There is no record of any application for the custody of any children having been made by you or any of your colleagues, so the police are completely at a loss to understand how they came to be resident in the house—or why, given that they were resident in the house, they don't appear to have attended school or to be registered with a doctor, or...."

"This is a waste of time," Hemans interrupted. "If you're just going to pretend that you don't know anything, I think I'll wait for the formal interrogation, when my lawyer can decide how little I ought to say."

"I spoke to one of the children in the aftermath of the fire," I told him, abruptly. "She seemed to believe that she wasn't the product of a human womb. Did you tell her that?"

"We told her the truth about her origins," he answered.

"And what was the truth?" I asked.

"That she was the product of a scientific experiment."

"An illegal experiment?"

"Certainly not. Neither I nor any of my colleagues has ever transplanted any human genes into any other animal. We have been exceedingly careful to work within the existing law."

"But you haven't published any of your work," I pointed out. "You haven't applied for any patents. Even by private sector standards, that's unusually secretive."

"We haven't published because the work wasn't complete,"

Hemans retorted, "and now, thanks to your murderous interference, it never will be. We haven't applied for any patents because we aren't ready. Not that it's any of your business—or anyone else's. Rawley, Brad, and I were able to finance this project ourselves."

"The police didn't set fire to the house," I pointed out. "It isn't their fault that your equipment and records were destroyed. You did that yourselves."

"No we didn't," Hemans lied. "The fire was an accident—the result of the confusion generated by the raid."

"Your work wasn't merely self-funded," I pointed out, not wishing to pursue that particular red herring. "It was clandestine. You've made every possible effort to keep it secret. You seem to have been using children as experimental subjects—children of whom there is no official record of any kind. Even if they were your own children, that would be illegal. If they aren't...there's a great deal that requires explanation."

"And you already know what the explanation is, so we'd make better progress if you cut to the chase."

"I'm sorry," I said, "but I don't know any such thing. I don't know that the story the girl gave me was anything but a pack of lies, cooked up to make your work seem much more successful than it was. We can't interrogate the dead, so we have no way to know whether the individuals identified by genetic fingerprinting as pigs in human form were capable of speech, let alone rational thought. I'm certain in my own mind that the scene in the cellar was staged—how else would the three of them have been able to disappear, given that the exit they were ostensibly aiming for was blocked?"

"Maybe they found another," Hemans said. "Who did you talk to?"

"She called herself Alice."

"We all called her Alice," he assured me. "She's not among the dead, then? And she did get away from the gunmen?"

"They *will* find her," I told him. "Whoever and whatever she is, she can't hide. Wherever she went, there'll be a trail. This is the twenty-first century. Nobody can hide for long."

"That includes the people chasing her," he pointed out. "It's one thing to surround a house in the middle of a wood for one night only, and quite another to conduct a nationwide manhunt for weeks on end. How many are you looking for?"

"How many were there?"

He still didn't smile, but he knew that that was one of the best cards he held up his sleeve. If we'd been fooled into thinking there were at least seven, when there were really only four, we might keep searching for a long time—and he was right about the difficulty of hiding a nationwide manhunt, whether that was the right word for it or not.

"Why did you do it?" I asked him, abruptly. "It's such a strange thing to attempt. Why did you even try?"

"You're a geneticist yourself, Dr. Hitchens," he replied. "You, of all people, should understand."

I thought I did. I thought that now was the time to show him that I did. "If you really did do it," I said, "I can only conclude that it was by accident. I can't imagine that you had the least idea when you started out just how successful your experiment in Applied Homeotics would be. I can only suppose that you started out trying to figure out what the limits of embryonic plasticity were, and that you wouldn't have dared to superimpose a human anatomical template on the pig embryos if you had realized that it would work so spectacularly. Once you found out what the babies were actually capable of, you must have been thrown into a quandary, unable to decide what to do next—so you simply carried on, monitoring their development in secret, not knowing when or how to stop. You must have been grateful when the police finally made their move, taking the matter out of your hands."

He looked at me with what seemed to me to be a new respect. "You keep saying *if,*" he pointed out, "but you don't really believe there's an if, do you? You know perfectly well that Alice is the real thing."

"I don't *know* it," I told him, truthfully. "You're the one that *knows*. How clever is she, do you think?"

"Not so very clever," he told me, feigning slight reluctance. "Precocious, but not so very far from the norm. Only human. But her parents *were* pigs, Dr. Hitchens. We did do it—and we're prepared to defend ourselves in any court you care to haul us into. We're prepared to defend it all the way. I like your label, by the way. *Applied Homeotics* sounds so much more dignified than Brad's *homeoboxing*. If you know that that's what it is, you must also know that it isn't going to go away. Not now."

Hemans didn't just mean that he and his colleagues were prepared to defend the legality of their experiment and the merits of their new biotechnology. He meant that they were prepared to defend the humanity of its first products. Maybe he *was* just a little bit grateful to have his hand forced, but he had decided long ago exactly how he would play it when the forcing started. He might have fallen into a godlike role by accident, but he had accepted the responsibility that went with it. Our side hadn't, yet. Our side had gone in blind and trigger-happy. That wasn't my fault, but I'd have to carry the can along with everyone else if things continued to get more and more screwed-up.

"I also know that it can't be *merely* a matter of tweaking development times," I said. "Pigs might have homologues of ninety-eight-point-six per cent of human genes, but that still isn't enough. Whatever you told Alice, you had to make up a substantial fraction of the remainder. Maybe you copied the sequences from a contig library, used YACs, to multiply them and then delivered them into the embryo by retrovirus, but that doesn't make it legal. Human sequences are human sequences, even if you build them base by base, and when you transplanted them into pig embryos you broke the law."

"We didn't transplant anything," Hemans insisted. "We didn't break any laws. Put us in the dock and we'll prove it. But you don't want to do that, do you?"

"That depends," I hedged—but his lip curled again, and I knew that I had to play the game more openly than that. "You have to give me more," I went on. "You have to give me some idea of what you actually did, if you didn't transplant the human sequences."

"Why should I?" he countered, bluntly.

I wasn't speaking for myself, but I had to make the offer. "Because we might still be able to put this thing away," I told him. "We might not be able to unmake the discovery, but we might be able to save ourselves from its consequences, at least for a while."

"No," he said, wearily as well as firmly. "We can't. We thought about it—Rawley, Brad, and I—but we decided that we couldn't. We're not policemen, Dr. Hitchens, we're not politicians, and we're not lawyers. We couldn't put it away, and we still can't. Not because it wouldn't do any good, although it wouldn't, but because it simply wouldn't be right. We're not going to cooperate, Dr. Hitchens. We're going to take it to the bitter end. They're human, and every ovum produced by every animal on our farms and in our zoos is potentially human. That's the way it is, and we can't just ignore the fact. We can't make any deal that doesn't make the whole matter public."

"You were the ones who never published," I pointed out. "You were the ones who kept on working in secret."

"It *wasn't finished*," he told me. I was sure that he wasn't trying to wriggle out of it.

"If you're telling the truth," I told him, "it never will be. But you still have to convince me of that."

He was still looking at me with faint disgust, because of what he thought I'd become, but in the end he had to loosen up. Like me, he didn't have any alternative.

* * * * * * *

Even when we'd reviewed the tape and gone through it step by step, the senior Special Branch men and most of the Home Office staff still didn't get it.

"Okay," said the Unit's top man, "so the one you talked to was smart and kind of cute—but she isn't ever going to get to court, let alone to daytime TV. She's a pig. An animal. We *can* send her to the slaughterhouse. We can get rid of them all, if we decide that's the appropriate thing to do."

"We wouldn't necessarily have to go that far," one of the junior ministers put in. "Once people know what she really is, that will color everyone's view of her. It doesn't matter how cute or clever she is, nobody is going to make out a serious case for making any more like her. Let's not throw the baby out with the bathwater here."

What he meant, of course, was "let's not throw the bathwater out with the baby." He figured that there might be useful purposes to which the technics might be put—secret purposes, of course, if the legal advisors decided that the whole area was legally out of bounds, but government-approvable purposes nevertheless. He was thinking about designing ultra-smart animals for use as spies and soldiers. He'd probably been a fan of the wrong kind of comic books in his youth. He wasn't thinking *Boy's Own Adventures*; he was thinking *Reality Is What You Can Get Away With*.

The permanent under-secretary knew better, of course. "She was right about the records," he observed, reflectively. "The fact that we failed to recover them makes it a mystery. As soon as the rumor spreads that you can turn animal embryos into pass-able human beings with standard equipment and a chicken-feed budget, everybody and his cousin will be curious to know how it's done. We left it far too late to make our move—and I'm talking years, not weeks. We should have applied the new laws as soon as we had reason to believe that they'd been broken."

"Without the records," I said, quietly, "there's no way to be sure that even the new laws *have* been broken. And that makes it an even better mystery."

"She's a *pig*, Hitchens," the plain-speaking policeman pointed out. "She's a pig that looks like a little girl. If that isn't illegal genetic engineering, what is?"

"If Hemans is telling the truth," I said, "Applied Homeotics isn't genetic engineering in the legal sense at all. He had to make up most of the missing one-point-four per cent somehow, but if he'd simply tried to transplant or import it he'd probably have failed in exactly the same way that most other attempts to transplant whole blocks of genes have failed. Assuming that what he told me was true—and I'm inclined to believe him—his way is *much* better, and it's not against the law. If this ever gets to court, we might have to hope that the back-up records really have been destroyed—because if they haven't, and Hemans, Rawlingford, and Bradby can use them to mount a successful defense, we're going to look *really* stupid."

"That won't happen," the permanent under-secretary said. "If they want any kind of life after acquittal, they'll make a deal. They'll give us their secrets *and* they'll sign a non-disclosure agreement. The real question is whether other people will be able to duplicate their work anyhow, guided by the knowledge—or even the rumor—that it's possible."

"Who but the wackos would want to?" asked the chief inspector. "Do you really think the world is full of people who want to turn out imitation human beings? Even the worst kinds of animal liberation lunatics aren't about to start clamoring for every piglet's right to walk on two legs and wear a dress. This is the real world. Some animals are a hell of a lot more equal than others, and we're them, and that's the way it's going to stay."

It was time to cut through the bullshit to the real heart of the matter. "You're not taking Alice seriously enough," I told them. "You haven't listened properly to what she and Hemans said. Suppose she's right. Suppose she isn't a pig pretending to be a human. Suppose she really *is* a human."

"She's not," the policeman said, flatly. "Genetically, she's a pig. End of story."

"According to her," I pointed out, "genetics doesn't enter into it. Human is as human does—and her brothers and sisters were the ones who got gunned down because they didn't believe that their fellow men would open fire on a bunch of unarmed children. Without her school records, and until she consents to be tested again, we can only guess at her IQ, but on the evidence of my conversation and Hemans' assurances I'd be willing to bet that it's a little bit higher than the average teenager's. You haven't yet begun to consider the implications of that fact."

"*If* pigs in human form are smarter than real humans, that's all the more reason for making sure that all the world's pigs stay in their sties," the man from Special Branch insisted. The minister was content to listen, for the time being.

"If Hemans is telling the truth," I went on, disregarding the policeman's interruption, "he and his colleagues didn't need to transplant any genes to make her human. DNA-analysis of the dead bodies supports that contention. The difference between a human being and a chimpanzee, as Alice pointed out, is very small. The most important differences are in the homeotic genes—the genes that control the expression of other genes, thus determining which cells in a developing embryo are going to specialize as liver cells or as neurons, and how the structures built out of specialized cells are going to be laid out within an anatomical frame. If you have an alternative control mechanism that can take over the work of those controlling genes, they become redundant—and as long as the embryo you're working with has the stocks of genes required to make all the specialized kinds of cells you need, you can make *any* kind of an embryo grow into any form you required. You could make human beings out of pigs and cows, tigers and elephants, exactly as Alice said—and *vice versa*."

"That's bullshit," the policeman said. "You've said all along that they had to make up the difference. We have to have the extra genes that make us human."

"That's true," I agreed, wondering how simple I could make it, and how simple I'd need to make it before he could understand. "And until today I'd assumed, just as you had, that the extra genes would have to be transplanted, or that they'd have to synthesized from library DNA and imported—but that almost never works with whole sets of genes, because mere possession of a gene is only part of the story. You have to control its expression—and that's what Applied Homeotics is all about. We've become so accustomed to genetic engineering by transplantation that we've lost sight of other approaches—but Hemans and his friends are lateral thinkers. We didn't get to be human by having genes transplanted into us—we *grew* the new genes *in situ*. Only a few million of the three billion base pairs in the human genome are actually expressed, but it's an insult to the rest to call it junk DNA, the way we used to. Most of it is satellite repeat sequences, but in between the satellites there are hundreds of thousands of truncated genes and pseudogenes, all of them in a constant state of crossgenerational flux because of transposon activity.

"Pigs might only have homologues of ninety-eight-point-six per cent of our genes, but they also have homologues of almost all the protogenes making up the difference. Those protogenes are not only present within the pig genome, they're mostly in the right sites. Hemans, Rawlingford, and Bradby didn't need to transplant any human DNA—all they had to do was tweak the pig DNA that was already in place. And as Alice said when she had me trapped in Wonderland, if you can do it to a pig, you can do it to a cow—and given that the common ancestor relating us to rats and bats seems to be more recent than the one relating us to pigs, you can probably do it to a hundred or a thousand other species."

"It still sounds like bullshit to me," the policeman repeated, as if he were some obstinate DNA satellite hopelessly intent on taking over an entire genome.

"You might not like its implications, Chief Inspector," I said, tiredly, "but that's not enough to make it bullshit. I don't know *exactly* how Hemans did it, because he isn't going to tell us until he gets some guarantees, but I already know how I'd go about trying to copy the trick, now that I know that it can be done. Transforming and activating the protogenes is probably the easy part, given that every sequencer in the world is avid to learn how to write as well as read the language of the bases. I'm pretty sure I could figure out a way to do that. If I could also figure out a way to delay an embryo's phylotypic stage—that's the moment at which the control of an embryo's development is transferred from the maternal environment to the embryo's own genes—I might be able to stop the homeotic genes kicking in at all. Given that the onset of the phylotypic stage is much later in some species than others that doesn't seem be any great hurdle to leap. A careful inspection of the research Hemans, Rawlingford, and Bradby published before they got together at Hollinghurst Manor suggests that they were probably using human maternal tissue as a mediator in the embryonic induction process. That's not genetic engineering, of course—there's no law against interspecific transplantation of mature tissues or the use of human somatic cells in tissue-cultures. Believe me, sir: Applied Homeotics is a whole new field of biotechnology. None of the existing rules apply."

"So you're telling me that every fucking farm animal in the realm—not to mention every household pet—is potentially human?" The Special Branch man was looking at me with as much contempt and distaste as Hemans had, but with even less justification.

"No," I said, patiently. "I'm telling you that the embryos they produce as parents are now potentially human. It still adds a whole new dimension to the ethics of animal usage, but we don't yet know how far that dimension extends. We can be reasonably sure that birds and reptiles don't have the required stocks of protein-template genes, and some of the smaller mammals probably don't have them either, but the question of where the limits of potential metamorphosis actually lie is a minor one. The point is that unless we're the victims of a monstrous hoax, humanity is determined almost entirely by the development of the embryo. If so, Hemans is right. Alice and all her kind are as human as you or I. An even more important question, of course, is what this kind of technology might allow us to make of human beings."

I paused for effect, but nobody jumped in with an exclamation of astonishment. They were all waiting, guardedly, to see what came next.

"We, after all, are merely *nature*'s humans," I told them. "We're a product of the rough-and-ready process of natural selection, and control of the expression of *our* genes has been left to other genes. Homeotic genes were never an ideal solution to the problem of embryo-formation—they were just the best improvisation that DNA could come up with on its own. Alice's humanity is the product of relatively unskilled artifice—and the evidence we've so far seen suggests that relatively unskilled artifice might already be the slightly better maker of men. If it isn't, then it certainly will be, just as soon as we bring our ingenuity fully to bear on the problem.

"The genie's out of the bottle, gentlemen. We can pass all the laws we like against the genetic engineering of human beings, and we can make sure, if we care to, that what Hemans, Rawlingford, and Bradby have actually done to pig embryos will in future fall within the scope of those laws—but that won't alter the fact that human beings and the world they have made are imperfect in more ways than any of us would care to count, and that Hemans, Rawlingford, and Bradby have found a new way to allow us to set to work on those imperfections. If Alice is telling the truth, we've already passed through the looking-glass, and there's no way back. You might be able to stop the animals walking and talking, but you won't be able to stop the people. If a mere pig can be a better human than any of us, *imagine what our own children might become, with the proper assistance!*"

The minister and his junior nodded gravely, but that was just the legacy of good schooling by their image-consultants. The chief inspector looked dumbfounded. The permanent under-secretary was the only one who was keeping up, after his own crude fashion. "You're talking about building a master race," he said, reflexively. If in doubt, hoist a scarecrow.

"I'm talking about D-I-Y supermen," I told him, frankly. "I'm talking about something that can be done with standard equipment on a chicken-feed budget, after a little bit of practice on the family pet. I'm talking anarchy, not mad dictators. If you intend to make a deal with the Three Musketeers, you need to know what cards they're holding. It's still conceivable that they're bluffing, and that Alice was just feeding us a line, but I can't believe that—and if they're *not* bluffing, the old world has already ended. The GE-Crime Unit will catch up with the runaways eventually, but it's already too late. Their story has been told, and *will* be told, again and again and again."

Nobody told me I was crazy. The policeman might have lacked imagination, but he wasn't stupid enough to continue to argue that his reflexive prejudices were worth more than my educated judgment. "We could still shoot the lot," he muttered— but he knew, deep down, that it wouldn't do the trick, even if that option could be put back on the agenda.

"What *can* we do?" asked the permanent under-secretary, who had already moved reluctantly on to the next stage.

I knew that it wouldn't be easy to persuade him, but nobody ever said that working for the Home Office was going to be easy. The instinct of government is to govern, to take control, to keep as tight a hold on the reins as humanly possible.

"Basically," I said, "we have two options. We can be Napoleon, or we can be Snowball. Neither way will be easy— in fact, I suspect that all hell has already been let loose—so I figure that we might as well try to do the right thing. For once in our lives, let's not even try to stand in the way of progress. I know you're not going to be grateful for the advice, but my vote is that we simply let them all go and let them get on with it."

"Let public opinion take care of them, you mean," the junior minister said, still trying his damnedest to misunderstand. "Let the mob take care of them, the way they take care of child molesters."

"No," I said. "I mean, let artifice take its course. Let the pioneers of Applied Homeotics do what they have to, and what they can. Even the pigs."

It *wasn't* easy to persuade them, but Hemans and his collaborators had a battery of lawyers on their side, as well as reason and stubbornness, and in the end, the situation simply wasn't governable, even by the government. Eventually, I made them see that.

They weren't grateful, of course, but I never expected them to be. Sometimes, you just have to settle for being right.

* * * * * * *

By the time I saw Alice again she was twenty-two and famous, although she never went anywhere without her bodyguards. She came to my lab to see what I was working on, and to thank me for the small part I had played in winning her precarious freedom.

"You did save my life," I pointed out, when we'd done the tour and had time to reflect.

"That was Ed and Kath," she admitted. "They were the ones who picked you up and dragged you down the stairs. All I did was hit you with the axe when you tried to grab it."

"But you hit me with the flat bit, not the edge," I said. "If you'd hit me with the edge, I'd be dead—and so, I suspect, would you."

"They really wanted to kill us all," she said, as if it were still very hard for her to comprehend.

"Only some of them—and only because they didn't understand," I told her, hoping that it was the truth. "None of us understood, not even Hemans, Rawlingford, and Bradby, although they'd had longer to think about it than anybody else. None of us really understood what it meant to be human, because we'd never had to explore the limits of the argument before—and none of us understood what scope there was for us to be more than human. We simply didn't realize how easy it is to be creative, once you have the basic stock of protein-producing genes—and protogenes—to work with. Maybe we should have, given what we knew about the diversity of Earthly species and the unreliability of mutation as a means of change, but we didn't. We needed a lesson to bring it home to us. How does it feel to be accepted as human just as the species is becoming obsolete?"

"My children will have the same chances as anyone else's," she pointed out. I wasn't so sure about that. She was now as human as anyone else, in law as well as in fact, but there were an awful lot of people who hadn't yet conceded the point. *My* children, on the other hand, really would have opportunities of which I had never dreamed ten years before; the people who wanted to reserve the privileges of creativity to imaginary gods wouldn't be able to stop my making sure of that.

"I was sorry to hear about Hemans," I said. Hemans had been taken out by a sniper eight months before. I had no reason to think that he and Alice were particularly close, but it seemed only polite to offer my condolences.

"Me too," she said. "It always upsets me to hear about my friends being shot."

"What happened at the manor really wasn't a conspiracy," I told her, although I'd never been *entirely* sure. "It was a genuine mistake. It's in the nature of Armed Response Units that they sometimes make mistakes, especially when they're working in the dark."

"I remember Dr. Hemans saying the same thing, afterwards," she admitted. "But some mistakes work out better than others, don't they?" She wasn't talking about the wayward ways of mutation. She was talking about the freak of chance that made me go on when I should have turned back, and the one that had made Ed and Kath pause to pull me out of the fume-filled corridor and down the cellar steps to safety. She was talking about the freak of chance that had made me go on when things got tough at the Home Office, blowing my career in government in order to make sure that nobody could put a lid on it even for a little while, and that the government couldn't even make a convincing show of governing the unfolding situation. She was talking about the mistake that Hemans and his colleagues had made when they decided to try something wildly ambitious, and found that it succeeded far too well. She was talking about the fact that science proceeds by trial and error, and that the errors sometimes turn out to be far more important than the intentions.

"Yes they do," I agreed. "If that weren't the case, progress wouldn't be possible at all. But it is. In spite of the fact that every significant advance in biotechnology is seen by the vast majority of horrified onlookers as a hideous perversion, we do make progress. We keep on passing through the looking glass, finding new worlds and new selves."

"You've been practicing," she said. "Do you really think you can talk yourself back into the corridors of power?"

"Not a snowball's chance in hell," I admitted. "But I did my bit for the revolution when I had the chance—and there aren't many of nature's humans who can say that, are there?"

"There never used to be," Alice admitted. "But things are different now. Human history is only just beginning."

THE LAST SUPPER

I had reserved the table at Trimalchio's way back in January, three months in advance. It was Tamara's birthday treat, and I figured that it would also be the perfect occasion to ask her to marry me. I wanted the circumstances to be as favorable as possible to maximize my chances of success. Rumor has it that a lot of celebrities were clamoring to get in, not because they had any inkling of what was about to happen but simply because it was Saturday night—and ever since Jerome had joined the hallowed ranks of superstar chefs Trimalchio's was *the* place to be seen—but Jerome wasn't the kind of man to start canceling reservations in order to accommodate TV personalities. He was a man of honor.

We had to run the gauntlet when we arrived, of course, but we weren't in the least frightened. We didn't feel that we were in any real danger from the anti-GM brigade who were baying for Jerome's blood. They were very noisy, of course—their cause had been on the skids for years, and the hard core had responded by becoming even more fanatical and dogmatic—but they knew from bitter experience that attacking customers qualified as a instant PR disaster. The only people in physical danger were the members of the increasingly vociferous counter-demonstration: Jerome's most ardent fans. For every banner proclaiming that he was a "Frankenstein Chef" or a "Kitchen Devil" there was one proclaiming him to be the messiah of the new gastronomy. There were even a few innocently hyperbolic placards carrying forward a grand old south London tradition that went way back to the 1960s and the first rock superstars, which simply said: JEROME IS GOD.

I found the sprint from the taxi quite exhilarating, although Tamara was a little bit annoyed that none of the paparazzi bothered to aim a flashbulb in our direction. I assured her that she looked as good as any of the models who were distracting their attention, and apologized for the fact that mere riches didn't make me as newsworthy as the sons of hereditary peers. She did look wonderful. Her peacock-blue evening dress and pastel hosiery were smart in the old sense as well as the new: a perfect refutation of the fashion-dinosaur argument that no matter how useful and hygienic they might be, active fibers would never look as good as ancient silks and velvets.

We didn't get the best table, of course. I suppose anyone who was there to be seen would have reckoned it the worst, and there was a distinct frown on Tamara's face as we were shown to it, but it suited my purposes very well. I wanted to be in a quiet corner, where Tamara and I would have eyes only for one another. We didn't have to worry about being unable to catch the waiter's eye—the staff at Trimalchio's was the best in London and it wasn't as if we had any choices to make. Jerome's clients were expected to eat and drink exactly what he provided and be grateful, and that was fine by us.

When she had first read about him in the Style section of the *Sunday Times*, Tamara had been as fervent in her support of Jerome's insistence on a set menu as she was of his determination to experiment with the best Genetically Modified foodstuffs that the world had to offer. "The man is a great artist," she had assured me, way back on New Year's Eve, in the course of what was then a purely hypothetical discussion. "He plans a meal as a perfect *ensemble*. He leaves pick-and-mix to the sweetie counter in Woolworth's, where it belongs. I was at uni with one of the geneticists he works with, and the firm has regular dealings with his suppliers. A lot of the GM-chefs are content to use modern substitutes for the ingredients in traditional recipes, but Jerome's a genuine inventor. He's right at the cutting edge of food science, and that puts him at the cutting edge of biotech itself. There'd be no point in offering his customers a choice of dishes because he uses so many ingredients that none of his clients—even his regulars—have ever had the opportunity of tasting. Even if they've encountered the raw materials, they can't possibly have the slightest idea what a master chef can do with them."

"I'm not sure I like the sound of that," I'd said at the time. "Individual tastes do differ—one man's meat and all that."

"Don't be silly, Ben," she'd said. "Faddy eating is the sign of a bad upbringing. Your petty prejudices are quite irrational. They have nothing to do with matters of *individual taste*."

I loved her very dearly. It would only have spoiled our mood to press the point that, however irrational it might be, there were certain foods I simply hated, especially anchovies and escargots, and certain others to which I strongly suspected that I might be allergic—including mussels and locusts, no matter what modifications had been made to their genomes.

"A great chef is a great artist," Tamara had added. "His customers have to have faith in him. He has every right to demand that they trust his judgment."

"I guess you're right," I had admitted, as the seeds of my plan had taken root. As we took our seats and the waiter handed Tamara a card headed SUPPER: DIRECTORY OF COURSES I crossed my fingers, hoping that if anything turned up that I didn't like I would either be able to stomach it in spite of my inclinations or dispose of it surreptitiously. The one thing I couldn't do, of course, was leave it on the plate. Newspaper reports alleged that Jerome was wont to emerge from his kitchen wielding a heavy ladle in response to that kind of insult. I could certainly expect a negative answer to my proposal if we were asked to leave in mid-meal—and the bored paparazzi inevitably took a great and exceedingly unflattering interest in anyone coming out of Trimalchio's in advance of the sated and spiritually-uplifted crowd.

* * * * * * *

Our table was lit by two candles—molded in GM-tallow, of course—and decorated by a discreet bouquet of flowers set in a tiny vase. I couldn't put a name to the flowers, but that was hardly surprising. Jerome only used originals. It was entirely possible that there was at least one species in the array that had only existed for a matter of weeks and would become extinct that very night.

The *aperitif* was as clear and colorless as water, but its texture suggested that it was a complex organic cocktail. When I remarked that I found it refreshing but oddly tasteless, Tamara explained that that was the whole point. It was intended to restore the "virginity of the tongue" by clearing away the lingering legacy of past experience.

The *hors d'oeuvres* were served in little silver dishes mounted on the heads of rampant chimeras formed from some kind of acrylic plastic. The workmanship was exceptionally fine; you could almost see the individual scales in the chimera's hind-parts. I didn't bother to point this out to Tamara in case she took it as another example of what she called "nanotechnologist's disease." "The trouble with you, Ben," she had said during the big row we had had after Christmas, "is that you're obsessed with *tiny* things. With you, it's not just a matter of not being able to see the wood for the trees—it's a matter of not being able to see the forest for the cracks in the bark of a fallen twig." For much the same reason, I didn't bother to point out the marvelous intricacy of the patterns engraved in black and white on the skins of the olives. Tamara made up for my reticence by waxing lyrical about the technical difficulties that Jerome's geneticists had had to overcome in order to ensure that the honeyed poppy-seeds used to season the roast dormice could be grown *in situ*, within the flesh of the living animal.

The dormice were a trifle too sweet for my taste and the olives too oily, but I did like the little toroidal sausages—although I might have liked them even better if they hadn't been wrapped around black figs. Tamara loved all of it, to the extent that she ate at least twice as much as me. I didn't mind. It was her treat, and it's not every day that a woman reaches her twenty-fifth birthday *and* receives her fourth proposal of marriage. I had wondered whether it was worth quipping that it was a lot better than receiving her twenty-fifth proposal on her fourth birthday, but I'd abandoned the plan because she would only have looked at me as if I were mad. "It's a joke," I would have said, the way I always did. "Is it?" she would have replied, implying that if there were such a thing as a joking test I would probably have failed it nearly as often as I'd failed my driving test.

The possibility of being out-eaten didn't arise again, of course, because the other courses were served in carefully measured individual portions on separate plates. The possibility of being out-drunk remained—the decanters containing the first white wine were brought out in advance of the second course—but Tamara was sufficiently old-fashioned to think that it was a gentleman's duty to pour, so I was confident that I could share it out with as much exactitude as my slightly unsteady hand could contrive. I was so nervous that I would have liked an extra glass to settle me down, but I also wanted to make sure that Tamara was as mellow as possible by the time the big moment arrived, so scrupulous even-handedness seemed politic as well as polite.

"Happy, darling?" I asked, as we paused with our glasses to savor the bouquet of the wine.

"Ecstatic," she assured me. She closed her eyes for a while, saying: "I'm trying to make the most of the pleasures of anticipation, so that they'll be redoubled by those of satiation."

"Me too," I assured her, although I was thinking about the ring in my pocket rather than the food.

* * * * * * *

The second course was what I'd normally have thought of as a starter, although the *hors d'oeuvres* had been far too substantial to qualify as a mere tease. It looked like an unusually coherent terrine, but there was no trace of token green stuff except for a light sprinkle of chopped herbs. The central blob was surrounded by a ring of eggs smaller than a quail's and the whole thing was bedded on what looked like unleavened bread.

According to the directory the blob was compounded from the "vulva" and "sumen" of a virgin sow—some kind of fancy pork, I deduced. The herbal seasoning was allegedly *laserpitium*, although a dutiful footnote pointed out that because no one now knew what plant the *laserpitium* of the ancients had been, the name had been considered free for application to an entirely new herb devised by Jerome's geneticists.

All in all, it didn't taste too bad. I wouldn't go so far as to say that I *liked* it, but it was on the sunny side of tolerable.

"Brilliant," Tamara said, as she finished. "Magical, even. I thought it would just be the taste, but it isn't, is it? You can actually feel the food settling into your stomach, can't you? It's as if this is what our alimentary systems have been crying out for ever since the first cooking fires were lit."

Tamara had strong feelings about the folly of the anti-GM brigade. "Everything we now think of as human nature is the product of the primal biotechnologies," she was fond of saying. "Anyone who thinks that biotechnology is an offence against nature is delusional as well as stupid." The *primal biotechnologies*, in the jargon of her trade, were cooking and clothing. Both innovations, in Tamara's firmly-held but not-quite-conventional view, had been introduced by women; according to her, the entire panoply of "masculine hardware"—including all the stone, ceramic, and metal tools in whose evolution old-fashioned male archaeologists were wont to trace the progress of preliterate societies—had been nothing more than a series of technical tricks developed to serve the imperatives of the primal biotechnologies.

Tamara further contended—and how could a mere technical trickster like me disagree with an ace biotechnologist?—that the entire history of civilization had followed the same pattern. Everything men had ever made or done had been devised to serve the insatiable demands of the "feminine imperative"—a valiant but inadequate tribute to the twin maternal devices that had broken nature's cruel yoke and set humankind on the road of intellect and artistry. My colleague and ex-friend Steve Semple had once opined that that was exactly the kind of thing a mad domineering bitch might be expected to say to a lovesick puppy, but he was just jealous.

I had once—and only once—made the mistake of pointing out to Tamara that in the modern world the "primal biotechnologies" seemed to have been hijacked by men, who still supplied the great majority of the twenty-first century's finest chefs and couturiers in spite of the victories of late twentieth-century feminism. "The greatest ambition of the male of the species has always been to cultivate as much effeminacy as testosterone will permit," she informed me. "How many great chefs and couturiers are straight, do you think? The trouble is that those unlucky souls who can't measure up to mature standards of effeminacy tend to express their defensive masculinity in a frank refusal to learn to cook or dress themselves properly."

There was none of that at Trimalchio's, of course. By that time I knew exactly which topics of conversation were safe and comfortable, and I was able to steer the chat in all the right directions. Tamara was happy that night, and when she was happy she was breathtakingly beautiful. People like Steve were incapable of understanding a woman like her, and resentment transformed their lust into hostility. I, on the other hand, loved her as honestly and as absolutely as anyone could. If she were ever going to marry anyone, I thought as I gulped my first mouthful of the red wine, it would definitely be me—and for all her affectations of independence, she needed love and stability just as much as anyone else.

* * * * * * *

Ever since I had first glanced at Jerome's directory of courses I had known that the third would be the most substantial challenge to my constitution. There is not a dessert in the world that can intimidate me, but when it comes to *entrées* I candidly admit that I am what Tamara was wont to call "a Stone Age meat and two veg man." I love the roast beef, potatoes, and carrots my mother used to make, with or without the Yorkshire pudding, and I see no need to apologize for the fact.

I had been hoping all week that I might strike lucky and catch Jerome in a traditional mood, taking what comfort I could from the knowledge that my wishes were likely to be at least partially granted. Jerome was well-known as a great fan of the potato. He'd been waxing lyrical on its virtues for ten years, and had presumably been doing so even before he got heavily into GM cuisine. The so-called "degradation of the potato" had always been the favorite object of his particular version of the fiery anger that is every great chef's prerogative and duty. When Columbus first reached the Americas, he told the world, there were six hundred different species of potato distributed from the heights of the Andes to the plains of Patagonia, and all but a handful had been driven to extinction by chip-addicted dullards. One of the key projects he had set his scientific collaborators was to recover and then to surpass the natural variability of the potato—so it's hardly surprising that the main course on that epoch-making evening was accompanied by no less than three different kinds of potato, one served mashed, one boiled, and one sautéed.

Having been granted that, how could I then complain about the fact that they were accompanying tentacles of young giant squid stuffed with mutton-brains?

I found, once I'd steeled myself to try it, that the flesh of young giant squid wasn't nearly as rubbery as the kind of calamari my mother used to foist on me when she wasn't in a roast beef mood. The engineers modifying squid species were still engaged in a headlong dash to produce the biggest living organism ever, so the culinary possibilities of the species had been virtually relegated to the economically-important but crudely utilitarian realms of pet food production. Jerome was one of the first people to figure out that the tender meat of very young individuals had possibilities undreamed of by geneticists fixated on issues of size, and I had to admit that he had a point.

As it turned out, I had slightly more difficulty with the stuffing. My maternal grandmother had an aunt who'd died of the same strain of CJD that was implicated in the infamous beef ban of the 1990s and Gran was always insistent—in spite of all the scientific evidence that later came to light proving that the cattle had caught it from us, not the other way around—that it had been scrapie-infected sheep that had been the source of the trouble. According to her, mutton-brains were just about the most dangerous foodstuff in the world. "No good will come of it!" she'd cried, when the proven effectiveness of GM-mutton-brains as an intelligence-enhancer in infants had delivered the first effective left hook to the jutting chin of anti-GM prejudice. Alas, her protests hadn't prevented Mum from feeding it to me throughout my teens, as if quantity might somehow make up for the fact that she'd missed the window of real opportunity by a good ten years.

At the end of the day, though, the stuffing was something I *could* eat, and I tucked the lot away without bothering to enquire too carefully as to the contents of the sauce, which were conveniently disguised by esoteric French and Latin in the directory. When I washed the last mouthful down with the last of the red wine I felt positively triumphant—as if my success in dealing with the food were an infallible omen of success in the evening's greater enterprise.

"Wasn't that simply extraordinary?" I said to Tamara.

"Marvelous," she confirmed.

"I suppose we ought to feel slightly guilty about snatching good mutton-brain out of the mouths of the tinies who derive such benefit from it," I said, "but I can't. I can feel it doing me good, even though I'm way too old."

"You're right," she said. It wasn't a phrase that passed her lovely lips very often, so I was delighted to hear it. "The wine sets it off perfectly, don't you think? To think that our parents used to value wine for its age! Do you think there'll ever come a time again when this year's vintage isn't the finest ever?"

"My Mum and Dad used to drink that *Beaujolais nouveau* stuff," I remembered.

"Vile red ink!" she retorted. "It might have helped in some small way to pioneer the change of attitude necessary to introduce GM wine, but no true connoisseur would have touched it. *This* is entirely different. Entirely!"

"Oh, absolutely," I said, as the third decanter was deposited in the middle of the table. "Who knew what true intoxication was in those days? Who understood the real subtleties of psychotropic artistry?"

"We owe Jerome and his disciples a tremendous debt," she confirmed. "When I think about those demonstrators outside— the antis, I mean, not his supporters—it makes me want to cry. They're dogmatists of the worst stripe, incapable of seeing sense—the stuff of which witch-hunters and inquisitors are made. Did you see that item on last night's 'Sky News' about the chef in New York who was shot?"

"Yes I did," I confirmed. "Yet another martyr to the cause of progress. There's always a mindless mob, isn't there? It's as if the lunatics just moved two doors down the road on the day the last abortion clinic closed. It's not as if there isn't an effective system of monitoring and control, is it?"

That was a slight mistake. I should have known better than to use the word "effective."

"Well, yes it is, actually," Tamara snapped. "We got saddled with far too many bad laws in the first decade of the new millennium, and far to many of them are still on the statute book. There's far too much insistence on formulaic testing. That obsolete monitoring system has become a millstone around the neck of the nation's scientists—bioscientists, I mean. You specialists in inorganic nanotech don't know how lucky you are not to have to deal with all that shit."

Mercifully, the arrival of the dessert cut the lecture short.

* * * * * * *

I had been looking forward to what I still insisted, if only privately, of thinking of as "pudding." The dessert on offer on that fateful night at Trimalchio's was one of those ingenious dishes that take advantage of the fact that ice-crystals are poor absorbers of microwave radiation and poor conductors of heat. This allows ingenious ice-cream sculptures to contain nested compotes of fruit heated to a temperature that can easily burn the mouth of an unwary diner. Needless to say, there were no such fools present at Trimalchio's that evening. We all knew that the art of eating such concoctions was all in the timing. Even Tamara knew how to manage the various components of the dessert as she dissected its complex architecture, savoring its gradual dissolution as well as its medley of tastes.

It is, I suppose, one of the great ironies of GM cuisine that it remains subject to the basic elements of the sense of taste. Although the gastronomic employment of saltiness and bitterness has always been relatively subtle, there is a certain inevitable crudity about sweetness. The only natural substance on which genetic engineers have not yet managed to improve is sucrose, and there is thus a sense in which the dessert is the most "primitive" part of any modern meal. In my personal opinion, however, the miracles that the engineers have wrought in cultured animal-flesh are outweighed by those applied to soft fruits. I would gladly have swallowed a few garlic-laden snails or risked the effects of a few deep-fried locusts in order to have the privilege of having Jerome's raspberries and blaeberries melt on my tongue.

The dessert wine was equally fine. Even Tamara said so, although if it had been something I'd brought home from the hypermarket the merest glance would have been enough to convince her that it was too syrupy. It's slightly absurd, now that slimness is a straightforward matter of somatic management, that so many willowy women still profess to dislike the taste of sugar, but in Tamara's case the idiosyncrasy was authentic. She was never one to follow fashion blindly.

"The perfect end to a perfect meal," was Tamara's judgment, as she laid her spoon aside for the final time.

"The evening's not over yet," I told her—but she seemed to have no suspicion of my intended meaning. She might even have made some remark about not having forgotten the coffee had it not been for the fact that Jerome chose that moment to make his entrance into the dining-room.

I had no inkling at first that anything was wrong. Reports I had read in the newspapers had said that the great man often came into the dining-room when his own work was concluded, in order to receive the grateful thanks of his clients. Routine or not, though, every eye in the place was upon him from the moment he stepped into view. When he raised his arms slightly to ask for silence, all conversation was instantly hushed.

"My friends," he said, in a tone whose evenness can only have been maintained with the utmost effort and dignity, "I fear that I have some bad news for you. It seems that Trimalchio's will be closing its doors tonight, never to reopen."

This statement was greeted with a collective gasp of astonished horror, but no one said a word. We simply waited for Jerome to continue.

"I have been informed that officers from New Scotland Yard are on their way to arrest me even as we speak," he told us. "It seems that a man I trusted—a *sous-chef* who has long been one of my most trusted confidants—has provided the police with an extensive dossier on my recent activities, including an itemized list of ingredients that I have used in my kitchens despite their lack of a certification of safety from the Ministry of Food Technology. I must confess that I have never made more than tenuous efforts to conceal the fact that I have used technically-illicit materials whenever I felt that my recipes required them. Those of you who know my methods well will know that I have never served anything to my customers—my guests, as I have always thought of them—whose effects I have not tested to the full on my own digestive system. I am, and always will be, perfectly confident that my judgment of a foodstuff's value and safety is worth infinitely more than any MFT certificate, but the fact remains that I have broken the law and that the evidence my former disciple has given to New Scotland Yard will ensure that I am held to account for my transgressions."

A few cries of "Shame!" were heard at this point, but Jerome raised his hand again to silence them.

"It is, of course, highly unlikely that I shall be required to serve a prison sentence," he continued, "and I have more than enough money to pay any reasonable fine, but you will all understand that the matter of my punishment is not so simple. The law, as it presently stands, will require that I be banned for life from owning or working in a restaurant, or from any significant involvement in commercial catering. In short, ladies and gentleman, the result of my inevitable conviction will be a virtual death sentence. This body will continue to live, but its soul and vocation will be extinguished. After tonight, Jerome will be no more. The meal you have just eaten is the last master-piece I shall ever create.

"In a few minutes I will pass among you, as has often been my pleasure, to shake you all by the hand and thank you for coming here tonight. I know that each and every one of you, whether you are numbered among my dearest friends and most loyal customers or whether you are visiting Trimalchio's for the very first time, will be as sorry to hear this news as I am, but I beg you to be brave, and not to make a sad occasion sadder by weeping. I would like to be able to treasure the memory of these last few moments of my life as Jerome, and I hope that you can help me to do that. I hope, too, that you will take away memo-ries of your own that you will always treasure; we are, after all, true collaborators in the great enterprise—may I say the great *crusade?*—that has been Trimalchio's. If you will indulge me, I should like to say a few final words about my mission before the police arrive."

Indulge him! His audience was rapt, hungry for every word.

"No one here will be surprised to hear me say that the

Promethean fire that first raised humanity above the animal was the cooking fire," Jerome went on. "The seed of Godhood was sown within humankind on the day when it was first decided that the raw, bloody, and meager providence of nature was inadequate to the needs of a creature possessed of mind—and hence of taste. No one here will be astonished to hear me quote with unqualified approval the old saw that *we are what we eat*. When the first agriculturalists and herdsmen set out to modify the genomes of other species by selective breeding, for culinary convenience, they also began the modification of their own flesh by the alteration their own selective regime. When I say that we are what we eat, I do not simply mean that the flesh of our captive plants and animals has become our flesh, but that we have internalized the consequences of our own biotechnologies. Our first human ancestors placed themselves in the slow oven that we call society, carefully dressed themselves with the seasoning that we call culture, and set their sights firmly upon that perfect combination of manufactured tastes that we call civilization.

"You and I are fortunate, my friends, to have lived in interesting times—not because we have witnessed the imbecilic wars and witch-hunts whose casualty-lists I am about to join, but because we have been present at the dawn of a new era in human nutrition: the era of nutritive augmentation. Just as the clothes we wear nowadays are active assistants in the business of waste-management, patiently absorbing all the organic by-products of which the body must be rid, so the food we shall eat in future will be active within our bodies. The foodstuffs of tomorrow will not simply be broken down into the elementary building blocks of our resident metabolism; they will work within us in far more ambitious ways, to equip our flesh with new fortitude and new versatility. I have tried, in my own humble way, to make some beginnings of this kind. I promise you, my friends, that you will be better off for the meal you have eaten this evening in more ways than you had anticipated. Even before I learned that it would be my last I had determined to excel myself, and when I learned of my betrayal, I increased my efforts. The effects will, I fear, be subtle, but I hope that they will be detectable long after the constituents of any ordinary meal would have been thoroughly digested, excreted, and evacuated. I hope that they will help you to remember me, and to remember me kindly. Thank you all—and farewell."

He made his tour of the room then. There must have been camcorders in the building, and I dare say that three out of every five diners probably had digital cameras secreted somewhere about their persons, but no one attempted to take pictures. It was an essentially private and personal occasion. To make a record of it would have been too closely akin to admitting the loathsome paparazzi.

When Jerome came to take my hand in his I knew that fate had already spoiled my grand plan—how could I possibly propose to Tamara now?—but I also knew that he was not at all to blame. I tried my utmost to keep the tears from my eyes as I gripped his fingers and thanked him profusely for everything that he had done for me and for the world, but I'm not sure that I succeeded.

Tamara certainly didn't: had it not been for her smart foundation her cheeks would have been streaming when she whispered: "Maestro!" and allowed him to kiss her naked hand. "You will return," she said. "I know it! Thousands, if not millions, will see to it that the ban will be lifted. Trimalchio's will open again, and a thousand years of glorious evolution will begin! We shall not rest until the population of the whole world is convert to our cause."

"Thank you, my child," he said.

The officers from New Scotland Yard had already arrived by then, but they waited dutifully until Jerome had completed his circuit before they led him away.

* * * * * * *

I left it until the following Saturday to ask Tamara to marry me. She refused. I had felt fairly sure that she would, just as I had felt fairly sure that she would have accepted if I had been able to seize the more propitious moment. Nothing I could say a week after Jerome's arrest made any difference. When I told her, in frank desperation, that I had booked into a Harley Street sex clinic to have the full treatment—tongue as well as penis—she merely shrugged her shoulders.

"In Mexico," she pointed out, "pioneers are already busy converting the semen of rich Americans into what Jerome called a *nutritive augmentation*. What use are mere playthings when possibilities like that are visible on the horizon? How many times have you heard me argue that marriage is irrelevant in a world like ours, when ectogenesis will soon relieve the womb of its role in the reproductive process and dieticians will make sure that all children are raised successfully? It's not you, Ben—you know perfectly well that I've turned down others. I love you dearly, even though you are so absurdly old-fashioned—but I couldn't love you half as much if I didn't love the ideals of progress even more."

She was right, according to her own lights. I *was* old-fashioned, perhaps to the point of quaintness if not absurdity. I still am—and I see nothing wrong with it. Such things are a matter of taste, after all, and the world would surely be a poorer place if we couldn't take some pride in the arbitrary idiosyncrasies and mannerisms that form our individual personalities.

Tamara and I remained good friends, but it was inevitable that we eventually drifted apart. In the end, I married Monica, and I still think that the marriage was reasonably successful, within its limitations. We both grew out of it, but that doesn't mean that it has to be reckoned a failure.

The last meal ever served in Trimalchio's did leave the kind of lasting impression for which Jerome had hoped. The antis were outraged when they heard what he'd done, and the tabloids were full of scare stories for months afterwards about our having dined on "living food" and "living wine" that would "devour our inner being" as we struggled to digest it, but it wasn't like that at all. The active cells could have been flushed out of our alimentary canals in five minutes if we'd cared to ask our doctors to flush them but, so far as I know, not a single person who was at Trimalchio's that night even went so far as to take advice from a GP. We had faith in Jerome, you see. We trusted him not to harm us, and we were confident that if the active cells—which weren't really any more "alive" than a new set of Marks & Spencer underwear—had any perceptible effect at all, it would definitely be beneficial.

I was always pretty fit, but I think I've been even healthier since I ate that meal. I know there's more of a spring in my step, more zest for life. I'm more confident, too. It's almost as if a weight that I didn't even know I was carrying has been lifted from my shoulders.

All that's a bit vague, I know, but there are some specifics I can point to. I'm no longer allergic to mussels, and I've developed quite a partiality to locusts in bitter chocolate. I've doubled my bench-press record and I've knocked five seconds off my best time for fifteen-hundred kilometers. I'm also becoming far more adventurous. As soon as the divorce settlement has been formalized—assuming that it doesn't prove to be *too* ruinous— I'm thinking of taking a little trip to Mexico. If fate has decreed that I'm to be a swinging single for the rest of my life, I might as well try to make the most of the opportunities.

If all goes well, the only thing I'll need to make my future happiness complete is for Trimalchio's to re-open. Maybe I haven't been as active in that cause as I ought to have been, but I've never been the zealot type, and I figure that I did my bit simply by taking Tamara to the restaurant. It's rather ironic that if it hadn't been for my botched proposal plan, the movement would lack its most brilliant leading light.

Anyhow, with or without my help, that's bound to happen soon. The old world is already dead; it's merely a matter of waiting for the enemies of progress to admit that it's high time for the new one to begin.

THE FACTS OF LIFE

1. December 2020

Benjy Stephens carefully peeled off the sterile gloves before standing back to scrutinize his handiwork through the glass wall of the terrarium. He surveyed the central mountain with a careful and critical eye, and saw that it was well done—or well enough done, at any rate.

Four flat blocks of no particular shape sat atop one another, the biggest at the base and the smallest at the apex. He had smoothed the edges of the steps, but not so much as to create too many shallow slopes. It would be possible for motiles to migrate from one level to the next—and hence from one thermal regime to another—but such migrations wouldn't be so easy that the environments merged into a seamless spectrum.

He had decked the exposed faces of the four blocks with appropriate combinations of primary producers. Their distribution would change fairly rapidly over the next few weeks as they grew to cover the entire territory, but ought to have settled down after a couple of months. Benjy knew that there would be a strong temptation to introduce the motiles too soon, while the pp populations were still in flux, but he was an old hand now and he was confident that he had patience enough to wait until the moment was ripe.

He heard a loud crash from the room directly below his own, and felt the faint reverberation as something slammed into the wall. The muffled voices, which had been periodically raised for some time, grew in volume yet again.

In scientifically detached fashion he noted that Monica was at full screech now, and that the row must therefore be close to its climax. She would have been the one who had hurled whatever it was that had hit the wall; she was always the first to resort to missile warfare. Benjy wondered what on earth it had been that she had thrown; the thump had been far too solid to be mere crockery but too light to be a chair. Surely she couldn't have torn the vidphone free of its connections!

There was no point wondering what the row was actually about. What were they ever about?

May came in, without knocking. If ever Benjy had had the temerity to enter *her* room without knocking, she'd have complained in no uncertain terms—she had inherited her mother's screech and knew how to use it to devastating effect—but it would not have occurred to her to extend him a similar courtesy. She was only six months older than he was, and he had recently caught up a little of the difference in height and weight that had always been to her conspicuous advantage, but because he *looked* two years younger than he actually was, May and everyone else treated him as the baby of the family.

"Christmas sucks," she said. "Two p.m. and everything's gone to hell. You got the right idea, kid—hide out until new year." She came to stand beside him, peering into the new terrarium curiously.

"What hit the wall?" Benjy asked.

"What do you think? The tree, of course. Good thing it's a hundred per cent synth. Even the lights stayed on. Your old man's a real bastard, you know—which maybe wouldn't matter so much, except that he's such a *careless* bastard. What's the point of going to all the trouble of paying *cash* for something if you keep the fucking *receipt?*"

"What did he buy?"

"Just trash—but it was fancier trash than he bought for Mom, and way more expensive. I mean, Jesus, you'd think a guy who'd been through it all before would be wise to *that* one. Christmas is stressful enough even when all the associated hypocrisy is decently covered up. You got this one set up in record time, didn't you? Nice mountain. When do the critters go in?"

Down below the screeching crescendo continued to build, with occasional punctuation by a deeper voice. Benjy couldn't make out what his father was saying, but Monica's contribution to the discussion was clearly audible, if somewhat muddled by alcoholic incoherence. "If you care so much more about her than you do about me," was the gist of it, "then why don't you get the hell out and shack up with *her?*"

"The end of February," said Benjy, absent-mindedly. "Maybe mid-March."

"*March?*" May echoed, incredulously. "You put all this together in eight hours and you aren't going to *use* the thing till March?"

"The primary producers have to settle down," he told her. "It's not necessary for them to reach true equilibrium, but if I put motiles in any earlier than that, the whole system would go straight into tachytelic mode. I'm going to use the new tank to set up a test-case for Gause's Axiom, and there's no hope of breaking the rule unless the pp distribution over the four thermal regimes is stable enough to allow the two kinds of motiles to establish themselves securely while their numbers are low."

"Don't try to show off with *me*, kid," May said, acidly. "I'm your sister, remember. I got my first tank the same day you got yours, Christmas 2017—only I put away my mutaclay with all the other *childish things* when I started my periods, because I'm not a case of arrested development. Now, you want to tell me that again, in plain English or would you rather talk about the divorce rate?"

Benjy knew that he must be blushing fiercely, but he tried to take control. There was no use protesting about any of the inaccuracies in what she said, not even the one about her being his sister. Actually, even though his father was married to her mother, they weren't related by blood at all, both being relics of former relationships.

"Gause's Axiom says that two species with the same ecological requirements can't co-exist in the same ecoarena," he said, mildly. "It's considered to be obsolete in respect of natural organisms—there are several counter-examples in nature and the results of several contradictory lab experiments were published more than fifty years ago. So far, though, it's held up with respect to mutaclay organisms. If you put two motile species that feed on the same range of pps into the same terrarium, one always drives the other to extinction within a matter of six or eight months—a couple of hundred generations. So the literature says, anyhow. Even in the universities, no one's managed to stabilize a situation like that. In principle, though, anything that DNA can do mutaclay ought to be able to do too. DNA got a couple of billion years start, but it didn't have the kind of help mutaclay has."

"Some help!" said May. "Postgrads serving their time in second-rate colleges and teenage boys hiding away in their rooms because they can't be bothered to grow up, all playing at being God. What makes you think you can do it if the college guys can't?"

"Anybody can set up experiments," said Benjy, keeping his temper under strict control. "Mutaclay's cheap and the price of the tanks has come way down since they were the big Christmas fad of '17. University labs might do things on a much bigger scale, but there are tens of thousands of amateurs running operations like mine. Anybody can work at the cutting edge, if they're prepared to put in the time, because it's all so new. Nobody knows what can and can't be done because it's all still to do. The world record for keeping an ancestral line of motiles going is only seven years, and that's in a classic bradytelic set-up. I've got two horotelic lines that have clocked up four hundred days." He pointed as he spoke at Tank Two and Tank Three. Tank One—the one he had received with his first kit—had long ago been relegated to the lowly status of breeder tank. It was where he grew his primary producers: the thermosynthetic organisms that were mutaclay's "plants."

"This is in danger of becoming an obsession, you know," said May, loftily. "You're hiding out from reality in here. There's a world, you know, *out there*." She pointed at the window, which Benjy kept curtained at all times lest sunlight shining on the walls of the terraria should upset the internal temperature-regimes.

Downstairs, something else hit the wall—something considerably lighter than the Christmas tree. It was probably a bottle. The row had reached its final phase.

It was perhaps as well, Benjy thought, that the march of progress had consigned breakable bottles to the dustbin of history. He became tense, waiting for the sound of something heavier hitting the floor. The march of progress hadn't done as much for the human body as it had for bottles; people could still get badly hurt when things got this far out of hand. Mercifully, that sound never came; instead there was the slam of a door, followed soon after by the slam of another. Monica gave voice to one last screech. It was his father who had retreated, as per usual.

"No prizes for guessing where *he*'s going," said May, bitterly, as they head the sound of the garage door rolling up on the cylinder.

"He'll be back," said Benjy, faintly.

"Oh, sure," said May. "And by that time, she'll be maudlin drunk and full of apology. She'll forgive her darling Jim—again—and he'll make the usual soothing noises. But it won't be the end, will it? Christmas is peak time for divorce petitions, you know—not to mention suicides and domestic murders. Like I say, it really *sucks*. Not that you care—you got what you wanted."

Benjy asked for new mutaclay equipment every year, birthdays as well as Christmas. This year he'd got an assay kit, which produced paragene spectra by chromatography, as well as the new tank. It would make a big difference to the kinds of data he could collect. May hadn't ever supplemented the kit she'd got back in '17. In fact, she hadn't managed to sustain her own mutaclay populations through the summer of 2018. Her tank had gone tachytelic through sheer neglect, and she hadn't been able or willing to take the measures necessary to prevent mass extinctions. By the time she'd offered Benjy anything he could salvage, it had all been reduced to junk. In that first season of fashionability, the manufacturers had sold millions of kits with the slogan MUTACLAY IS REAL LIFE; few of its purchasers had realized the that the chief implication of that sentence was that in the fullness of time, it rotted down into mere dirt.

"I care," Benjy protested, feebly. "I don't want your mom to be unhappy any more than you do. I don't want you to be unhappy."

"I'm not unhappy," May retorted, as if he'd accused her of something disgusting. "You think I give a shit whether they break up? I've been through it all before. It's easy when you know how."

Benjy had been through it all before too, but he didn't remember much about it. He'd been six years old, so meek and mild that he just went where he was taken, did what he was told to do, and just waited to see what would happen. He could hardly remember what his mother had looked like. He hadn't seen her in ten years; she never wrote to him or called, not even at Christmas. Five years had passed before his father had married Monica, but Monica had been straight out of one marriage and into the other, so May had been eleven and twelve while the turbulent change-over was transacted, and she remembered everything. She still got Christmas presents from her father, too—better presents than she got from Monica and Benjy's dad, except perhaps for that first terrarium and the supply of muta-clay. Even then, she'd probably preferred the cheaper gift she got from her real father on the grounds that it wasn't "educa-tional." May wasn't a big fan of education.

"They won't break up," said Benjy, without much conviction. "Monica will forgive him, just like you said, and he'll be sorry. He'll try to make it up to her. It'll be okay."

"Oh sure," said May, here voice dripping venomous scorn. "She'll forgive him and he'll be sorry...only they'll both be pretending. Maybe he'll dump the girlfriend, because he's sick of her anyway, and play happy families for at least a fortnight before he makes some new connection...but then the pretence will wear thin, until it's threadbare...and it'll all flare up again. What's that big word you're always using that means things going down the toilet double quick? Tachytelic, right?"

"That's not really what it means," said Benjy, unable to resist the provocation. "It refers to any situation that encourages rapid natural selection. It doesn't *necessarily* lead to ecocatastrophe and extinction. It's just that...."

"It's just that poor bloody mutaclay, even with the help of little godlings like you, can't ever seem to keep things going when that kind of crunch comes. Good thing, hey? If it could keep right on going, getting better and better every day in every way, it'd soon end up smarter than *you* are."

Benjy was tempted to carry on trying to explain, but he knew how futile it would be. May didn't want to understand; she just wanted an excuse to mock. As she was so fond of telling him, she was growing up, becoming an adult. She was learning the skills of adult discourse. Anyhow, he thought, at the metaphorical level what she'd said was probably more intelligent than she realized. There *was* a sense in which their parents' marriage had moved from a horotelic to a tachytelic phase. It had become more and more unstable, more and more vulnerable to wayward changes in the social environment. Its daily routines had begun to mutate more rapidly. Was it, Benjy wondered, doomed to extinction?

Benjy silently considered the further implications of the metaphor, conscientiously reminding himself that he shouldn't be tempted to read too much into it. Even straightforward comparisons between mutaclay's artificial genetic systems and DNA could be misleading.

Conventional wisdom, Benjy knew—and his own experience had given him no reason to doubt it—held that populations of mutaclay organisms were easy to maintain indefinitely in tanks where the conditions remained absolutely stable. Such easily-maintained populations, however, inevitably slipped into brady-telic mode, with each species maintaining an optimum genome. In such conditions the mutation rate tended to decline to negligibility. It wasn't nearly so easy to maintain mutaclay species—especially motiles—in conditions that varied, even when the variations were slow or cyclic. Although the matter was fiercely disputed by rival claimants, the world record for maintaining a mutaclay ecosystem in tachytelic mode was little more than a year: about four hundred generations. Such processes of rapid evolution had so far thrown up nothing more "advanced" than oversized spirilli. No mutaclay organism had yet contrived to invent cell membranes.

The great majority of DNA organisms, by contrast, had been forced to exist in tachytelic mode for hundreds of millions of years, and some of them had done very well out of it indeed. On the other hand, DNA species were said to be going extinct at the rate of several thousand a day, and the world was full of prophets who did not hesitate to declare that the turn of *Homo sapiens* would come within a few generations, long before that of the brown rat or the German cockroach. In the end, even DNA might be reduced all the way to the bacterial level...maybe even to the point that wild mutaclay might be able to give it a fight. Surely, Benny thought, human relationships behaved more like DNA than mutaclay—but what exactly did that imply about their resilience and mortality?

"It'll be okay," Benjy said, eventually, when May didn't bother to supplement her acid observations with anything more substantial. "People can get along, if they only put their minds to it. They don't really mean to hurt one another—Dad and Monica, I mean."

"You really are wrapped up in cotton wool up here, aren't you?" said May. "You really haven't a clue what it's all about. Why do you think they invented Christmas, hey? One lousy day out of three hundred and sixty-five when we're supposed to try our level best to be nice to one another—and fail miserably every fucking time! Do you think we'd have to try so hard, if we *didn't really mean to hurt one another?*"

Benjy winced. "I don't...," he began.

"No," she countered, without even waiting for him to finish. "You're too busy trying to prove Gause's fucking axiom false to notice that other people even exist. Unfortunately, whatever mutaclay worms can do if you treat them right, men and women *can't* co-exist for long in the kind of tank they call a *marriage*... and the sooner you figure out that those are the facts of real life the better. Not that I'll be sorry to see the back of *you*, Benjy—next time, maybe I'll get a brother with balls."

As she delivered the last sentence, she turned on her heel and walked out. He didn't know why; it certainly wasn't fear of his being able to frame an adequately nasty reply. Maybe, he thought, she was trying to preventing his noticing that she had tears in the corners of her eyes. He felt an unexpected pang of affection for her, and wished that he could help.

Calmly and carefully, Benjy lifted the lid on to the new terrarium. Then he checked the electrical leads carrying the current that would warm the substrata from which the primary producers drew their energy-supply. Finally, he switched on the tiny pinpoint lamp that would keep one half of the mountain-slopes perpetually flooded with warm white light, while the other side was in shadow.

* * * * * * *

When Benjy retired to his bed that night—by which time Jim Stephens had returned, the prophesied reconciliation had been effected according to schedule, and all seemed calm again—the little daystar set in the new terrarium seemed to shine uncannily bright in the near-darkness as it presided over the newborn world. It seemed to Benjy to be as full of promise as the star of Bethlehem.

"It'll be okay," he told himself, as he laid his head contentedly upon his pillow. "It's all going to work."

2. April 2021

Benjy drew the blade of the scalpel along the fourth side of the last of the squares that were scheduled for replacement, then laid the instrument aside. He used two sets of tweezers to worry the square loose from the underlying plastic. He lifted it very carefully, trying to keep the mat of mutaclay "vegetation" as flat as possible. The motiles tended to cling hard if disturbed, but he wanted to avoid the possibility of any falling back into the tank. The odd one or two wouldn't make any real difference, but he took a perfectionist pride in his ability to manage the experimental procedure with maximum efficiency.

He laid the square in a Petri dish, and put the lid on before taking up the virgin square of primary producers that he'd taken from Tank One. He set the replacement patch in the bare space, matching the edges minutely so that they'd eventually knit together with the minimum of difficulty.

He had replaced the lid of the tank, and was just swinging the magnifying glass into place so that he could begin the preliminary eye-count of the motiles on the first of his samples, when the door of his room burst open. As it slammed shut again, the whole house seemed to vibrate with the impact.

"Don't *do* that!" he complained, turning wrathfully around—but when he saw May's face he bit his lip. It wasn't just the tears—he was used to those. This time there was more: a split lip, angry red marks on the cheek, and a bluish bulge beneath the left eye that would surely turn black with time. He calculated that it must have taken at least three blows, one of them more solid than an open hand could readily have delivered. He felt ashamed of his own clinicality, and rose from his seat in order to go to her.

She sat down on his bed, drawing her legs up and huddling sideways against the wall. She glared at him as he came towards her, and he faltered. Within the last few months she seemed to have developed an aversion to his touch—an aversion that he found rather wounding, although they had never really been close in a physical sense. In the end, the hesitation stopped him in his tracks. He stepped backwards again and sat down on the chair, half-turning it so that it faced the bed instead of the desk. He felt even more ashamed of the warm glow of lust that lurked somewhere inside him than he had of his clinical analysis of the situation. Surely the sight of her injuries should make him feel protective, not sexy? What kind of person was he?

"Crazy bitch!" May spat the words out between half-strangled sobs. "Crazy fucking *bitch!*"

"What happened?" asked Benjy, only just stopping himself from adding the fateful words *this time.*

"As if it's my fault!" The sense of injustice in her voice was so evidently real that Benjy had little doubt that for once it really hadn't been May's fault—whatever *it* was.

May rubbed her eyes, as if to squeeze the tear-ducts shut. Her knuckles came away stained with purple, leaving ugly streaks and blotches behind. She tested the tender swelling beneath her eye with the tips of her fingers, and they too came away stained. She cleaned them in perfunctory fashion by using the hem of her short black skirt as if it were a handkerchief. Benjy averted his eyes from the additional expanse of thigh exposed by the gesture. May was wearing tights patterned with a hologram design that made it look as if colored flowers were growing in her pale flesh.

"I'll get a cloth or something from the bathroom," Benjy said, leaping to his feet again.

"I don't need...," she said—but he was already moving to the door, and he had no intention of stopping. He wanted to *do* something, and if she wouldn't let him cuddle her, he could at least help her clean up. Anyway, he thought, it would give her a chance to calm down, to pull herself together, to become slightly less troublesome to his eye and his restless mind.

* * * * * * *

By the time Benjy came back into his room, carrying a hand towel whose corner he had carefully wetted with lukewarm water, May was sitting a little more comfortably. He handed the towel to her, and she used it with reasonable efficiency to clean up the mess around her eyes. When he reached out to take it back, intending to finish the job neatly, she wouldn't let go of it. He went back to the chair again.

"It's not my fault," she said, in a low voice, which was almost steady. "Why does it always have to be my fault. He's *your* father."

"What did he do?" Benjy asked, innocently.

"Do? He didn't *do* anything. D'you think I'd let him touch me? I'd take a fucking knife to him before I'd let him *touch* me. It's not my fault. It's nothing to do with how I dress or how I walk or how I smile. How can I help the way he *looks* at me, for Christ's sake? Anyway, it's not the way he looks at *me* that pisses her off—it's the way he looks at *her*. Is *that* my fault? Is it?"

"No," said Benjy, grateful that he wasn't called upon to be anything but honest. "It's not." He was glad to be entirely on May's side. Monica shouldn't hit her, especially not for a reason like that.

It was true, he knew, that his father had begun to take more notice of May, and to look at her in a different way—he had made remarks to Benjy, sometimes accompanied by a coarse chuckle that Benjy found utterly distasteful—but that wasn't May's fault. As May said, it had nothing to do with the way she dressed or acted. It was just nature; *human* nature, his father would have said, though his father had an odd notion of "humanity."

Benjy understood the situation well enough, in terms of evolutionary logic. When the females of a species reached childbearing age, they naturally became attractive to the males, who naturally found newly nubile individuals more attractive than those nearing the end of their reproductive usefulness. Humanity had nothing to do with it. If anything, *humanity—*

meaning sentience and intelligence and the ability to place oneself imaginatively in the shoes of others—ought to be able to override such crude and basic impulses, elevating the demands of social obligation over the raw force of instinct. So Benjy thought, at any rate. On the other hand, though....

"It's not you she's mad at," Benjy told May, scrupulously. "It's not even my father, really. She's angry with herself."

"Well I wish she'd hit herself, then! I wish she'd take a fucking overdose of those stupid pills she lives on, and let us all off the hook."

May stood up and looked around. Having failed to find what she was looking for—a mirror, he guessed—she came over to the desk and leaned over, squinting at her reflection in the glass wall of Tank One. "Shit!" she murmured, prodding her swollen lip with a slender forefinger.

Benjy refrained from pointing out that Monica's tranquilisers were genetically-engineered metaendorphin derivatives, so easily degradable that she could swallow a truckload without doing any serious damage to her liver or her kidneys. Their only unfortunate side-effects were reduced sensitivity to the body's own inbuilt endorphins and a tendency to abrupt let-down effects, which—as in Monica's case—could result in exaggerated mood-swings.

"I really don't think he is having an affair, you know," Benjy said. "I think he's telling the truth when he says it's over."

She rounded on him. "Did you emigrate to Cloudcuckooland or were you drafted?" she asked, snidely. Her hand had fallen on one of the Petri dishes, and she picked it up, peering at the square section of mutaclay inside. Then she looked at the carefully-drawn map of Tank Four's terrain that was presently spread out on the lid of Tank Three, and studied the intricate map of squares that he'd inscribed upon it. "What're you doing now?" she asked, contemptuously. "Playing war games with your little worms?"

"Not exactly," he said, gravely. "I'm testing Gause's Axiom. If I'd simply dropped two populations of motiles into the tank and left them to it, one or other would be bound to drive the other to extinction when the overall population pressure became too great.

"Because there aren't any mutaclay predators yet, there's nothing to keep the motile populations in check unless the experimenter intervenes by imposing an external death-rate—but the death-rate has to be in some sense arbitrary, because it mustn't be done in such a way as to produce the desired result by design. So, every seventy-two hours I remove three randomly-selected squares of motile-infested primary producers and replace them with squares taken from the breeder tank. Sometimes it takes out more of one of the competing species, sometimes the other, but in the long term the harvesting regime should allow both populations to equilibrate, more-or-less. If I'm right about the likely outcome, that is. It'll be interesting to see, though, what happens to the mutation rates—in the pps as well as the motiles. I think it's a horotely-type situation, so they should stay pretty close to normal; if they go tachytelic, of course, the whole operation could crash."

"And what do you do with these?" she asked, holding up the Petri dish.

"I do a population count on each one. By eye initially, although that's rather crude and inaccurate even though the motile species I'm using are distinctive enough to permit it. To check the data I use the assay kit to compare the paragene clusters of the various species. That way I can track the mutation rates as well as the raw numbers. I file all the data with Mutaclay, Inc. and the State University—it's an officially registered experiment."

"Since when?"

"Since just after Christmas—I sent the details by e-mail a few days after I first set it up. They passed the design at the end of January and I started filing the results as soon as the motiles went in."

"Benjy, you're fifteen years old. How the hell do you get to run an *officially registered experiment?*"

"Anybody can register their work," he told her, proudly. "There aren't any age limits. As long as the design is properly vetted and the data gets filed regularly, the experiment stays on the register. They can send people round to check up, of course—I guess they do that whenever an experiment begins to produce interesting results, although they probably have routine inspections too. The monthly bulletins often have pictures of kids younger than me who've generated significant new strains or whatever. I haven't had any official reaction since I started sending stuff in, but it's a long-term experiment and it's early days yet. If it's still going strong in June or July, it might attract some attention."

"I see," said May, sceptically. "Mutaclay, Inc. markets their gunk as an educational toy, and all of a sudden they have a huge coast-to-coast r-and-d division. Very clever. Do they *pay* these cute kids who develop *significant new strains?*"

"Of course not. This isn't technology, May, it's *life*. It's not a business, it's *creation*: the ultimate art."

"Like I said before," May opined, setting the Petri dish down again, "it's Cloudcuckooland. You have to play this cutting-out and counting game every third day, you say? Are you crazy, or what? I mean, I know it doesn't play havoc with your social life because I know you haven't *got* a social life, but hasn't it occurred to you that some day soon you're going to want a little more than *all this?* Some day, Benjy, you're going to have to get out there and start doing all the things that *people* do, like drinking and popping and gambling and seducing members of the opposite sex. Some day fairly soon—and I know it's a hellish thought, but there it is—you're going to have to begin the process of turning into something like your father."

Benjy knew that he had to refrain from making the obvious reply, so he refrained from saying anything at all. He just looked at her, reproachfully. He was surprised when she turned away, because she didn't usually give way. Was it possible that *she* was blushing?

"What is it?" he asked, reaching out to take her arm.

She knocked his hand away. "Don't *touch* me!" she hissed, meeting his eyes again, but with a very different expression, whose implication filled him with embarrassment.

"I didn't mean...," he protested, but trailed off.

"Not *just* like your father," she said, in a malevolent whisper. "You might aim a *little* higher than that!"

"I only...," he began, but stopped again, because he knew in his heart of hearts that he did want to look at her, and to touch her, and that his dreams were not entirely innocent, and that the corollaries of his knowledge that she was *not*, after all, his real sister were, however natural, not at all comfortable.

He *had* only wanted to help, to be reassuring, to be generous... but he couldn't honestly claim that his motives were *entirely* pure.

"It's okay, May," he said, when he was sure that he could finish a whole sentence. "It'll all work out. Dad and Monica are just going through a bad patch. It'll all settle down." His hands were balled into fists, pressing into his thighs. She, meanwhile, had reached up to fondle her bruised cheeks again.

"Crazy bitch has no right," she said. "Next time, I'll let her have it right back again. Why the fuck should *I* have to take the blame?"

Three were tears in the corners of her eyes again. Benjy's fists unwound, and he reached out with both arms—not insistently, but invitingly, stopping half way.

"Please," he said. "Don't be...."

She wouldn't accept the invitation. She wouldn't let him hold her. She pulled away, retreating towards the door—but this time, *she* was apologetic.

"It's okay," she said. "I'll be fine. Just...get back to your bugs. Do what you have to do. Don't worry about me." There was no bitterness left in her voice now. She had said what she had come to say, accomplished whatever it was she had set out to do. Benjy watched her until the door closed behind her.

All was silence down below; peace had descended yet again upon the household.

* * * * * * *

When he was done with the magnifier, Benjy swung it back into its resting-position. Then he picked up the three Petri dishes and carried them to the desk, where the assay kit sat beside the dead computer screen. He picked up the keyboard and deposited it on top of the VDU to give himself more room in which to work. Then he set about preparing the chromatograms, with practiced efficiency.

While he worked he couldn't help remembering what May had said way back at Christmas-time about the relevance of Gause's Axiom to the ecoarena of marriage, and wondering how the added complexity of a second generation complicated the issue. Mutaclay motiles didn't yet have that kind of problem; all the lines so far evolved reproduced by binary fission—multiplying by division, as the old joke had it—and hadn't yet produced, anywhere in the world, a progressive mutant capable of anything resembling sexual intercourse.

Someday, of course, it was bound to come, but even with the aid of the meddling attentions of hundreds of thousands of conscientious God-experimenters these things took time.

When he was done with the preparations, he set the chromatograms up to develop. Then he took the Petri-dishes downstairs and put them in the freezer. An hour at low temperature was enough to remove the semblance of life from the mutaclay and reduce it to mere raw material: "soil" that could be "fed" to the primary producers in Tank One and thus recycled.

Benjy was careful never to waste any of the artificial organic substance, but he knew how necessary it was to build death into the eternal process, because he understood well enough how vital it was to the business of change and progress. He knew from the literature and from experience that if you tried to keep everything in a tank alive, the growing strain on the ultimate limiting factor—living space—would eventually precipitate disaster. The key to long-term stability was control, and one of the most significant modes of control was induced mortality.

"But human nature isn't like that," he told himself, as he crept back up the stairs. "*Human* nature is better than that; it doesn't need to break things in order to sustain them."

It was such a neat turn of phrase that he wanted to preserve it, and to share it, but he knew better than to knock on May's door—or his father's—without a much better excuse than that, and there was no way he could sneak it into the e-mail report updating his data. If you wanted to stay on the official register you had to be very careful to stick to the facts.

Sticking to the facts was the hallmark of the true scientist, the *modus operandi* of the scrupulous engineer of artificial life. Benjy wanted to be reckoned a true scientist. He was determined to stick to the facts, just as hard as he could.

3. August 2021

Benjy stared at the graph displayed on the computer screen, wondering whether it meant failure or an altogether unexpected form of success. The assistant professor from the university who'd come over in July to check his experimental set-up had not been very forthcoming on the subject, but the data hadn't been anywhere near as clear at that point in time.

"Wait and see how it develops," she'd said. "It could be just statistical scatter."

It wasn't statistical scatter. The latest paragene assay was quite unambiguous; one of his two original populations was undergoing a speciation split. But if he now had *three* species with the same ecological requirements in the same ecoarena, how did that relate to Gause's Axiom? If one of them became extinct, would that count as a confirmation, or would *two* have to die out to sustain the rule? Or did the fact that speciation was happening mean that the two descendant species *didn't* have the same ecological requirements? *How* was speciation happening, given that there were no strong boundaries between the different thermal regimes in the tank?

He didn't know the answers to any of those questions. He didn't even know how to go about trying to find answers. Nor were those the only questions relevant to the progress of the experiment. Given that the mutation rates of both motile species had been hovering close to the upper limit of horotelic mode for some little while, the speciation event could easily throw the whole system into tachytelic mode. On the other hand, it *might* actually bring about a relative stabilization: a relaxation towards the norm. Which would actually happen, and what would the implications be, in either case?

Benjy knew that if he called the Mutaclay Helpline they'd only tell him to carry on filing his results. This wasn't the kind of problem the program was set up to deal with. The assistant professor, Doctor Shane, might be able to come up with a few reassuring noises, if she were in the mood, but when she'd visited she'd made it abundantly clear that checking up on amateurs working from home was only one step up from grading freshman papers, just something she had to do as part of her departmental workload. She'd given him a number where he could reach her, but she hadn't looked as if she expected him to use it.

"Well, hell," he murmured, finally, "science would be a dull business if nothing unexpected ever happened. Things come right out of the blue sometimes. That's life." All the same, he thought, it would be a bit of a bummer if his first major enterprise came apart after two hundred and twenty days. Two hundred and twenty days was a big slice out of the life of someone who was only pushing sixteen. He couldn't relish the thought of having to start all over again.

* * * * * * *

Benjy was startled out of his long reverie by a polite knock on his door.

"Yeah?" he called, expecting that it would be May summoning him downstairs to join the others and make his all-too-modest contribution to the pretence that all was well in Happyfamilyland—but it wasn't May. When the door opened it was Monica who came in. That was highly unusual; ever since he'd begged her to stop coming in to "tidy up," she'd hardly set foot in the room.

Considering that it was after seven in the evening she seemed surprisingly sober.

"Hello Benjy," she said, demurely. "May I sit down?"

"Sure," he said, getting up to offer her his one and only chair. She ignored the gesture and sat down on the bed, so he turned the chair to face her and sat down on it again.

"I think we need to have a serious talk," she said, ominously.

"I've nearly finished," he told her. "I've just got to file the results of today's count and I'll be down. I didn't think we'd be eating so early. I'm not exactly *late*."

"It's about your father, Benjy," she said, very earnestly. "He's not home yet—but he's not at work, and the dispatcher says that he didn't go out on any jobs this afternoon. I think you're old enough now to know what that implies, Benjy."

Benjy felt that his jaw was hanging loose, and shut his mouth rather too abruptly. His stepmother crossed and uncrossed her legs uneasily, and put on an ingratiating smile. It looked slightly grotesque, but it was not ineffective. Was it normal, Benjy wondered, to be so hyped up by testosterone that even your own stepmother came to seem provocative?

"I've been a good mother to you, Benjy," Monica said, still speaking in that strange ultra-careful way, "haven't I?"

"Yeah, sure," he said, hoping he didn't sound as dubious as he felt.

"You've been happy here, haven't you? You and May get along *so* well. I mean, this has always been a real family, hasn't it? This is everything you could want in a *home*."

"Sure," he said, again, hoping his tone didn't sound too luke-warm.

"I want you to know that we're all proud of you," she went on, her voice now showing just the faintest trace of an alcoholic slur. "We're all real pleased about the way you've applied your-self to this clay stuff. It's not like it's a career or anything, but it shows you have real sticking power, and that's an important thing to have. If you're to succeed in life, Benjy, you have to have sticking power. I only wish Jim knew that as well as you do. I only wish you could make him see it as well as you do. Because if your father had sticking power, everything would be all right Benjy. Everything."

Benjy had the uncomfortable feeling that he knew exactly what response his father would make to the news that Monica wished he had more sticking power. *Everything would be all right, Monica,* he'd say, *if only you had a little* less *sticking power—if only you didn't stick so fucking hard to your booze and your pills and your obsessions. If only you could loosen up, Monica, and give me a bit of space, everything would be A-fucking-one.* Benjy was all too well aware that a very different response was required from *him.*

"Maybe something unexpected came up," Benjy said, unen-thusiastically. "Dad does odd jobs for friends sometimes—he even does jobs for cash without telling the boss. The dispatcher wouldn't know about that—but maybe he has his suspicions, and maybe that's why he tried to give you a wrong...."

"That's very loyal of you, Benjy," said Monica, punctili-ously, "but it isn't true. He's got another woman, Benjy. He's screwing around. And I think you ought to be aware, Benjy, that it's eating me up inside. It's chewing us all up...the whole family. It's destroying us: our life, our home, our future. I've tried everything I know to get him to stop, to make him see sense, but he just won't see sense. And I've got May to think of, Benjy.... I've got *her* life, and *her* future to think of."

"I'm sorry," said Benjy, because he didn't know what else to say. Did she actually expect him to volunteer to take his father to one side and have a man-to-man chat with him? Did she really expect *Benjy* to be able to put Jim Stephens straight on matters of duty and obligation? Could she possibly expect that his father would take the least little bit of notice of him, even if he tried?

Alas, life just wasn't that simple.

"That stuff's very delicate, isn't it?" she said, nodding her head in the direction of the four terraria. "It's wonderful, really, they way it runs off the household electricity supply, just like all the appliances."

"It doesn't use the current directly," he said, uneasily. "The electricity just heats up the elements inside the blocks. Mutaclay primary producers are thermosynthetic, you see, not photosynthetic the way plants are. They can use the radiant heat from the pinlamps, but they grow much better on a heated substrate—the ceramic blocks making up the mountain in Tank Four function just like the hob on the stove, really."

"You couldn't just load them into a truck and move them someplace else, could you?" she said, pretending—but not very hard—to be making innocent conversation. "They'd all *die*, wouldn't they?"

He realized, a little belatedly, what she was getting at. "I don't think Dad wants to *move out*," he said, warily. "He hasn't said anything to me about it. I don't think you need to worry about *that*."

She seemed to be fighting a temptation to grin wolfishly. "That's not the *relevant issue*," she said. "The relevant issue is that his screwing around is making things intolerable for May and for me, and if it doesn't stop...well, the option of remaining here might cease to be open to him. How long has that precious experiment of yours been running now? Ever since Christmas, right? It really means something to you, doesn't it?" She was still trying to speak conversationally, but not succeeding. *So it's blackmail and not plaintive persuasion after all*, he thought.

Paradoxically, blackmail seemed easier to take aboard than cajoling and wheedling. He no longer felt that he was being invited to betray some essential loyalty. He tried to put on his best expression of child-like innocence, intending to retaliate in kind.

"Dad always said that the house was half ours and half yours," he said, wonderingly. "Could you really just *throw us out?*" He was assuming, of course, that the answer was *no*.

"Nobody wants to throw anybody out, Benjy," she said. "That's not what we want at all. What we want—what we *all* want, Benjy—is for life to be pleasant and harmonious. We want to be a family, Benjy, pulling together the way families do. And we all have to do our bit to help, don't we? Nobody can just sit on the sidelines, staying out of it. Everybody has to *join in*. That's what life is all about: pulling together, joining in, helping out. That's what families are *for*."

The door opened again, and Benjy's father walked in. He barely glanced at Benjy before turning to stare at Monica. "What the hell is going on here?" he asked.

"Benjy and I were talking," said Monica. "Is there something wrong with that?"

"What about?" His tone was aggressive, but not quite angry.

"About his experiment. You ought to take more interest in his experiment, Jim. That Shane woman from the university who came out last month was very impressed with it, wasn't she, Benjy?"

"I know all about his experiment," Benjy's father lied. "Who was it bought him the mutaclay and all those goddam tanks? I've given him every encouragement, haven't I?"

"All right," said Monica, standing up and moving past him to the door. "There's no need to get upset. We were only talking. I *am* the boy's mother, after all."

Benjy could see that it was on the tip of his father's tongue to issue a denial of the last point, and was strangely grateful to see the impulse strangled.

It was not until the door had closed and the sound of Monica's footsteps had receded that Benjy's father turned around to face him.

"So," he said, with an evident effort. "How's the experiment coming along?"

"I'm not sure," said Benjy, glad not to have been asked a more difficult question. "Something kind of unexpected cropped up, but in a way that might be good. It confuses the original plan, but it might make the whole thing more interesting. You see, one of the two motile species is becoming *two* species—maybe because the distribution of the competitor has somehow divided its members into two almost-distinct groups...." He trailed off as it became obvious that his father wasn't really listening.

"You know," said Jim Stephens, "that woman is really letting herself go. Do you remember how *pretty* she used to be. It's not just the tranks and the booze...hell, it's an *attitude of mind*. I'm afraid she's not much of a mother to you, Ben—not any more." His father had taken to calling him "Ben" lately, or even "Benboy," as if to emphasize the fact that he was growing up. According to his father's way of thinking, although he had never actually said so, "Benjy" was evidently not a name befitting a grown man.

"She's okay," Benjy said, defensively.

"And that daughter of hers is growing into a real bitch. Monica ought to set a better example, she really ought."

"May's okay," said Benjy. "She's just...."

"A prick-teasing bitch is what she is," his father said, firmly, "And there ain't no justice in *that*." He grinned at his own feeble play on words, and looked hard at Benjy, expecting an echo. Benjy managed a faint smile.

"Don't get any ideas, though," his father went on. "She's too much for a little guy like you. She'd eat you up and spit you out. Find something easier for practice. Got to get out there, though—won't find nothing sitting on your butt in here. It's high summer, for Christ's sake. Forget the sludge-tanks for a while—run around a little; play some ball. Too many kids sit home looking at those goddam screens and playing with those goddam keyboards all day long. You gotta get *out there*."

Benjy feared that this might be a prelude to one of his father's favorite speeches, about how electronic brains were all very well, but at the end of the line there had to be *moving parts* to get the job done. Jim Stephens made his living servicing the mechanical parts of various kinds of industrial and household robots, and was perversely proud of the fact that he took over where what he called "the software so-called engineers" had to leave off.

"It's okay," Benjy said, deciding that it would be diplomatic simply to ignore the greater part of what his father had said. "I'm almost finished. I won't be late for dinner. I promised Monica. I just have to do this *one thing.*"

"I know the feeling, kid," his father said, with another of those grins. "I know the feeling. Don't mind your Mom too much— women always come a bit unstuck when their looks begin to go. Nothing to worry about. It's all under control."

"I like Monica, really," Benjy said, cautiously. "May too. It's all okay. I just wish everything could be a little *smoother....*"

"Don't I know it," said his father. "All those tranks and *still* she's got a temper like a polecat. But her bark's worse than her bite, and her throwing arm ain't dangerous in spite of all the practice she puts in. Don't let her worry you too much—like I say, everything's under control."

Benjy knew that there was no point trying to make himself any clearer. His father was in too ebullient a mood. In fact, he was in the kind of mood that May had lately taken to calling— but not within her mother's hearing—"freshly-laid."

"I'll see you in a few minutes," Benjy said, doggedly, trying hard not to make it sound like a dismissive instruction. "I've just got to file this stuff—it's important to keep a full record."

"That woman from the university really was interested, huh?"

"Not *that* much," Benjy confessed. "But she did say that the college people liked my design enough to duplicate it in the lab. They're running a couple of months behind, so it's too early to say whether they'll get speciation too, but it'd be real interesting if they did."

"Sure," said Jim Stephens. "Sure it would. But remember what I say, now. You're only young once—time to be old when you're old. You only got one life." Having delivered this advice, in his best paternal tone, he left.

* * * * * * *

Benjy wasted no time at all in collating and packaging his results and sending them off to Mutaclay's and the university's data-banks. By the time it was all done he felt much better. Monica's visit and its aftermath had faded into unimportance.

Maybe, he thought, someone running a similar experiment was keeping tabs on his results week by week. Maybe someone would get in touch with him by e-mail, wanting to discuss the implications of the recent development. Maybe this would really lead somewhere, get his name and picture into the bulletin. *Benjamin Stephens, a young mutaclay engineer from a small north-eastern town, has produced an interesting and unprecedented situation while mounting an experiment to prove that Gause's Axiom does not necessarily apply to mutaclay populations in the laboratory any more than it applies to DNA-organisms....*

In the great community of mutaclay enthusiasts there were no insurmountable barriers of age or status, so if anyone *did* take an interest in his work it was just as likely to be a full professor as some other hobbyist adolescent. The whole mutaclay enterprise was so new, so multidimensional, so rapidly moving forward, that *anything* might happen, to anyone....

"The possibilities," he whispered to himself as he finally left the room, valiantly making the best of his uncertainties, "are endless. Literally endless."

4. December 2021

Benjy removed the developed chromatogram and immediately reset the equipment for a second run. Double-checking the assay results was time-consuming, but Benjy had found that it wasn't tiresome at all—quite the reverse, in fact. The steady accumulation of his data had attained a momentum of its own, which seemed quietly magnificent. His technique was now honed to perfection; he felt that he could have gone through the whole process blindfolded if he had to. He took real pleasure nowadays from the deft efficiency of his hands as they dissected out and replaced the allotted squares of substrate, and he felt that the way the purple patches migrated across the chromatograms had a fluid grace of its own.

The last doubts were ebbing away now. It had become abundantly clear that there were now four motile-representative clusters where there had earlier been three. He felt that he had never in his life seen anything half so beautiful as the pattern of separation mapped out on the computer's time-lapsed series of images.

"It might be a freak," he said to himself, as he put the computer through its paces one last time, "but it's a *lucky* freak. This is the one-in-a-million precarious situation that *works*."

He winced at the sound of an unprecedentedly loud crash from below. *Jesus*, he thought. *That has to be the table! And it must have been piled high with stuff.*

The voices were very loud—so loud that he paused to wonder how he had been able to ignore them for so long. It wasn't so very mysterious; when he was concentrating hard he could filter out almost anything, and the sound of raised voices was hardly unfamiliar.

Now he had begun to pay attention he perceived that it was not just Monica's voice that had attained its maximum decibel level. His father was shouting at the top of his voice too, and the stentorian blast was colored by a brutal anger that Benjy could not remember ever having heard before.

Unfortunately, the moment he brought his concentration to bear on the question of what was being said the row broke up, leaving him none the wiser as to its details. He heard a door slam, and then heard footsteps on the staircase. They were his father's footsteps, and Benjy counted them uneasily, waiting to see where they would lead.

They led, as Benjy had feared, to the door of the room in which he sat, which flew open.

"An ouster!" yelled Jim Stephens. "The bitch has only hit us with a fucking ouster!" He was waving a piece of paper in his hand, which he thrust at Benjy as he crossed the room. Benjy took it, cringing as he did so from the force of his father's arousal. He saw that it was some kind of official document.

"What's an ouster?" he asked, querulously.

"It's a court order," his father said, still towering over him, abuzz with unsuppressed rage. "It's a court order throwing us out of our own fucking home."

Benjy looked down at the document again, trying to focus his eyes on the print. "What?" he said, dumbly.

"The bitch couldn't be content with filing for divorce," his father went on, the words still overloud and vibrant with bitterness. "Oh no—she couldn't just pack *her* bags like any other washed-up paper widow. She had to go the extra distance. You know what she's done? She's practically charged me with sexual molestation of a fucking minor! She's got an order ousting me from my own fucking house on the grounds that I'm endangering her fucking daughter! Can you believe it?"

The words were in focus now, and Benjy read through them as efficiently as he could, while the import of the information slowly sank in.

"She can't do this," he said, faintly. "She can't."

"Damn right she can't," said Jim Stephens. "You ever see me touch that girl? No! It's *perjury*, and there's no way in the world she can get away with it. No way. We're going to fight this, Benboy. We're going to fight it to the end. We'll be back, son, never fear. This is just the beginning. If the bitch wants a war, she can have a fucking war."

Benjy was still scanning the paper, looking at the slightly-blurred dates that had been filled in by an overaged ink-jet printer. "But Dad," he said, faintly. "This says we have to be out by *Christmas Eve!*"

Christmas Eve was less then ten days away.

"Isn't that just typical?" Jim Stephens retorted. "Throwing her husband and sixteen-year-old stepson on to the streets on

Christmas Eve. Doesn't that just say it all? Spiteful bitch!"

"You have to stop this," said Benjy, grimly. All the color seemed to have drained out of his voice. He sounded like an antique voice-synthesizer. *It can't happen,* he was saying to himself, under his breath. *It can't happen. Not like this.*

"I'll have us back in just as soon as I can, Benboy. We'll be in and *she'll* be out, just as soon as my guy can get a hearing. They served this thing on me at the office, and I was on the phone right away. It's clear cut—unless they have independent testimony from a witness, or medical evidence with a clear DNA-spectrum, their word ain't worth shit against ours. They can't get away with this kind of ambush by slander. We might be spending Christmas in a motel, son, but it'll just be a time-out."

"You don't understand," said Benjy, wondering why he sounded so absurdly mechanical. "I can't go—not even for a week. *I can't go.*"

Jim Stephens paused before replying to that, but whether he was thinking or just getting his breath back Benjy couldn't tell. Six or seven seconds passed before he said, "We can't get a hearing before Christmas, son. No way. The shark says we have to comply—he says if we're delinquent it'll count against us. He reckons we'll win all right, but he says we have to play by the rules and let the other side show up dirty. It won't be for long, son, I promise you. That bitch is going to get what's coming to her this time. I'll show her she can't mess around this way with *us.*"

Benjy scanned the document for the third time, to make certain that it said what he thought it said. It did—but that didn't make things any easier. He looked sideways at the assay equipment and the pinlamp that illuminated the slopes of the mountain in Tank Four. His cowardly instincts melted away beneath the force of a wholly conscious sense of dire necessity.

He took a deep breath, knowing that he needed courage now the way he'd never needed it before.

"I can't go, Dad," he said.

"We *have* to go, son."

"That's not true, Dad. This doesn't say that *I* have to go. It only says that *you* have to go. I have to stay, Dad. I can't leave the experiment. Not even for a week."

Benjy was painfully aware that his father had suddenly become ominously still and stiff. He watched in trepidation as Jim Stephens' gaze flickered back and forth between the tanks, the glowing computer screen, and his own upturned face.

"It can't be done, Ben," said his father, finally, in what was obviously meant to be a carefully controlled and scrupulously reasonable tone. "We have to stand together on this. We have to fight it two against two. You have to come with me."

"I can't," said Benjy, helplessly.

A single tremor ran across Jim Stephens' face, but his features were more rigidly controlled now than Benjy had ever seen them. "This is more important than your experiment," his father said—and now it was *his* voice that sounded synthetic, unreal. "This is our lives—yours and mine. This is our future, my fucking *reputation*. You can't stay here after *this*—it'd look like you were taking *her side*. It'd look like you believed what she's saying." He paused, and left it to his eyes to carry on. *You don't believe it, do you?* his eyes said, bleakly.

"It has nothing to do with what Monica says—with what anybody says," Benjy told him, earnestly. "I just can't leave the experiment. The mutation rate is borderline tachytelic, but the situation's still stable. The second of the two initial populations is undergoing speciation. Nothing like that has ever happened before, Dad. It's unique. The duplicate experiment Doctor Shane's students set up at the university settled into a much duller routine—just a straightforward falsification of Gause's Axiom, maybe not even that. It can't be left, Dad. If I miss just one count, just *one* cut-and-paste procedure, it'll destabilize. It'll break down—I know it will. No one else has ever done this, Dad—*no one*. Hell, Dad, *I can't just walk out and leave it!*"

His father was starting at him, utterly uncomprehending. "It's just a toy, son," he said, gently. He really was trying to be reasonable. "It's just fancy plasticine. It doesn't matter. We're talking about our lives here, our actual lives. I need you to help me out here, Ben. I need you to be on my side."

"It's *not* just a toy," Benjy insisted. "It's a kind of life. It's a kind of life at the very beginning of its evolution. It's trying to figure out how to become more complex, how to develop real cells, how to evolve into something better. It's not a toy!"

Benjy was watching his father's face, and he saw him switch off the argument and go into parental authority mode. It was just like that—like a change of mental gear. One moment there was a discussion going on, the next there was just an implacable wall. "Pack your bags, Benjy," said Jim Stephens, in a whiplash tone that forbade any possibility of rebellion. "No buts, no arguments. Just pack your bags. Pack your goddam mudworms if you think you have to, but pack. We're leaving first thing in the morning."

Benjy wished with all his heart that he could find the courage to say "No" out loud, but he knew it would make no difference even if he did.

Only actions could speak from now on. But what on earth was he going to do?

* * * * * * *

Benjy was still sitting at the computer when May came in.

"Look," she said, awkwardly, "I'm sorry. I really am. I didn't have any choice—and anyway, *he* started it. He's the one who's been screwing around. He brought it on himself."

"I just talked to Doctor Shane at the university," said Benjy, quietly. "I asked her if she could send someone out here every third day, to stand in for me and keep things going. She really wasn't interested—she really didn't *care*. Can you figure that? Is it because she thinks I'm just a kid? Or is it that even *she* thinks mutaclay is just smart dirt, just something to use for playing qualification-games? You have to talk to your mother, May. You have to tell her to stop this, to let us stay. I have to keep the experiment going."

"You think *I* can tell her that?" said May, incredulously. "You think *anybody* can tell her *anything* when she's in this kind of mood? Jesus, Benjy, you must know us better than that."

"This is more important than moods," he told her. "We have to make her see. *I* have to make her see, if you can't."

May laughed derisively. "Like you made your dad see?"

He looked her squarely in the eye. "I'm not going, May," he said, firmly.

"What're you going to do? Barricade yourself in?"

"If I have to," he said.

"Shall I ask your dad to fetch you a hammer and nails? What do you intend using? The bed-frame? Not the tables, surely— that would mean disturbing your precious experiment, wouldn't it?"

Benjy looked at the door, mournfully. It had a lock, but the lock was electronic and his father knew the code. Even if he reprogrammed it, his reprogramming could be overridden from the house's central system. He could push the bed up against the door, but that was about the best he could achieve. He knew that he wouldn't be given the chance to do anything more elaborate.

"I'm not mentioned in the court order," he said, in a low tone. "I don't have to go. He can't force me. I can get a lawyer of my own."

"My mother doesn't want you here, with or without your father," May said, bluntly. "She wants you both out."

"She asked for my help, once," he said. "She asked me to talk to him."

"If you did," May pointed out, "it didn't work. We're way past that now. She never loved you, you know. She never even liked you much. You were just something that came along with *him*. Everything she ever did for you she did for *his* sake. And now she's had her fill of him, she never wants to set eyes on you again."

It was true, Benjy thought. It was all true, and would have been abundantly clear to him all along if only he'd bothered to think about it—if only he'd bothered to look at it with the objective eye of a budding scientist.

"It's all a lie, isn't it?" Benjy muttered, resentfully. "He never laid a finger on you, did he?"

"Only because I'd cut it off if he did," she retorted. "He *wants* to—just the way you do. I don't have to tell any lies, Benjy. I just have to say what I've seen—what I see every day of the week, when he actually bothers to come home. What *you'd* see every day of the week, if you weren't always hiding up here, messing about with your fucking tanks full of fucking mud."

"He wouldn't *do* anything to you," said Benjy. "You know that. So does Monica."

"Nobody *knows*," she said, flatly. "These things happen. It's a fact of life. Men like your dad are dangerous, Benjy, and not just because they're incapable of keeping their promises. You'll be dangerous too, when you stop hiding yourself away every night, trying to figure the difference between one microscopic worm and another. You have the same faithless genes as he does, the same lying eyes. Even you can't be a kid forever, and when you stop, you'll be just another chip off the same old block."

Benjy stared at her, remembering that she'd come in so that she could tell him how sorry she was. What had deflected her into that tirade? Was it his fault? For the first time, he wondered whether they might be right, and whether *he* really might be the one who was wrong, the one who was mad. Suppose, he thought, they *were* right, and the experiment really *didn't* matter, and the mutaclay's achievement was just one more futile, fruitless, meaningless ripple in the primordial slime...what then? Did *anything* matter?

"I'm not going," he said, yet again—but for the first time, the words had an ominously hollow ring, as it finally penetrated to the inmost heart of him that he really didn't have the power to determine that.

There's nothing I can do, he thought, suddenly swamped by a wave of appalling desolation. *Nobody's going to take any notice; nobody's even going to listen. They're just going to blow it all away, without even thinking about it. It just doesn't matter to them. I don't matter to them. Nothing matters but their stupid determination to tear one another apart.*

Benjy came slowly to his feet, and looked at the ceiling of his room, and howled at the top of his voice: *"I'm not going! I won't go! D'you hear me, Dad...Monica? I CAN'T LEAVE THE EXPERIMENT!"*

He knew, even as he did it, how ridiculous it was. For years he had sat up here night after night, listening with half an ear to raised voices, knowing full well how stupid and futile it was to think that shouting something at the top of your voice could make it come true—and yet, when you came to the end of the line, what else was there?

What other way was there to rage against the fallibility of men and the viciousness of fate? He was only human, after all—only a kid. He couldn't *change* anything.

The echoes had hardly died away before Jim Stephens came back into the room. He was still outwardly calm; he had finished all *his* ranting and raving. He looked at Benjy with naked distaste—not with anger, not with hatred, just *distaste*.

"I changed my mind," he said, as though to nobody in particular. Then he walked over to the table, lifted the lid off Tank Four and reached in with his big, gnarled, unsterile hand.

One by one he wrested the four layers of the "mountain" from their bed, and one by one he hurled them across the room, each in a different direction. One by one they crashed into the walls, sending minute globules of mutaclay everywhere.

Jim Stephens wiped his hands on his shirt, turned to Benjy, and said: "Tidy up the mess, Ben. Then pack your bags. It's over. We're leaving. We aren't coming back. You and I, we have to get on with the rest of our lives." As he strode out of the room again he cast a single malevolent glance in May's direction, and hissed: *"Bitch!"* He was gone by the time she managed to lift a rude retaliatory finger.

"Nice guy, your dad," she said to Benjy, with feeling.

Benjy didn't reply. He was dumbstruck. He just stared at he wreckage of his experiment. *Three hundred and fifty-eight days,* he thought, numbly. *Nearly three hundred generations of the motiles. Two new species. And it all comes to this. Five seconds of destructive wrath. Five seconds, and everything wiped out.*

There were no tears in his eyes. Desolation didn't permit tears. The enormity of the event was too great to be encompassed by any simple, childish, tear-jerking emotion.

"That's life," said May, after a little while, perhaps not quite as sarcastically as she had intended. "So it goes. When things get out of hand, there's no way of stopping it. When people can't get along any more, it all just comes apart."

There was no arguing with that.

Benjy, still desolate and speechless, made no reply. There was nothing to be said, let alone shouted. But he realized, slowly and silently, that the fact that there was nothing he could say didn't necessarily mean that there wasn't an answer.

What would a sentient dinosaur have felt, he thought, on the day when that rogue asteroid came hurtling out of nowhere? Two hundred million years of diversification, speciation, problem-solving...and all wiped out with a single casual flourish, by a bolt from the blue. Would it have cried, or laughed, or simply have shrugged its reptilian shoulders and said, "That's life. So it goes. Another world ripped to shreds. Dust to dust, ashes to ashes, back to square one."

He stared, helplessly, at the terrarium whose contents had been so recklessly scattered and smashed, and at the bright pinprick of warm white light that had shone upon the little world twenty-four hours a day for three hundred and fifty-eight days like the star of Bethlehem, full of hope and promise.

For a moment, there *was* a tear there. But then he let the light fill his eyes, and drive out all other sensation.

It doesn't have to be this way, he said, trying with all his might to invest the thought with the force and authority of divine revelation. *Whatever else is lost, the knowledge isn't. Just because things get out of hand, just because things get smashed, just because everything comes apart, it doesn't mean that it always has to be that way, now and forever. Whether it's care that does it or sheer blind luck, things can work, things can grow, things can change and still stay together. If only they get enough chances, things can work out in the end. We're here, aren't we? In all our awesome complexity, we're here, even though we started out as nothing but ambitious dirt, nothing but clever clay. And in the end, one way or another, we'll find a way to get it all together, to make things work. That's* life, *May. That's what* real *life is all about.*

He let he thought die away before he even tried to speak, and when he did speak, all he said was, "I'm sorry too."

"What?" said May, probably having forgotten that she'd offered an apology of her own.

"I said, I'm sorry too."

"Oh," she said, uncertainly.

He turned to her, and put out his arms, not tremulously but with real confidence, real determination.

She hesitated, but in the end she let him put his arms around her and bid her a proper farewell, on behalf of the past they had shared, the world they had not, and the life they never would.

HOT BLOOD

When I first went into the blood business I had no idea that vampirism would ever become fashionable, or that it would provide me with the opportunity to fulfill my mother's dying wish by saving my brother Frankie from a life of crime. When I built my first bloodshed in one of the less picturesque parts of the Pennines and stocked it with four hundred genetically-modified swine, the business was a simple matter of producing designer blood for xenotransfusion. Biotech companies were busy engineering animals whose blood was far better for patients in need than anything that could be leeched from human donors, because it was augmented with various kinds of healing aids as well as being guaranteed free of inconvenient viruses and prions.

It might have been a profitable business even then, if I hadn't been squeezed from every side. Every time I got my head above water the relevant taxes would rise, or the interest on my loans would be hiked, or the stocks I'd removed to the breeding pens would become obsolete, or some franchise consultant with a bee in his bonnet about economies of scale would convince me that I'd never get ahead if I didn't expand. Even so, I'd probably have stayed completely honest if it hadn't been for Frankie's evil influence.

Frankie had always been the hot-headed and hot-blooded one: the compulsive taker of short cuts, the fanciful wheeler-dealer. He had started his criminal career when neither he nor the century had yet attained their twenties, working for a cigarette-smuggler in Huddersfield. Frankie's luck being what it was, the bottom fell out of that racket mere months after he had decided to go independent—but Frankie's luck being what it was, he was just in time to catch the leading edge of the great plantigen panic of '29. For the next five years he hawked genetically-enhanced potatoes and carrots out of the back of his van from Manchester to Doncaster, cutting a tidy profit even on the rare occasions when the veg was carrying the subtle merchandise he claimed. His so-called fleet grew from one van to twenty—eleven of them refrigerated—before fate and a couple of dissatisfied customers caught up with him, at which point his newly-acquired wealth melted like snow in July into the black hole of his medical expenses.

The doctors fixed him up all right—better than new in many ways—but that only made it harder for Frankie to learn the lesson that experience had been trying to teach him. While they were picking the bullets out of his back, they had to pump no less than forty-one liters of designer blood through his system, and while he was laid up for a further six weeks regenerating his pulverised kidneys, they had to give him another fifty-six liters to provide "resident stem-cell stimulation, nascent tissue reinforcement, and analgesic support," plus twelve more to compensate for "dialysis wastage." At any rate, that's what the bill said—and who among us nowadays has the guts to challenge a flesh mechanic's accounts?

I suppose, looking back, it's no wonder that Frankie came out of hospital with a very healthy regard for the value of genemod pig's blood. Given that he was Frankie, it was also no wonder that he came out with a brand new girl friend: a senior staff nurse with contacts—not the kind that you put in your eyes—and the bulkiest breast-enhancements I ever saw. Human mammary glands aren't very useful as bioreactors—on that particular playing-field the cows will always win hands down—but there's a certain kind of woman who reckons that the fringe-benefits more than make up for the low rent, and Janis was definitely that sort of woman. Frankie, alas, was always that sort of woman's man, and to make matters worse he was going through a phase when he felt that his image couldn't be complete unless it included a "moll."

Frankie and Janis came to stay with me for a week following his release from medical captivity. He told me on the phone that he needed a few days' rest and recuperation in the "deep countryside" but I knew there had to be more to it than that. I even suspected that there'd be trouble, but I could hardly turn him down, could I? He was my brother, and he never ceased to remind me, with a suitably satirical cackle, that blood is thicker than water.

I was mildly surprised that he asked me to show him the bloodsheds—I had three by that time—and very surprised that he got through the tour without throwing up, but he never had time to feel queasy when his mind was on money.

"You know, Jeff," he said to me, as he crunched the crackling he'd carefully moved to the side of his plate while he ate his dinner, "this place could be a little gold-mine if you could only bring yourself to stretch the regs a bit."

"No it couldn't," I told him. "The Ministry comes down like a ton of bricks on anyone who sets up unlicensed stock. If you're thinking of importing black-market pigs from China, forget it. Most of them are dodgier than those King Edwards you used to shift by the sackload, and even the ones with genuine supplements have genetic fingerprints that stick out like a sore thumb when Mr. Maff pays a routine call. I'm thirty-two expecting to live to a hundred-and-twenty, and I aim to keep my license clean for at least another fifty years."

"You mistake my meaning, little bro," he said, putting on a pseudo-parental manner even though he was only eighteen months the elder and hadn't ever taken care of me even after Mum's death. "Replacing your stock with illegal immigrants would be a bad move, I quite agree—but there's more than one way to skin a piggie. I never realized until I had to grow a new pair of kidneys how good a little fresh blood can make you feel. It was a real tonic, I can tell you—but I couldn't help feeling, towards the end, that the medics were being just a little bit *mean*."

"Not according to the bill they stuck you with," I pointed out.

"Not *quantitatively* mean," he said, having obviously been practicing his pronunciation. "*Qualitatively* mean. There was a possibility of addiction, they said, so they had to thin out the analgesics. Those little red cells were stuffed full of all kinds of nutrients, antibiotics, and collagen-precursors, but when it came to the feel-good factor, they felt just a little bit anemic, if you follow my drift."

I followed his drift all right. The genetic fingerprints recorded by the Ministry's field-testing devices are a little bit blurred: they're reliable as far as detecting which genes are present, but they're not much good at estimating the level of their activity. What Frankie had in mind—thanks, no doubt, to a crash course in elementary genetics administered by Janis, the senior staff nurse—wasn't anywhere near as crude as smuggling patent-busting pigs. What he had in mind was tweaking the expressivity of the genes with which my fully-licensed Ministry-approved pigs were already fitted so as to alter the product-balance. He was suggesting that I should increase the concentration of the morphine-analogues in the blood my pigs were producing.

"Don't you think the hospitals would notice if their patients were boosted into orbit?" I asked, although I already knew what he was going to say next.

"Don't be daft, Jeff," he retorted. "What would be the point of selling it on to hospitals at list price? Fact is, not all the blood that's sold to hospitals ends up in the patients—not *current* patients, at any rate. Some of it gets sold on via the back door, mostly to people who've got a taste for it, but also to people who've heard how good it is and would like to acquire a taste for it. It's a growing market, kiddo. It won't be as big as the plan-tigen bubble, but it won't turn turtle the way that one did. The situation is crying out for someone to cut out the middleman and take the product direct from the farm to the consumer."

"And Janis knows how you can do that, I suppose?" I said.

"Bang on," he informed me. "And guess who happens to have seven refrigerator-trucks sat in the garage doing bugger all?"

"Haven't they been repossessed?"

"The other four were," he admitted. "The ones I still have were acquired through unorthodox channels. As their existence was always semi-official, at best, they sort of slipped through a hole in the receiver's net."

Frankie went on to explain, in great detail, exactly how he and Janis could fix it up for an engineer to call around and collect a few dozen embryos from my breeding sows. He'd remove them to some university lab—the only way the government can hold down higher education expenditure is to turn a blind eye to the details of their entrepreneurial adventures—and tweak the genes controlling the expressivity of the genes on the artificial chromosomes. He wouldn't switch anything off, because the therapeutic value of the cocktail accounted for at least a part of the demand, but he'd pump up the volume of the products that had "recreational value." Then he'd send them back to be reared; with luck, enough of them would beat the attrition rate to establish a breeding population.

If I could step up the production of my industry standard pigs even slightly, the gradual drop in production distributed through existing channels as I moved the new stock into the bloodsheds wouldn't look suspicious. The product of the re-enhanced animals would be loaded into Frankie's trucks and spirited away to a destination I didn't need to know anything about, and my cut would be payable on a weekly basis, in hard cash. The Treasury had been trying to develop a cashless economy for the best part of half a century, but the people wouldn't tolerate it. The man in the street loves his fiddles, and without cash, fiddling would become a hackers' monopoly—and the only thing the man in the street hates more than the Inland Revenue is the hacker who can pick his pocket from the other side of the world.

I took some persuading, but in the end went for it. Maybe I was weak, but I was getting sick of always having to run faster just to stay in the same place. I was also getting just a little bit tired of always being the sensible one. To cap it all, and despite the occasional hallucinatory image of Mum spinning in her grave, it really did seem like a good idea—a better one than I had ever expected from Frankie the cockeyed optimist.

* * * * * * *

Everything went well for the first couple of years. In fact, it went extremely well. The tweaker was an ace, and I reared two boars and a sow from the first batch of re-enhanced embryos. They were not only fit but fertile, and my breeding population increased rapidly. Frankie had been absolutely right about the growth-potential of the market, and I'd been in the business long enough to have learned a wrinkle or two about stretching production, so my regular production didn't suffer at all. The extra work was hard, of course, but I was used to working sixteen-hour days, and it was a temporary problem. As my cash-flow improved I was able to hire another full-timer and two more part-timers, reducing my own hours by a third.

During '35 and '36 I expanded my "special herd" from two dozen to two hundred, and then to three hundred. I had to add an extra bloodshed to my premises and take in more standard-ized stock, but the rate of innovation had slowed somewhat and there was no need for a large-scale replacement program. I not only passed all four of the half-yearly Ministry inspections but survived a surprise visit from the Animal Welfare Squad. The random geneprintings sampled a couple of dozen re-enhanced animals along with a hundred and fifty others, but all the smudges were well within the tolerance-limits of Mr. Maff's portable equipment.

In the meantime, ever-increasing quantities of cash rolled in. By Christmas '36 I was able to get a couple of cosmetic enhancements of my own, and a whole new wardrobe of clothes that were smart in both senses of the word. I was beginning to get out a lot more too—so much, in fact, that in the spring of '37 I ended up with a girlfriend. Melanie was an engineer in the food industry, who had recently graduated from routine work on cereal-based whole-diet manna-powders to exploratory research in the relatively underdeveloped field of "texture management." Melanie was *much* nicer than Janis, because she'd never gone in for any kind of personal enhancement and wasn't the sort of woman who'd hire herself out as a bioreactor in any case.

Alas, when things first began to get sticky, Janis turned out to be not very nice at all. With her nurse's salary, her milk income, and her cut of the bloodrunning business she was clearing a tidy sum, but she was one of those people whose appetites increase as they're fed, and who can't tolerate the slightest setback. When our sales leveled off, and then began to slide, she put pressure on Frankie, demanding that he put pressure on me to increase production further and faster.

Actually, it wasn't really a production problem. Obsolescence doesn't affect illicit trade as much as legitimate business, but progress always marches on. When her contacts explained to her that better products were coming on-stream, she started banging on about starting over with a new set of re-tweaked embryos. I was reluctant to do that, partly because it would be expensive and troublesome, but also because I felt that I'd already got what I needed out of the illicit operation. It seemed to me that the hot blood had got me over the hump in my career, and that I could now make a go of the business without its support. I was quite happy to let the sideline cool off gradually and wither away—but I could tell that Frankie wasn't yet ready to go legit, and never would be while Janis' bosom was a millstone round his neck. So I procrastinated, figuring that time and increasing competition might settle the question.

For once, it was me who was being the cockeyed optimist.

All the while she was applying pressure to us, apparently Janis was also putting pressure on the people she was supplying to hike their retail prices, in order to facilitate a similar increase in the wholesale price. They couldn't do it. The market was still expanding, but it was also diversifying, in more ways than one. It wasn't just a matter of competing products but of competing organizations. Many of them were small independent operators just like us, but as the size of the market grew it attracted other kinds of people. When the old pros began to muscle in on the racket and the principle of natural selection came into force, the business evolved into something quite different and much more dangerous.

I had to explain to Frankie—although he, of all people, should have understood the logic of the situation—that we were getting out of our depth. If we were to keep going at all, I told him, the only sensible course was to keep our own operation small and unobtrusive, and to accept the creeping obsolescence of our product as a blessing that would help to persuade the new operators that we could not offer them any serious competition. Maybe Frankie tried to explain all this to Janis, but if so, the message got lost somewhere along the chain of transmission.

"You're out of touch, Jeff, stuck way out here on the moors," she explained to me, when Frankie brought her out to the farm to celebrate the second anniversary of our first big pay day. "The queues for elective surgery are growing longer every day, partly because new techniques in cosmetic somatic engineering keep rolling off the production line but mainly because you can't take the face and body God gave you into any interview anywhere in the city and walk out with a job. There isn't anyone in the country under forty who hasn't spent a vacation on the wards in the last couple of years—and that's not counting the sick, the injured, and the reproductively challenged. Just because the panic's over doesn't mean that the Eight Plagues have shot their bolt, and '36 was the biggest year ever for Extreme Sports. Everybody and his cousin has tasted xenotransfusion blood by now, and even the ones who get it while they're comatose come out the other end feeling that something is missing from their lives. This market is going to be *huge*, and we're in on the ground floor. All we have to do is *keep up*. Hell, in ten years time it'll probably be *legal*. It's the opportunity of a lifetime, Jeff, and we have to seize the day. We have to update our stock, and we have to step up production."

"Even if I did update the stock I couldn't build another shed," I told her, exercising my first line of defense. "I just don't have the land."

Her answer to that, of course, was to buy more—but our profits weren't *that* big, and ours wasn't the kind of business plan you can take to a bank.

"I can get you the money," she said. "I have contacts."

"So what you want me to do, Janis," I said, sarcastically, "is to borrow money from one lot of gangsters so that Frankie and I can go head to head with another lot of gangsters in a bloody turf war?"

The sarcasm was wasted, because that was exactly what she wanted to do.

So far, I'd managed to rig things so that my staff didn't know what I was up to, although they must have figured out that I had to be into *something* dodgy. Even those I'd only been able to take on with the aid of under-the-table cash were neighbors I'd known since I first moved to the area, who reckoned my operation was a thoroughly good thing for the local economy. I'd always treated them well, by their admittedly-meager standards, and they had a tradition of not blabbing to "the authorities" that went back to the nineteenth century and beyond. If I bought more land and built more sheds, though, I'd be seen as a man of disruptive ambition rather than one who had accommodated himself to the existing scheme of things. If I hired any more new staff I'd have to bring them in from further afield. Keeping the lid on the bigger operation would be a much trickier affair. A further issue, of steadily-increasing importance, was Melanie. She didn't know, as yet, that I was doing anything I shouldn't have been, but our relationship had matured to the point where I didn't want to keep secrets from her—and she was certainly smart enough to know that I couldn't expand on the basis of my honest business. So there were all kinds of powerful reasons why I had to say no to Janis, and that's what I did.

Unfortunately, Janis wasn't the sort of girl to take no for an answer.

Three weeks later I had a visit from two extremely well-dressed gentlemen who were extremely keen to lend me a lot of money, and very eloquent in explaining the reasons why I ought to take it.

I said no to them, too, as politely as I could.

I knew that Janis had exposed us to exactly the kind of attention I was desperate to avoid, but I clung to the hope that the smart men wouldn't consider it worth their while to persist. Unfortunately, and however paradoxical it might be, it's often the most unprincipled people who cling hardest to those points of principle they do uphold. Three days later, one of Frankie's vans was hijacked ten minutes after leaving the farm. The driver wasn't too badly roughed up, but the van and its cargo disappeared into thin air.

I summoned Frankie to a family conference and told him flatly that I wasn't prepared to go to war to defend the illicit side of my business, because losing—or even a hard-fought draw—would undoubtedly cost me everything. I also reminded him about Mum and the probability of her resting uneasily in her coffin. He told me that he was disappointed to hear me using such underhanded tactics, but that he understood where I was coming from. He promised to have a stern word with Janis and set her straight.

Three days later a second van was hijacked. This time, Frankie—following a plan whose details he hadn't thought to confide to me—was "riding shotgun." The driver and one of the hijackers ended up shot in the head, with their brains completely mashed, but even though two of the five remaining hijackers suffered painful injuries they were sufficiently businesslike to make sure that Frankie only ended up in hospital, facing stupendous medical bills and a *real* blood habit.

I spent that night slaughtering pigs. It took me until three in the morning to kill all the ones I needed to kill, and it required all of Frankie's remaining refrigerator trucks to ferry the carcasses to a semi-legal chop shop. Whether any of the crackling found its way to the side of one of Frankie's plates, hoarded for a climactic treat, I don't know.

I had to close down one of my sheds, but at least I'd made my position clear. Janis' friends decided that they, too, had made their point.

* * * * * * *

By the time the doctors brought him out of the induced coma, Frankie was flat broke again, but his lights were all switched on and his heart was back in the right place. Another week passed while he was suspended in a tank, conscious but not able to do much except watch subsurface TV, but once they hauled him out of the gel and into a bed he was allowed visitors. The first words out of his mouth were the ones that told Janis she was history. She didn't like it, especially because he did it in front of Melanie and me, but we figured that her threat-cum-promise that he'd live to regret it was so much hot air.

"It's time to give up the life of crime, Frankie," I told him. "I know you're over forty now, but we're living in the twenty-first century. It's not too late to start over. It's what Mum would want."

"I can't," he said, miserably. "You have no idea what it's like. I'm hooked, Jeff. Those bastards knew exactly what they were doing. It's not so much a matter of suffering the withdrawal symptoms—the doctors will pull me through that, at a price. It's all in the mind. Once you've tasted *real* blood, you can never be content with the stuff in your veins. You're way too straight to understand, but I'm committed to the dark side, as a customer if not as a supplier. If I can't work for myself, I'll have to work for *them*."

He meant that he had to earn his fix, and that if he couldn't do it as an entrepreneur he'd have to do it as a foot soldier. Even as a small-time entrepreneur his life-expectancy had looked shaky; as a mere foot soldier he'd be lucky to survive ten years.

"You can come and work for me," I said. "Or rather, for Melanie and me. The newest generation of enhanced swine produce shaggy coats at a phenomenal rate as well as super-abundant blood, and she's setting up a factory in my empty bloodshed to process the shearings."

"Process them into what?" he wanted to know. "Silk purses?"

"That's ears, not fleeces," I told him. "No, what we're aiming to do is to produce the ultimate in dietary roughage."

He looked at me as if I were mad. "What?"

"Dietary roughage." I didn't normally trouble Frankie with technical details, but for once I let my enthusiasm carry me away. "You see, the trouble with whole-diet products is that although they provide all the nutritional requirements of the human body, they don't entirely agree with the human digestive system. Whether you take them in liquid form or bulk them out artificially as porridge they don't have the kind of textural spectrum that your gut feels comfortable with. What the world needs right now is effectively-designed roughage, which has no nutritional value whatsoever—except for the flavorings and maybe a few trace-elements that are inconvenient in solution—but which fills the comfort-gap and the oral reward-gap that mannas leave unsatisfied. You might think that's easy, but it isn't. To get the necessary textural flexibility you need a very carefully-balanced blend of cellulose-analogues and keratin-derivatives. The engineers have been trying for decades to persuade plants to do the work, but there are problems with lignin-spinoff as well orchestrating a keratin-deposition system. It turns out that it's far more convenient to translocate the cellulose-analogue gene-set into pigskin. Melanie's right at the forefront of the field, and with my talent for coaxing extra production out of the stock we reckon we can steal a march on the opposition. The new products don't require refrigerator-trucks for transportation, and they're absolutely one hundred per cent legal."

"And what would I do?" he asked, plaintively. "I don't know the first thing about food tech."

"Yours would be a management position," I assured him.

"One that would pay enough to supply my need for you know what?" he said, miserably.

"Absolutely," I said. I thought—rightly—that there'd be plenty of time later to explain, in more private surroundings, that although I'd slaughtered the right number of pigs, in case anyone was taking a precise count, not all of them had been re-enhanced. I still had a small breeding population of happy-chemical supermanufacturers. I wasn't selling their produce, and I had no intention of doing so in the foreseeable future, but I certainly had more than enough to supply a few family members and close friends, should the need arise. Being the cool-headed one, if not the cold-blooded one, I always like to keep my options open, especially when I'm under excessive pressure to close them down.

Ironically, it turned out that Frankie's need for illegal substances wasn't quite as desperate as he had anticipated while he still lay inactive in his extremely expensive bed. Once he had thrown himself into his new job—which was a perfectly real job, with opportunities for career-progression as well as a healthy supply of responsibilities—he found that his dependency decreased by slow but inexorable degrees. By the time another year had passed, he was as fit as a flea, and by no means as obsessed with blood. Instead, he had become obsessed with every aspect of dietary roughage: its production, its design, and its marketing.

"It's criminal that this stuff should be legal," he said to me, when we had a little party to celebrate the second anniversary of our new joint venture. "I mean, it sounds stodgy but in fact it's pure fun. People love the stuff. They can eat it to their heart's content, savoring every texture, every flavor, and suffer not a single side-effect. It does *nothing*."

"Not exactly—and not for long," Melanie told him, a trifle severely. "It makes much more sense to accommodate some of the nutritional responsibilities that have previously been consigned to soluble manna-powders into a robust structured matrix. But that'll only be the start. It also makes sense to transfer some of the medical responsibilities that are currently provided by xenotransfusive blood. Bit by bit, products that are currently expressed in the blood-manufacturing cells of Jeff's pigs will be expressed in the follicular roots as well—or even instead."

"That's an engineer's point of view," the new Frankie told her, "but doing what's possible—even what might seem perfectly rational, to a superstraight person like you—isn't necessarily the right way to go. I think it would be a crying shame to start loading our stuff with useful functions, when what we could do is keep working on the fun aspects. It isn't as if the world's short of useful things. Hell, there are so many useful things around that we've forgotten what a wonder it is to have things around us that have no earthly use whatsoever. Trust me on this one, Mel—let's not confuse the issue by trying to make roughage into another kind of manna. Leave the demand-management to me, and I'll make us all three times as rich as we would be if we played it your way."

"What do you think, Jeff?" my wife-to-be asked me, loyally.

"Let's just take it one step at a time," I said, in my careful fashion. "Who knows what trends the new year will throw up?"

To tell the truth, I was still a bit worried about Frankie reverting to type, and I didn't like to hear him using phrases like "three times as rich." It turned out, though, that I had never spoken a wiser sentence in my entire life.

* * * * * * *

The new roughage was a big hit, not because anybody really needed it, but because it *felt right*.

The revolution in human eating habits that had alienated us from our innate digestive technology had happened long before modern times. It dated back at least to the invention of agriculture, and probably to the invention of cooking. We'd made astonishing progress in the interim, in terms of gastronomy as well as nutritional science, but there had always been a little something lacking: a small loophole in our satisfaction. It wasn't until the ingenuity of biotech engineers was brought to bear on the roughage problem that most people realized the problem existed—but once they discovered that it not only existed but had been solved, they took to the stuff like ducks to water.

Our early involvement in roughage production would have made us modestly well off even in the absence of other trends, and there was a period when Frankie urged me to get out of the blood business altogether so that we could concentrate all our resources on our most profitable hairlines. I wouldn't do that, partly because of my habitual cautiousness and partly because I figured that while our animals had no option but to have blood flooding their veins as well as hair fountaining out of their skins, we might as well make the most of both.

It was perhaps as well that I stuck to my guns, because it turned out that Janis had been right. By the mid-forties the illicit blood business had grown to such awesome proportions that it made no political sense to maintain its illegality. Not only were the laws in question criminalizing an absurdly high percentage of the population, but organized crime was getting out of hand *again.*

This time, even parliament and the police understood that the sensible response to that kind of situation was to call off the dogs. Consumer blood became legal in June '48, and the whole economic spectrum in which we operated was transformed, so to speak, at a stroke. Vampirism was all the rage by Halloween; no cocktail party was complete without a dozen bottles of the best, and the dossers in the city streets were buying it by the bucketful.

Suddenly, the demand for re-enhanced pigs far outstripped the supply. Anyone with a potential breeding population, no matter how it had been acquired, might as well have been in possession of a goose that could lay golden eggs. Under the protection of a temporary amnesty, I came clean about my secret sties and gave the little darlings the go-ahead to breed like rabbits.

Vampirism couldn't have become so popular, of course, if it hadn't been for the new roughage. Manna could supply the nutritional requirements of a vampire, but a digestive system that was already out of sorts because it wasn't entirely comfort-able with manna would have thrown a real wobbly under the further burden of orally-consumed blood. Thanks to the new roughage, though, the human gut could be perfectly at ease with itself while the palate enjoyed the plethora of delights produced by all the new kinds of blood that erupted on to the market.

Some hardened users, of course, remained adamant that the only proper way to take blood was straight into a vein, but the march of progress went on regardless. There was an aesthetic component to blood-drinking, which went far beyond the taste sensations that could be as easily satisfied by manna and roughage. Vampirism was a style thing: a matter of image. You might think that a practice that permeated every stratum of society wouldn't be much use as an image-maker, but it isn't so. Thanks to the ceaseless endeavors of twentieth-century film-makers, there were vampire icons available to suit every pocket and every idiosyncrasy. If there were a thousand kinds of blood, there were nearly as many accompanying rituals of consump-tion.

I knew that it couldn't last, of course, but I was fully prepared to ride the fad while the product was hot. There had never been a better time to be in the blood business, and I was determined to make the most of it. Mr. Maff the Regulator was still a blight upon the land, of course, because even civil servants can spot a golden opportunity, but a number of backhanders changed pockets and twice as many scrupulous eyes were turned in other directions, and for eighteen glorious months we were on top of the world. There wasn't a gangster in sight, because the gangsters were doing what gangsters always do in that kind of situation, and trying their level best to go legit.

Melanie and I got married in February '50, and Frankie was thoroughly convincing in the role of best man. By this time he was embarked upon a new and atypically healthy relationship of his own with Melanie's cousin and fellow food technologist, Suzanne. The honeymoon was a sheer delight, and fate smiled on us long enough to let all but a day of it elapse before we were urgently called home.

We were informed by the policeman who summoned us that Frankie had been waylaid while exiting Suzanne's apartment by a vengeful and crazy Janis, who was drugged up to the eyeballs on seriously dodgy blood derived from pigs illegally imported from China. She had shot him four times.

Fortunately, although Janis had aimed at Frankie's heart, the weight of her unwieldy weapon had dragged the trajectories of the bullets downwards, and all four had ended up in his abdomen. The doctors told me that when he had been stretchered in, he had told them not to bother to patch up the holes this time, so that the next lot could just pass right on through.

The bills were horrendous, but we could afford them—and we still had plenty of change to spare. When Frankie came out of the tank, he was still in a passably good mood.

"You see, Jeff," he said to me, as if he were proving a point, "it wasn't my criminal tendencies that kept getting me into trouble after all. It's just that I'm the kind of guy who gets shot up occasionally, whether he's going straight or not."

Suzanne wasn't impressed by this display of bravado. "Frank," she said, with the air of a person who meant exactly what she said, "I forbid you to do this again—*ever.*"

"Okay, Suze" he said, with surprising docility. "You're the boss."

"No," I reminded him, gently. "*I'*m the boss. But if you can possibly help it, I'd rather this was the last time. There are only so many times you can regrow a kidney and still produce workmanlike piss."

"No problem," he said. "If the worst comes to the worst I'll hire myself out as a bioreactor in order to get them re-enhanced."

"No you won't," said Suzanne. I realized then that Mum would have been proud of Suzanne, and proud of me for making Suzanne possible. The government had helped, of course, but the ultimate credit for Frankie's reformation was down to me.

Frankie, sensing that Suzanne had the measure of him, and that it was more accurate than he'd ever have liked to admit, switched to safer ground. "How's business?" he asked.

"Pretty good," I assured him, gladly. "The vampire fad has begun to fade out, but the medical side of the blood business is steady enough. Melanie and Suzanne have some really hot ideas for a new set of hairlines and the techs at the supply company have decided that there might be something useful to be made out of those cute little curly tails pigs have, so there's no danger of things becoming boring. There'll be plenty to occupy your mind when you're fit again, and plenty to do to get your muscles back in shape. You'd better recover quickly, though—we can't get by without you for much longer."

"Thanks, bro," he said, with enough genuine feeling to warm the cockles of a younger brother's heart and allow a dutiful mother to rest easy in her eternal sleep. "It's good to know that some things never change."

THE HOUSE OF MOURNING

Anna stared at her thin face in the mirror, wondering where the substance had gone and why the color had vanished from the little that remained. Her eyes had so little blue left in them that they were as grey as her hair. She understood what had become of her well enough to know that a disruption of the chemistry of the brain was bound to affect the body as profoundly as the mind, but the sight of her image in a soul-stealing glass reawakened more atavistic notions. It was as if her dangerous madness had wrought a magical corruption of her flesh.

Perhaps, she thought, it was hazardous for such as she to look into mirrors; the confrontation might be capable of precipitating a crisis of confidence and a subsequent relapse into delirium. Facing up to the phantoms of the past was, however, the order of the day. With infinite patience she began to apply her make-up, determined that she would *look* alive, whatever her natural condition.

By the time she had finished, her hair was tinted gold, her cheeks delicately pink, and her lips fulsomely red—but her eyes still had the dubious transparency of raindrops on a window-pane.

Isabel was late, as usual. Anna was forced to pace up and down in the hallway, under the watchful eyes of the receptionist and the ward-sister. Fortunately, she was in the habit of dressing in black for everyday purposes, so her outfit attracted no particular attention.

The ward-sister was there because there was a ritual to be

observed. Anna couldn't just walk out of the hospital, even though she was classed as a voluntary patient. She had to be handed over in a formal fashion, to signify that responsibility was being officially transferred from one sister to another. Not that Isabel really was her sister in a biological sense, any more than the ward-sister was; she and Anna had simply been parts of the same arbitrarily-constructed foster-family. They were not alike in any way at all.

When Isabel finally arrived, in a rush, with all her generous flesh and hectic color, the ceremony began.

"You must remember that this is Anna's first day out," the ward-sister said to Isabel. "We don't anticipate any problems, but you must make sure that she takes her medication at the appointed times. If she shows signs of distress, you should bring her back here as soon as possible. This emergency number will connect you with a doctor immediately."

Isabel stared at the number scrawled on the card as though it were the track of some mysterious bird of ill-omen.

To Anna, the sister said only: "Be good." Not "Have a nice time" or even "Take it easy," but simply "Be good." *It's better to be beautiful than to be good*, Anna thought, *but it's better to be good than to be ugly*. She had been beautiful once, and more than beautiful—so much more as to be far beyond the reach of Saint Oscar's ancient wisdom, but now there was nothing left to her except to be good, because her more-than-beauty had gone very, very bad.

Isabel, of course, had no idea that Anna was on her way to a funeral, and that her role was merely to provide a convenient avenue of escape. Anna waited until the car was a good two miles away from the hospital before she broached the subject. "Can you drop me at the nearest tube station," she said, lightly, "and can you let me have some money?"

"Don't be silly," Isabel said. "We're going home."

Isabel meant her own home, where she lived with a husband and two children, paying solemn lip-service to the social ideal. Anna had seen Isabel's husband three or four times, but only in the distance. He was probably one of those visitors' partners whose supportive resolution failed at the threshold of Bedlam—many in-laws preferred to wait in the grounds while their better halves attended to the moral duty of comforting their afflicted kin—but it was possible that Isabel had forbidden him to come in and be properly introduced. Few women relished the prospect of introducing their husbands to whores, even whores who happened to be their sisters—legalistically speaking—and whose sexual charms had been obliterated in no uncertain terms.

"No we're not," Anna said. "That's just something I had to tell the doctors, so they'd let me out. If I'd told them the truth, they'd have stopped me, one way or another."

"What truth?" Isabel wanted to know. "What on earth are you talking about? I'll have you know that I've gone to a lot of trouble over this. You heard what the nurse said. I'm responsible for you."

"You won't be doing anything illegal," Anna told her. "I'll get back on time, and nobody will be any the wiser. Even if I didn't go back, nobody would blame you. I'm the crazy one, remember. How much cash can you let me have?"

"I don't have any cash," Isabel told her, as she drove resolutely past Clapham South tube station without even hesitating. "I don't carry cash. Nobody does. It's not necessary any more."

That was a half-truth, at best. At the Licensed House where Anna had worked, the clients had used their smartcards, and the transactions had been electronically laundered so that no dirty linen would be exposed to prying wives or the Inland Revenue. The streetwalkers who haunted the Euroterminal and the Bull Ring had smartcard processors too, but their laundering facilities were as dodgy as their augmentations, and most of their clients paid in cash. It was all a matter of safety play.

"You can still *get* cash, can't you?" Anna said, innocently. "Walls still have holes, just like spoiled whores. Don't worry about missing Clapham South. Vauxhall will be fine."

"Just where the hell do you think you're going, Anna?" Isabel demanded, hotly. "Just what the hell do you think you're going to do?" That was Isabel all over: repetition and resentment, with plenty of hell thrown in.

"There's something I need to do," Anna said, unhelpfully. She had no intention of spelling it out. Isabel would protest violently just as surely as the doctors would have done. Unlike the doctors, though, Isabel was easy to manipulate. Isabel had always been scared of Anna, even though she had always been two years older, two inches taller, and two stones heavier. Now that Anna was a shadow of her former self, of course, it was more like four stones—but that only increased Anna's advantage.

"I won't do it," Isabel said, although the hopelessness of her insistence was already evident.

"I can do anything I like," Anna said, reflectively. "It's one of the perks of being mad and bad—you can do anything you like, and nobody's surprised. I can't be punished, because there's nothing they can take away that I haven't already lost. I could do with a hundred pounds, but fifty might do in a pinch. I have to have cash, you see, because people with scrambled brain chemistry aren't allowed smartcards. Fortunately, there'll always be cash."

She knew that there always would be cash, despite the fact that it was technically redundant. As long as there were outposts of the black economy that weren't geared up for laundering, there'd be cash—and everybody in the world was engaged in the black economy in some fashion, even if it was only token tax-dodging.

"I don't like being used," Isabel said, frostily. "I agreed to take you out for the day because you asked me to, and because the doctors thought it would be a good idea—a significant step on the way to rehabilitation. I won't stand for it, Anna. It's not fair."

Since she was six years old, Isabel had been complaining that "it" wasn't fair. She had never quite grasped the fact that there was no earthly reason for expecting that anything should be.

"There's bound to be a cash-dispenser at Vauxhall," Anna said. "Fifty would probably do it, if that's all you can spare. I've lost track of inflation since they put me in the loony bin, but money can't have lost that much value in three years."

Isabel braked and pulled in to the side of the road. She was the kind of person who couldn't drive and have a fit at the same time. Anna could tell that her sister was upset because she'd stopped on a double yellow line; normally, she'd have looked for a proper parking-place.

"What the hell is this about, Anna?" Isabel demanded. "Exactly what have you got me into? If you're using me as an alibi while you abscond from the hospital, I've a right to know."

"I'll be back on time," Anna assured her. "No one will ever know, except your husband and children. They'll probably be disappointed that they aren't going to meet your mad, bad, and dangerous-to-know foster-sister, but they'll get over it. You can bring them in one day next week, to make up for it. I'll be as nice as pie, psychochemistry permitting."

"*What is this all about?*" Isabel repeated, pronouncing each word with leaden emphasis, as if to imply that Anna was only ignoring her because she was too stupid to know what the question was.

"There's something I have to do," Anna said, nobly refraining from adopting the same tone. "It won't take long. If you won't give me the fifty pounds, can you at least let me have enough for a Travelcard. I have to go all the way across town to zone four."

Anna knew as soon as she'd said it that it was a mistake. It gave Isabel a way out. She should have hammered on and on about the fifty until she got it. In the old days, she'd never have settled for a penny less than she'd actually wanted, whatever kind of client she was dealing with.

Isabel reached into her purse and pull a handful of coins out of its dusty depths. "Here," she said, as if to say, *It's all you're worth, you stupid, fouled-up slut.* "If you want to go, go—to hell if you want to—but if this goes wrong, just don't try to blame me. And take your medication." Long before she arrived at the last sentence, she had reached across Anna to open the passenger door, so that she could mark her final full stop with one of those dismissive pushes that Anna remembered all too well.

Anna submitted to the push and got out of the car, even though she was only vaguely aware of where she was. She waited until Isabel had driven off before she asked for directions to Clapham Common. It was a long way, but not too far to walk, even for someone in her debilitated condition. The value of the coins was just adequate to buy a Travelcard—which was perhaps as well, given that she'd have to make her own way back into town after the funeral.

She wondered if things might have been different if she'd had a *real* sister, but she decided that they probably wouldn't have been.

* * * * * * *

It wasn't difficult to find the church from Pinner tube station. It was larger than she had expected. She was glad that the funeral announcement in the *Guardian* had given both time and place; so many didn't, because the people who placed them were afraid of being burgled while they were at the ceremony. She waited until everyone else was inside before she sidled in, but she didn't escape notice. Several people turned around, and whispers were exchanged.

When the service was over and the pall-bearers carried the coffin out, Anna moved behind a pillar, but the people who filed out behind the dead man knew perfectly well that she was there. She didn't go to the graveside; she stayed in the shadow of an old horse chestnut tree, watching from thirty yards away. She couldn't hear what the vicar was saying, but that didn't matter. She could have improvised her own service if she'd wanted to, complete with appropriate psalms. Every bedside locker on the ward had a Bible in the top drawer, and boredom had made her dip into hers more frequently than she liked to think. She knew that according to the book of Ecclesiastes it was better to go to the House of Mourning than the House of Feasting, but she wasn't sure that Ecclesiastes had been in a position to make a scrupulous comparison, and he hadn't mentioned the House of the Rising Sun at all, although it would have made a better play on words if he had. Ecclesiastes had also offered the judgment that a good name was better than precious ointment, but Alan certainly wouldn't have agreed with him on that point.

Anna had no difficulty picking out Alan's wife, although she'd never seen a photograph. She was a good-looking woman, in a middle-class Home Counties sort of way. Her name was Christine, but Alan had usually referred to her as Kitty. Anna was mildly surprised that Kitty wasn't wearing a veil. Weren't widows supposed to wear veils, to hide their tears? Not that the woman was weeping; grim forbearance seemed to be more her style. Anna judged her—on the basis of an admittedly superficial inspection—to be a kind of upmarket Isabel, who probably did believe, with all her heart, that a good name was infinitely to be preferred to any kind of balm that cunning cosmetic engineers could devise.

In the grip of a sudden surge of anguish, Anna wished that Isabel hadn't been so tight-fisted. If Isabel had given her a hundred pounds, or even fifty, she'd have been able to bring a wreath to add to the memorials heaped about the grave. So far as she could judge at this distance, most of the mourners had gone for natural blooms, but she would have selected the most exotic products of genetic engineering she could afford, to symbolize herself and the crucial contribution she had made to Alan's life—and, presumably, his death.

Anna had no doubt that the accident hadn't been *entirely* accidental; even if it hadn't been a straightforward deceptive suicide, it must have been a case of gross and calculated negligence.

When the ceremony was over and done with, the crowd around the grave broke up, its members drifting away in all directions as though the emotion of the occasion had temporarily suppressed their sense of purpose. When the widow turned towards her, and shook off someone's restraining hand, Anna knew that the confrontation she had half-feared and half-craved was about to take place. She wasn't in the least tempted to turn and run, and she knew before the woman paused to look her up and down that *this* was what she had come for, and that all the sentimental rubbish about wanting to say goodbye was just an excuse.

"I know who you are," the widow said, in a cut-glass voice, which suggested that she took no pride in her perspicacity.

"I know who you are, too," Anna replied. The two of them were being watched, and Anna was conscious of the fact that the dissipating crowd had been reunited by a common urge to observe, even though no evident ripple of communication had passed through it.

"I thought you were in hospital, out of your mind." The widow's voice was carefully neutral, but had an edge to it that suggested that it might break out of confinement at any moment.

"I am," Anna told her. "But the doctors are beginning to figure things out, and they can keep me stable, most of the time. They're learning a lot about brain chemistry thanks to people like me." She didn't add, *and people like Alan.*

"So you'll soon be back on the streets, will you?" the widow enquired, cuttingly.

"I haven't worked the streets since I was sixteen," Anna said, equably. "I was in a Licensed House when Alan met me. I can't go back there, of course—there's no way they'd let me have my license back after what happened, even if they could normalize my body chemistry. I suppose I might go back to the street, when I'm released. There are men who like spoiled girls, believe it or not."

"You ought to be quarantined," the widow said, her voice easing into a spiteful hiss. "You and all your rancid kind ought to be locked up forever."

"Maybe so," Anna admitted. "But it was the good trips that got Alan hooked, and it was the withdrawal symptoms that hurt him, not the mutant proteins."

A man had joined the widow now: the fascinated crowd's appointed mediator. He put a protective arm around the widow's shoulder. He was too old to be one of her sons and too dignified to be a suitor ambitious to step into the dead man's shoes; perhaps he was her brother—or even Alan's brother.

"Go back to the car now, Kitty," the man said. "Let me take care of this."

Kitty seemed to be glad of the opportunity to retreat. Whatever she'd hoped to get out of the confrontation, she hadn't found it. She turned away and went back to the black-clad flock that was waiting to gather her in.

Anna expected a more combative approach from the man, whoever he might be, but all he said was; "If you're who I think you are, you shouldn't have come here. It's not fair to the family."

Another Isabel, Anna thought. *You'd think someone like him would know better.* By "someone like him" she meant doctor, lawyer, or banker. Something *professional* in the non-ironic sense of the word. Alan had been a stockbroker, careful overseer of a thousand personal equity plans. She'd often wondered if any of his clients had shares in the company that owned the House. Like everything else in today's complicated world, it had been part of some diverse conglomerate; the parent organization's share price was quoted every day in the *Guardian*'s financial pages, under the heading "Leisure and Entertainment."

"I'm not doing any harm," Anna said. "You could all have ignored me, if you'd wanted to."

"I believe that was the gist of the argument that prompted the legalization of prostitution," the other replied, mustering a sarcastic edge far sharper than Kitty's. "It does no harm, they said, and anyone who disapproves only has to ignore it. When the cosmetic engineers progressed from tinkering with shape and form to augmenting bodily fluids, they said much the same thing. The new aphrodisiacs are perfectly safe, they said, it's all just for fun, they're definitely not addictive—and anyone who disapproves can simply stay away from the new generation of good-time girls, and let the fun-lovers get on with it. In the end, though, the rot crept in, the way it always does. It all went horribly wrong. Isn't it bad enough that we had to lose Alan, without having to suffer a personal appearance by his own particular angel of death?"

Anna felt something stirring in the depths of her consciousness, but the comfort-blanket of her medication was weighing down upon it. It was easy to remain tame and self-possessed while the doctors' drugs were winning the battle against her own perverted psychochemistry. "I'm sorry," she said, effortlessly. "I didn't mean to cause distress." *Like hell I didn't*, she thought, by way of private compensation. *I came here to rub your turned-up noses in it, to force you to recognize how utterly and horribly unfair the world really is.*

"You have caused distress," the man said, accusatively. "I don't think you have the least idea how much distress you've caused—to Alan, to Kitty, to the boys, and to everyone who knew them. If you had the least vestige of conscience, you'd have cut your throat rather than come here today. In fact, you'd have cut your throat, period."

He's a punter, Anna thought, derisively. *Not mine, and not the House's, but someone's. He fucks augmented girls, and the juices really blow his mind, just like they're supposed to, and he's afraid. He's afraid that one fine day he too might find that he just can't stop, and that if and when his favourite squeeze goes bad it'll be cold turkey, for ever and ever amen. Like every man alive his prayer has always been "Lord give me chastity but please not yet!"—and now it's too late.*

"I'm sorry," she said, again. The words were the purified essence of her medication, wrought by a transformation every bit as miraculous as the one that had run its wayward course within her flesh and her spirit. The real Anna wasn't sorry at all. The real Anna wasn't sorry she had come, and wasn't sorry she was alive, and wasn't sorry that this black-clad prick saw her as some kind of ravenous *memento mori*.

"You're a degenerate," the black-clad prick informed her,

speaking not merely to her but to everything she stood for. "I don't agree with those people who say that what's happened to you is God's punishment for the sins you've committed, and that every whore in the world will eventually go the same sway, but I understand how they feel. I think you should go now, and never show your face here again. I don't want Kitty thinking that she can't bring the boys to visit Alan's grave in case she meets *you*. If you have a spark of decency in you, you'll promise me that you'll never come here again."

The clichés begin to flow in full force, Anna thought—but even the medication balked at sparks of decency. "I'm free to go wherever I want to, whenever I wish," she asserted, untruthfully. "You have no right to stop me."

"You poisonous bitch," he said, in a level fashion which suggested that he meant the adjective literally. "Wherever you go, corruption goes with you. Stay away from Alan's family, or you'll be sorry." She knew that he meant all of that quite literally too—but he had to turn away when he'd said it, because he couldn't meet the unnaturally steady stare of her colorless eyes.

She stayed where she was until everyone else had left, and then she walked over to the open grave and looked down at the coffin, on to which someone had dribbled a handful of brown loamy soil.

"Don't worry," she said to the dead man. "Nothing scares me. Not any more. I'll be back, and I'll get that wreath one way or another."

She had no wristwatch but the church clock told her that she had five hours in hand before they'd be expecting her at the hospital.

* * * * * * *

Anna hadn't been to the Euroterminal meat-rack for seven years, but it didn't take long for her to find her way around. The establishment of Licensed Houses had been intended to take prostitution off the streets but it had only resulted in a more complicated stratification of the marketplace. It wasn't just the fact that there were so many different kinds of augmentation available, or the fact that more than three-quarters of them were illegal, or even the fact that there were so many girls whose augmentations had ultimately gone wrong or thrown up unexpected side-effects; the oldest profession was one that, by its very nature, could never be moved out of the black economy into the gold. Sleaze, secrecy, and dark, dark shadows were marketable commodities, just like psychotropic bodily secretions.

She didn't bother to try for a managed stand; she'd spoken the truth when she'd told her dead lover that nothing scared her any more, but she hadn't time to get into complicated negotiations with a pimp. She went down to the arches where the independents hung out. There was no one there she knew, but there was a scene in which she knew all of them—especially the ones who were marked like her. It didn't take long to find one who was a virtual mirror-image in more overstated make-up.

"I'm not here to provide steady competition," she said, by way of introduction. "I'm still hospitalized. I'll be back on the ward tomorrow, but I need something to get me through today. Fifty'll do it—that's only one substitution, right?"

"Y'r arithmetic's fine," the mirror-image said, "but y'got a lot of nerve. Demand's not strong, and I don't owe y'anything just 'cause we're two peas from the same glass pod. It's a cat-eat-cat world out here."

"We aren't two peas from any kind of pod," Anna informed her, softly, "Symptoms are all on the surface. They used to say that all of us were sisters under the skin, but we were never *the same*. Even when they shot the virus vectors into us, so that our busy little epithelial cells would mass-produce their carefully-designed mind-expanders, it didn't make us into so many mass-produced wanking machines. One of my doctors explained to me that the reason it all began to go wrong is that *everybody's different*. We're not just different ghosts haunting production-line machines; each and every one of us has a subtly different brain chemistry. What makes you *you* and me *me* isn't just the layout of the synaptic network that forms in our brains as we accumulate memories and habits; we tailor our chemistry to individual specifications as well. You and I had exactly the same transformation, and our transplanted genes mutated according to the same distortive logic, but fucking you never felt exactly the same as fucking me, and it still isn't. We're all unique, all different; we offered subtly different good trips and now we offer subtly different bad ones. That's why some of our clients became regulars, and why some got hooked in defiance of all the ads that promised hand-on-heart that what we secreted wasn't physically addictive. You don't owe me anything at all, either because of what we both were or because of what we both are, but you could do me a favor, if you wanted to. You're free to say no."

The mirror-image looked at her long and hard, and then said: "Jesus, kid, y'really are strung out—but y'd better lose that accent if y're plannin' on workin' down here. It don't fit. I was goin' for a cup of coffee anyway. Y'got half an hour—if y'don't score by then, tough luck."

"Thanks," said Anna. "I appreciate it." She wasn't sure that half an hour would be enough, but she knew she had to settle for whatever she could get.

She'd been on the pitch for twenty-three minutes when the car drew up. In a way, she was grateful it had taken so long. Now, she wouldn't be able to go back afterwards.

The punter tried to bargain her down to thirty, but the car was a souped-up fleet model whose gloss shouted to the world that he wasn't strapped for cash, and there was no one else on the line with exactly her kind of spoliation.

The client was a wise guy; he knew enough about the chemistry of his own tastes to think he could show off. It probably didn't occur to him that the doctors had taken pains to explain to Anna exactly what had happened to her, or that she'd been better able to follow their expert discourse than his fudged mess. Nor did it occur to him that she wouldn't be at all interested in the important lessons that he thought were there to be learned from the whole sorry affair. She didn't try to put him right; he was paying, after all, and the torrent of words provided a distraction of sorts from the various other fluxes generated by their brief and—for her—painful intercourse.

"That whole class of euphorics should never have been licensed, of course," he opined, after he'd stumbled through a few garbled technicalities. "It's all very well designing fancy proteins by computer, but just because something's stable in cyberspace doesn't mean it's going to behave itself under physiological conditions, and *physiological conditions* is a politer way of putting it, when we're referring to the kind of witch's cauldron you get up a whore's you-knows-what. They say they have programs now that will spot likely mutation-sites and track likely chains of mutational consequence, but I reckon they're about as much use as a wooden fort against a fire-breathing dragon. I mean, this thing is *out of control* and there's no way to lock the stable door now the nags have bolted. Personally, I'm not at all distressed—I mean, I've had all the common-or-garden stuff up to *here*. I never liked whores wired up for the kind of jollies you can get from a pill or a fizzy drink. I mean, it's just stupid to try to roll up all your hits into one. It's like praying mantises eating their mates while they fuck—no sense to it at all. Me, I like things spread around a bit. I like it sour *and* sweet, in all kinds of exotic combinations. People like me are the real citizens of the twenty-first century, you know. In a world like ours, it ain't enough not to be xenophobic—you have to go the other way. Xeno*philia* is what it takes to cope with today and tomorrow. Just hang on in there, darling, and you'll find yourself back in demand on a big scale. Be grateful that they can't cure you—in time, you'll *adapt*, just like me."

She knew that in her own way she *had* adapted, and not just by taking her medication regularly. She had adapted her mind and her soul, and knew that in doing that she had adapted her body chemistry too, in subtle ways that no genetic engineer or ultra-smart expert system could ever have predicted. She knew that she was unique, and that what Alan had felt for her really did qualify as *love*, and was not to be dismissed as any mere addiction. If it had been mere addiction, there wouldn't have been any problem at all; he would simply have switched to another girl who'd been infected with the same virus vectors but had proved to be immune—so far—to the emergent mutations.

The punter wasn't a bad sort, all things considered. Unusual tastes weren't necessarily associated with perverted manners. He paid Anna in cash and he dropped her right outside the door of Lambeth North tube station. It was, he said, pretty much on his way home—which meant that he could conceivably have been Isabel's next door neighbor. Anna didn't ask for further details, and he wouldn't have told her the truth if she had. There was an etiquette in these matters that had to be observed.

* * * * * * *

By the time Anna got back to the cemetery, the grave had been filled in. The gravedigger had arranged the wreaths in a pretty pattern on the freshly-turned earth, which was carefully mounded so that it wouldn't sink into a hollow as it settled beneath the spring rains. Anna studied the floral design very carefully before deciding exactly how to modify it to incorporate her own wreath.

She was a little surprised to note that her earlier impression had been mistaken; there *were* several wreaths made up of genetically-engineered exotics. She quickly realized, however, that this was not a calculated expression of xenophilia so much as an ostentatious gesture of conspicuous consumption. Those of Alan's friends and relatives who were slightly better off than the rest had simply taken the opportunity to prove the point.

When she had rearranged the wreaths she stood back, looking down at her handiwork.

"I didn't want any of this to happen," she said. "In Paris, it might almost pass for romantic—man becomes infatuated with whore, recklessly smashes himself up in his car when she becomes infected with some almost-unprecedented kind of venereal disease—but in Pinner it's just absurd. You were a perfect fool, and I didn't even love you...but my mind got blown to Hell and back by the side-effects of my own mutated psychotropics, so maybe I would have if I could have. Who knows?"

I didn't want it to happen either, he said, struggling to get the words through the cloying blanket of her medication, which was deeply prejudiced against any and all hallucinations. *It really was an accident. I'd got over the worst of the withdrawal symptoms. I'd have been okay. Maybe I'd even have been okay with Kitty, once I'd got it all out of my system. Maybe I could have begun to be what everybody wanted and expected me to be.*

"Conformist bastard," she said. "You make it sound like it was all pretence. Is that what you think? Just a phase you were going through, was it? Just a mad fling with a maddening whore who went completely mad?"

It was the real thing, he insisted, dutifully.

"It was a lot realer than the so-called real thing," she told him. "Those expert systems are a hell of a lot cleverer than Old Mother Nature. Four billion years of natural selection produced Spanish fly and rhino horn; forty years of computerized protein design produced me and a thousand alternatives you just have to dilute to taste. You couldn't expect Mother Nature to take that kind of assault lying down, of course, even if she always has been the hoariest whore of them all. Heaven only knows what a psychochemical wilderness the world will be when all the tailored pheromones and augmentary psychotropics have run the gamut of mutational variation. You and I were just caught in the evolutionary crossfire. Kitty and Isabel too, I guess. No man is an island, and all that crap."

I don't think much of that as a eulogy, he said. *You could try to be a little more earnest, a little more sorrowful.*

He was right, but she didn't dare. She was afraid of earnestness, and doubly afraid of sorrow. There was no way in the world she was going to try to put it the way Ecclesiastes had— *in much wisdom is much grief, and he that increaseth knowl-*

edge increaseth sorrow—and all that kind of stuff. After all, she had to stay sane enough to get safely back to the hospital or they wouldn't let her out again for a *long* time.

"Goodbye, Alan," she said, quietly. "I don't think I'll be able to drop in again for quite a while. You know how things are, even though you never once came to see me in the hospital."

I know, he said. *You don't have any secrets from me. We're soulmates, you and I, now and forever.* It was a nicer way of putting it than saying he was addicted to her booby-trapped flesh, but it came to the same thing in the end.

She went away then: back to the tube station, across zones three, two, and one, and out again on the far side of the river. She wanted to be alone, although she knew that she never would be and never could be.

The receptionist demanded to now why Isabel hadn't brought her back in the car, so Anna said that she'd asked to be dropped at the end of the street. "I wanted to walk a little way," she explained. "It's such a nice evening."

"No it isn't," the receptionist pointed out. "It's cloudy and cold, and too windy by half."

"You don't notice things like that when you're in my condition," Anna told her, loftily. "I'm drugged up to the eyeballs on mutated euphorics manufactured by my own cells. If it weren't for the medication, I'd be right up there on cloud nine, out of my mind on sheer bliss." It was a lie, of course; the real effects were much nastier.

"If the way you're talking is any guide," the receptionist said, wryly, "you're almost back to normal. We'll soon have to throw you back into the wide and wicked world."

"It's not as wide or as wicked as all that," Anna said, with due kindness and consideration, "and certainly not as worldly. One day, though, all the fallen angels will learn how to fly again, and how to soar to undiscovered heights—and *then* we'll begin to find out what the true bounds of experience are."

"I take it back," the receptionist said. "I hope you haven't been plaguing your poor sister's ears with that kind of talk—she won't want to take you out again if you have."

"No," said Anna, "I don't suppose she will. But then, she's not really my sister, and never was. I'm one of a kind." And for once, there was no inner or outer voice to say, *Don't flatter yourself,* or *Better be grateful for what you've got,* or *We're all sisters under the skin,* or any of the other shallow and rough-hewn saws whose cutting edges she had always tried so very hard to resist.

ANOTHER BRANCH OF
THE FAMILY TREE

The appeal hearing was set for the twenty-sixth of March, the day after my seventy-second birthday—which would have been Kathy's seventy-second birthday too, had she lived.

I couldn't contest the evidence. They'd taken root samples from the wall that was under threat and they had proof positive that it was my tree that was doing the damage, corrupting the foundations of the Manderleys' oh-so-precious house. It wasn't as if there could possibly be any mistake about the identification; there wasn't another tree like mine in the entire world. There never had been, and there never would be; its uniqueness was the most powerful card I could play up in court by way of fighting the destruction order—although I always intended to make my final defense on other grounds.

I honestly think that I might have carried it off, if we'd still had the jury system. They still had the jury system when Kathy and I were together; we'd grown up with it, and all the other quaint little institutions that made the mad, bad old days of the twentieth century. We would have grown up with it a good few years longer, had Kathy had the chance to keep on growing. As things turned out. the tree eventually grew in her stead; if it had only stuck to growing *up*, everything would have been fine, but trees grow sideways as well, according to their nature. A tree must have roots, and the roots must spread out as far as they need to and as far as they can, in search of water to nourish the crown.

In the mad, bad old days of the twentieth century, water was easier to come by, even for trees. People hadn't grown quite so expert—or quite so desperate—in capturing and plundering every accessible drop. In the old days, the trees in the avenue where Kathy and I lived with Mother and Father had to be sycamores, because they were the only ones tough enough to get by in that kind of urban environment. When the Water Reclamation Schemes came in, not long after I went to live with Uncle Michael and Auntie Steph, even the sycamores had to be replaced by genetically-engineered mosaics that were part-palm and part-euphorbia. When I first planted *my* tree, which appeared to uninformed observers to be a mere oak, I was assured by more than one passer-by that it couldn't survive, but it did. We Galtons have always been a tough family. We've never been ones to let ordinary difficulties stand in our way—or, for that matter, extraordinary ones like the foundations of other people's houses.

A jury would have been an ordinary difficulty. I could have appealed to a jury on compassionate grounds. Judge Humphrey Gerrard, on the other hand, was an extraordinary difficulty. To obtain a verdict from a judge, you have to make him see reason, and judges are not renowned for their ability to do that.

To make matters worse, Judge Humphrey—as his absurdly old-fashioned name suggested—was about the same age as I was. He would have looked even older, but he was wearing a wig—not the ceremonial kind, which had gone the way of juries, but the standard kind, which was still awaiting the long-belated day when my fellow wizards of biotechnology would finally get around to finding a cure for baldness. I knew that my being older than he was would make the situation even worse. These days, when everyone who doesn't stop a bullet can expect to reach a hundred and twenty, seventy-two shouldn't be reckoned old—but old attitudes die hard, especially among the old. When Judge Humphrey Gerrard looked at me, he didn't see a wizard of biotechnology; he saw a batty old woman who had no right to be wasting his time.

"I'm very sorry that this matter has arisen, sir," I told him, trying with all my might to sound humble and sincere. "It's unfortunate that my tree's quest for sustenance has taken her roots beyond the bounds of my own property, and even more unfortunate that she has come into contact with the foundations of someone else's house. I appreciate the fact that it's an old house, and I understand that its owners regard it as a precious object—but it is, at the end of the day, only a house. In this day and age, I cannot believe that any court in the world—least of all a British court—could, when faced with the decision as to whether a tree or a house should be sacrificed, condemn the tree."

"That seems to me to be a brutal simplification of the decision that I am required to make, Miss Galton," the judge riposted, lingering over the *Miss* as if to suggest that the implication of permanent singularity was somehow unnatural. "You are leaving out of account the fact that Mister Manderley's house is situated within the boundaries of his own property, where it has every right to be, whereas the roots of your tree have recklessly exceeded the bounds of your own, committing a serious—not to mention dangerous—trespass."

"What does a tree know of property rights?" I countered, attempting to sound pathetic rather than admonitory. "It is no fault of hers that she is ignorant of the boundaries inscribed by the law. A tree cannot *commit a trespass*; only creatures that know the meaning of sin can do that. A tree is innocent; she cannot be held accountable."

"No one is trying to hold the *tree* accountable, Miss Galton," the appalling Humphrey replied, allowing the ghost of a smile to play upon his lubricious lips. "The tree, like the ground upon which it stands, is your property. *You* are responsible for its trespasses. That is why *you* have been summoned to the court, while the tree continues to enjoy the bliss of its ignorance."

He raised his right hand to stroke his chin, luxuriating in self-satisfaction. I could see why judges number alongside grief counselors and traffic coordinators as favorite targets of hobbyist terrorists. I knew that I had lost, but I had to keep going.

"I could no more prevent the roots of the tree from following their inbuilt imperative," I said, with dignity, "than I could prevent the sun from rising in the morning. The fact remains: a tree is infinitely more precious than a house. A *unique* tree—and no one has disputed that there is not another tree like this one in all the world—cannot be condemned to death merely in order to save a house from the slight probability of collapse. The house can be restabilized, remodeled, or even rebuilt; if I could afford to pay for that to be done, I would do it gladly. If I could afford to pay for the entire Manderley house to be taken down brick by ancient brick and reassembled on another site, I would do it unhesitatingly. The fact that I cannot does not alter the point of principle. A house is a house and a tree is a tree; one is dead, the other alive."

"Both, however, are artifacts," Judge Gerrard replied, having put away his smile and dropped his hand to the oaken table before him. "Your tree is, as you say, unique—and that is because it is the product of genetic engineering. Its uniqueness is a mere matter of circumstance; you have, according to the evidence laid before me, worked throughout your life as a genetic engineer, and were once reckoned one of the country's foremost experts in modified cloning. My expertise lies in another area, but I am assured by the experts that have appeared before me that the reproduction of the tree that stands at the heart of this dispute would be a perfectly simple matter—much simpler, in fact, than the reproduction of the house, which has been handed down to Mister Manderley from his great-grandfather."

I opened my mouth to protest but he wouldn't hear me. That horrid right hand rose again, sternly forbidding me to speak while he hurried on.

"You might, if you so wished," he told me, not caring about any reasonable objection I might make, "grow a dozen or a hundred trees exactly like the one whose roots are threatening Mister Manderley's foundations. If you do, however, you would be well advised to plant them in situations where they could not threaten other people's properties. Given that, I cannot see what grounds you have for asserting that the tree in question is so very precious that it should be allowed to demolish Mister Manderley's house. I am, therefore, minded to confirm the destruction order that Mister Manderley obtained from the local authority."

In the mad, bad old days I could, of course, have appealed to the House of Lords, but New Britain has put away such childish things along with jury trials, ceremonial wigs, and the principle that the sanctity of the family should always outweigh the rights of property. Legally, the matter was ended, and there was nothing further I could say or do. Alas, the silence that fell as Judge Humphrey lowered his imperious hand was too tempting to resist.

"Anyone who attempts to fell that tree," I said, risking an unaffordable fine—and hence, perhaps, imprisonment—for contempt of court, "will have to do it over my dead body."

The judge presumably thought that it was a kindness to pretend that he had not heard the remark—or perhaps he simply thought that someone as old and batty as I could not possibly mean what I said. Nobody knows as yet how long we might live, with the aid of the technologies that I and millions of others have labored long and hard to provide, and we all hope that even a hundred and twenty years might be a mere beginning, but people like Judge Humphrey Gerrard are not yet used to taking people like me entirely seriously.

I suppose I shall have to help them to learn. That's the principal duty left to me, now.

* * * * * * *

What a joy it was to be a twin, when genetic science was in its infancy! Kathy and I were in demand from the moment we were born. We always felt, by virtue of the attention lavished upon us, that we had been born to greatness. Our mentors and investigators encouraged that notion by continually calling attention to the implications of family tradition conveyed by our august surname, although we were not actually descended from the great Francis Galton. "Another branch of the family tree, no doubt," was all that Doctor Burden said, when Mother raised the quibble.

It would not have mattered had we been born Smiths or Joneses or Patels in some inner-city wilderness. Nor would it have made a difference had we had plainer faces, or IQs of merely average dimensions. The researchers would have beaten a path to our door in any case, and begged or bribed their way into our affections, so that we might play our part in their psychometric rituals. The fact remained, however, that we were Galtons, and we were stars. The psychometricians loved us, or so it seemed to us—and Doctor Burden seemed to love us most of all.

Many of our assiduous testers were clinical as well as kind, telling us little or nothing about what they were at, lest our understanding prejudice the results of their enquiries, but Doctor Burden wasn't like that. Doctor Burden believed in informed consent, and he wanted us to understand everything long before we were really capable of understanding anything. Doctor Burden also had a talent to amuse, which we appreciated. We never really loved Doctor Burden, but we did believe that he loved us, and we always did our best to live up to his expectations.

Some of our fellow twin-pairs resented the intrusiveness of the research—the physical probing, the ceaseless inquisition, the relentless challenging of the intellect with puzzle after puzzle— but Kathy and I thrived on it. Our participation was never less than wholehearted. Mother used to joke, if my memory serves me right, that the first words we learned to speak were not "Mummy" and "Daddy" but "genes" and "environment."

I am reasonably certain that by the time we were seven years old we already knew, partly by observation of our fellows and partly by pestering Doctor Burden with our own ceaseless inquisition, that most pairs of identical twins tended to adopt one of two contrasting strategies in dealing with their existential situation. Kathy and I made a *choice* rather than happening on our own strategy by chance—and having decided that we wanted to be "overlapping" twins rather than "complementary" twins, we became utterly determined to overlap more fully, and more ingeniously, than any twins ever had before. The only person we told about our choice was Doctor Burden, because we knew that he would laugh instead of frown, and thought that he would love us all the more.

He did laugh; of that much, I can still be certain.

Complementary twins deal with their identicality by carefully differentiating themselves from one another. They divide up their potential, so that one becomes the extrovert twin and the other the introvert, one the sporty twin and the other the reader, one the arty twin and the other the mathematician, one the twin who dresses in blue, the other the twin who prefers brown. Complementary twins are careful to forge separate identities, to become different people. They are the majority, although other people often fail to notice or appreciate their endeavors, being far more intent on spotting coincidences.

Overlapping twins, on the other hand, deal with their identicality by becoming interchangeable. They pool their potential and develop it in collaboration, happily flattering the expectation of the world that they will act, think and dress alike. In extreme cases, they develop private languages, make a habit of finishing one another's sentences, and deliberately set out to confuse anyone who tries to tell them apart. They regularly answer to one another's name and deny their own. They become helium atoms in a hydrogen world, two nuclei bound inseparably together. If they do so reflexively, they might become deeply disturbed, even psychotic—but if they do it carefully and consciously and cleverly, they might delight and fascinate the world.

It's not for me to judge the extent of our success, especially now, but Kathy and I certainly believed that we had contrived to fascinate the world. The coincidence-spotters delighted in our every contrivance, and we bathed in the glow of their delight, exchanging winks and nudges all the while with Doctor Burden, the sharer of our innermost secrets. Mother and Father had their reservations, of course, but they could not have interfered even if they had tried. Kathy and I were invincible.

I don't remember that Kathy and I ever formally *decided* to become geneticists ourselves. To have discussed the matter would have implied that there were other possibilities, and there were not. After all, no other ambition could have delighted our audience half so much.

Many pairs of complementary twins made the same decision, of course—it was obvious as the twentieth century gave way to the twenty-first that biotechnology would be the force that shaped the future, and that nothing else was really worth doing if you were young and had half a mind—but complementary twins always began by choosing divergent specialisms. When Kathy and I were thirteen, our friends were already deciding that if one of each pair were to be involved in mapping and sequencing the other must be involved in transgenic splicing, or that if one were to take an interest in computerized protein-design the other must investigate embryonic switching-mechanisms. It seemed obvious to everyone, however—not merely to Kathy and myself—that *our* mutual field would be cloning.

We knew, as we blew out the thirteen candles on our shared birthday-cake, that we would become experts in asexual reproduction. We knew, too, that our achievements in that field would be astonishing. We knew, without an atom of doubt, that we would do great things, and that we would do them together. What we didn't know—how could we?—was that I, and I alone, would slip on a patch of black ice outside the front gate on the third of January in the year two thousand and two, and break my shinbone against the unforgiving pavement edge.

I had to stay in the hospital overnight. Hurrying to visit me the next morning—spurred on, I cannot doubt, by Kathy's urgent demands—Father drove the family car into another expanse of that same black ice, and skidded into the path of a number thirty-two bus.

Mother died instantly, Father only a few hours later.

Kathy hung on for four long days—and they were, I can assure you, *exceedingly* long days—but in the end she died without recovering consciousness.

The person I had been died with her, and another was belatedly born.

* * * * * * *

When the bailiff had gone off in search of a further court order, the police set up barricades across the street, one up the hill and one down. The crowd behind them continued to grow, and the gawkers set about giving the police a great deal of grief. Every third adult and every second child had a video camera, and every one of them wanted to get closer. Zoom lenses and focused microphones can only accomplish so much; with so many competitors swarming around, whoever was going to sell their footage to the evening news was going to need an edge. When the time came, they would be avid for any favors I cared to throw their way.

You have to feel sorry for the police, nowadays; now that virtually all crime is machine-detectable, they have to devote the greater part of their time to suicides, sieges, and shooters. It's not the fun job it used to be.

For a few minutes, I thought the Chief Inspector was actually going to wrestle Old Mister Manderley to the ground, cuff him, and ship him off to the station, but it didn't quite come to that. Old military men always have an advantage when dealing with the police; they understand the power of a sharply-barked order. The gawkers protested, of course, even though Mister Manderley didn't have a camera or a mike, but their protests only allowed the Chief Inspector to repair his injured pride by rounding on them like a rabid rottweiler.

In the meantime, Mister Manderley marched right up to

my wrought-iron gates, shoved them open, and strode right in. For a moment I thought he might come all the way up to the tree, but he stopped by the sign I'd posted saying, DANGER: MINEFIELD. He was close enough to make himself heard. I moved a little further along the branch, clearing the foliage away so that he could get a clear sight of me—and, of course, the twin barrels of the shotgun.

"Can't we settle this between the two of us, Beth?" he said, posing as a reasonable man. "Do we really need this bloody circus?"

I couldn't remember whether he'd ever called me "Beth" before. Perhaps when he was young—but for the last thirty or forty years it had been "Miss Galton" on the rare occasions when he had had cause to address me at all.

"It's your circus," I reminded him. "Your court order, your bailiff. You can get rid of it any time you want to."

"You must know that you can't win," he said. "You can't sit up that tree forever, no matter how much food you've got stashed away up there. You have to sleep some time. Even if you really had sown landmines around the tree, you couldn't save the bloody thing. Now that the destruction order's been confirmed, the law will take it course regardless. Why not save everybody a great deal of trouble and come down?"

"There really are mines," I assured him. "They're the kind that send the force of the explosion upwards, so they'll blow the balls off anyone who comes too close, without hurting the roots of the tree at all. You're right about my having to sleep, of course—but while I'm hidden in the crown no one will know whether I'm awake or not, will they? If anyone treads on a mine, it'll wake me up soon enough."

"You do realize, I suppose," he said, the hurt in his voice suggesting that *he* was somehow the injured party, "that by threatening the bailiff with that gun you've placed yourself in a very dangerous situation? The police are now legally entitled to shoot you—which they could do very easily, at no risk to them-selves, with a high-powered rifle that has five times the range of that antique you're holding. If you so much as threaten to fire that thing, that's what they'll do."

"That's what it will take," I told him. "Until then, nobody touches the tree. Nobody."

He attempted, and failed, to contrive an expression of infinite sadness and compassion. "We've known one another a long time, Beth," he said. "I can remember the day you first moved in—what was it, fifty-eight, fifty-nine years ago? I would have been friends with you, if you'd let me. We all felt for you, you know, when we were told about what happened. We would have given you all the help we could, if you'd only let us. We could have been friends, you and I—and even though we weren't, we've always been good neighbors, haven't we? We've never quarreled before. I always thought we understood one another. We've got things in common, when all's said and done. I might not have understood the workings of grief when you first came to live here, but I came to understand them, didn't I? You *know* that."

I knew why Andrew Manderley had wanted to be friends when I first came to live with Uncle Michael and Aunty Steph. He'd been sixteen then, and I'd always been pretty enough. We had nothing in common then, and hadn't now. He wasn't a twin, and never had been. What *he* meant by things in common was that he'd suffered losses of his own, albeit much later. The Manderleys were a military family; he'd lost his younger son in the Middle East, in the so-called Second Armageddon, and the older—young Andrew—in Siberia, in the one and only Ragnarok. People still called him *Old* Mister Manderley, not so much because he seemed old, even to the old and attitude-hardened, but because they remembered *young* Mister Manderley, Andrew Junior—and his brother Peter, too.

"You don't understand anything," I told him. "We don't have anything in common. You'd kill a tree to protect bricks and mortar; I'd die before I let that happen."

"Nobody wants you to die!" he said, with a hint of screech in his voice. "I don't even want to kill the tree! I asked my expert whether there was any way we could shield the wall—dig a ditch on my side of the fence, amputate the roots that were causing the problem and put some kind of barrier in, but he said it would be a horrendous expense for no gain. He said the tree would die anyway—*will* die anyway—because it simply can't get the water it needs to keep on growing. Even if we let it alone, it'll be dead within fifteen or twenty years—the only difference will be that it'll take my house with it. That house was built *two hundred years ago*. It's three times as old as your precious tree. It's my home. It was my father's home before me and his father's before him."

"So what?" I said, brutally. "It won't be your son's after you, will it?"

He wasn't lying about what his so-called expert had told him, but his so-called expert was full of crap. I knew that the tree could go on for decades, maybe even centuries, if only she were allowed to extend her roots as far as was necessary.

"That's cruel, Beth," he said. I had to give him full marks for perspicacity—and patience too, given that he didn't lose his temper. "You inherited *that* house from your aunt—and Michael bought it when first he moved here, from someone else who'd bought it second-hand, or maybe fifth- or tenth-hand. You don't understand what it means to have a *family home*. Nobody does, these days—but I do, and *that*'s mine. I would have built that underground barrier fifty years ago, if I'd known then what your bloody tree was going to do. Your tree's the invader, you know, not my house. My house is where it's always been—it never sent out special forces to conduct an undeclared war on a friendly neighbor. Your tree is a creature of the era of plague wars and ecological attrition, but my house is a product of honest and honorable times, and if one of them has to go it will *not* be my house—even if I have to shoot you down from that branch myself."

"You won't have to do that," I assured him. "You're the son of a brigadier, grandson of a colonel-in-chief. People like you can always order others to do their dirty work. Even chief inspectors of police do what *you* say."

"You *can't win*, Beth," he said, as if repeating the magic spell might eventually make it work. "One thing a military man knows is that when you can't win, you might as well give in gracefully." Either he'd never studied military history or he took me for a perfect fool.

"If you want to kill the tree," I told him, "You have to kill me first."

For a moment, I thought that he was going to step past the warning notice, intent on marching all the way to the trunk and climbing up to pull me down, but he didn't. *He* knew the value of a tactical retreat. Maybe that was why he was the last of his line, having outlasted both his potential heirs.

I was glad to see him go, not just because he was gone but because I really didn't want to see him blown to Hell and back by one of the illegal mines that I really had planted all around the tree.

* * * * * * *

In the beginning, nobody was sure whether Kathy and I were identical twins or merely fraternal twins. The *merely* is mine, of course—Mother and Father wouldn't have minded one way or the other. Mother told us, when we were old enough to listen, that we hadn't been perfectly alike when we were born.

Later, Doctor Burden explained to us that its quite common for genetically-identical twins to diversify while still in the womb. Once fertilized ovum has separated, its two daughters are subject to all manner of random factors, which can assure one twin a larger share of the womb's resources. It often happens, in fact, that one twin outstrips the other so quickly and so extremely that she grows around her sister, who stops developing altogether. Sometimes, the twin enclosed in her sister's body can start to grow again, many years later, becoming a *fetus in fetu*. Fortunately, Kathy and I weren't as ill-matched as that.

Of the two of us, it was Kathy who was born the larger, the

stronger, the fitter—but I had caught up fairly rapidly. Even when things had evened out, though, it wasn't *obvious* that we weren't mere fraternals. There were other differences—differences of what Dr. Burden called "conformation."

It wasn't until the avid researchers had examined our DNA that they got what they wanted: the final confirmation that we were, indeed, genetically identical. Identicals are rarer than fraternals; it's the availability of identicals that determines experimental sample size. Fraternals get tested, of course, examined just as relentlessly as identicals, but only identicals fascinate and delight the world. Doctor Burden and his more careful fellows could not have loved us half so well—or even a tenth—had we been mere fraternals.

Kathy and I, of course, were slightly disappointed to find that we weren't quite as identical as our genetic make-up entitled us to be. Given that we had elected to be overlapping twins, always ready and willing to trade names and places, the fact that very observant people might be able to tell us apart seemed to us to be a handicap, and a betrayal of all that our genetic identicality had promised. We complained about it, to our one and only confidante.

"People read too much into the notion of identical twins," Doctor Burden told us, sadly—knowing, I now presume, how guilty he was of exactly that sin. "They pay far more attention to the similarities than the differences, but identical twins always have differences, and not just because of the differing effects of their environment."

"According to the Pope," we told him, "clones have only one soul. We're identical twins, so we're a clone. We only have one soul, so we *ought* to be identical in every way."

"The Pope's not a geneticist," Doctor Burden informed us, although we already understood *that*. "The idea that all members of a clone are bound to be absolutely identical is rather silly. Think of it this way: every human body is a clone, every cell of which has exactly the same genes as every other—but a liver cell isn't like a nerve-cell, and a skin-cell isn't like a blood-cell.

There are thousands of different kinds of cells, and what makes them different isn't having different sets of genes—it's having different subsets of genes switched on and switched off. You're twins and I'm not related to you, but your liver cells and my liver cells are much more similar to one another than your liver cells and your brain cells."

"But we both have liver cells and brain cells in exactly the same places," we pointed out. "We could still look exactly alike, and we should. Everything should switch on and off in exactly the same way—we're twins, after all."

"But they don't," he told us, cruelly. "Your genes do control the underlying switching process, but all kinds of other factors can get in the way—just like the factors which determined that Kathy was born slightly bigger than Beth. That difference diminished with time, but others increase. Your brains and livers aren't *exactly* alike, and nor are your faces. They could be a lot more different than they are—and I mean a *lot* more. The reason that humans look so very different from whales and ostriches has far less to do with the sets of genes we possess than with the way those genes are switched on and off as the embryos of humans, whales, and ostriches grow. It's theoretically possible—conceivable, at any rate—that two embryos could have exactly the same DNA in their cells, and thus be identical twins, and yet one might develop into a whale and the other into an ostrich, just because of different switching sequences. So it's not entirely surprising that you don't look *exactly* alike. The differences will probably become more noticeable as you get older. At present, only your mother and father and a few of us here at the Institute can tell you apart, but by the time you're my age, anyone who knows you well will probably be able to do it—if they can be bothered to stop looking for the similarities instead of the differences."

He was right, of course. We became very adept at playing to people's expectations—at cultivating identical mannerisms, adopting identical speech-patterns—but we always knew that the extent to which we shared the same soul was limited.

Everyone preferred to see the similarities, but *we* knew how much difference there was between us, and we were sensitive to every tiny increase in every dimension of difference. By the time we were thirty or forty, had Kathy lived, anybody and everybody would have been able to tell us apart, if they'd taken the trouble to pay proper attention.

We overlapped, but we were not *one*.

When Kathy's heart stopped, mine carried on beating. no matter how hard I willed it to cease—and it took me no longer to give up willing it than it took poor Kathy to die.

By the time I moved into the house next door to Andrew Manderley's precious family home, to live with Uncle Michael and Aunty Steph—who were Galtons, just as I was—I no longer wanted to die. I didn't want to be friends, with Andrew Manderley or anyone else, but I accepted that I would live, at least for a while. I even cherished the hope that I could repair the situation, if only I were clever enough. I thought that what had been done to me might yet be undone, that what had been taken away from me might yet be won back.

Even the cleverest of children can be a fool.

* * * * * * *

Unfortunately, I hadn't anticipated the cherry-picker. Somehow, fool that I was, I had forgotten to figure that particular possibility into my half-baked plans. I had stupidly assumed that the mines would make it impossible for anyone to extract me from the crown of the tree, even though I couldn't stay awake forever, without going to an *enormous* amount of trouble. Once the cherry-picker had been maneuvered into position by the big yellow lorry, however, I had to reconstruct the likely scenarios in my imagination.

It didn't take me long to figure that the cherry-picker was likely to blow my plan sky-high. I was still trying to work my way around that thought when the plot moved on—*their* plot, not mine.

When the rusty platform first swung over the garden wall and moved horizontally towards my lofty position I withdrew into the crown of the tree, hiding myself as best I could within its recently-renewed foliage. If only Old Mister Manderley had waited until May or June, I would have been much better able to conceal myself. On the other hand, if global warming hadn't made such a mess of the seasons, I might have seemed perfectly ridiculous amid branches that were virtually bare.

I assumed at first that the flak-jacketed man standing on the platform, clinging tight to the guard-rail, was a policeman or a soldier. Seeing that he had no gun—although there was no shortage of high-powered rifles behind Andrew Manderley's garden wall—I took him for a trained negotiator, come to make a final plea followed by a final threat. Even when I saw his face, and saw how old he seemed to be—even by today's elastic standards—I didn't recognize him. After all, I hadn't seen him for nearly sixty years.

When Kathy died, of course, all the testing had stopped. Once I was alone, I ceased to be of any real value as an experimental subject. No longer part of a fascinating pair, I lost the power to fascinate and delight the world. I lost my coterie of devoted admirers: the men whose loving interest had illuminated my closely-shared life.

"Hello, Beth," he said, while I still didn't know him. "They asked me to talk to you. They think that you're less likely to shoot me than any of your neighbors. I hope they're right. They also think that I might be able to figure out why you're doing this. I hope they're right about that too."

In the end, I guessed. His face, no longer handsome or loving, had become so unfamiliar that he might have been anyone at all, but I guessed.

"Hello, Doctor Burden," I said. "How's life among the clones? Still testing away?" I knew that he wasn't. The bottom had fallen out of that kind of research twenty-five or thirty years before. He knew that I knew, so he didn't bother to answer.

"Mister Manderley's root man showed me the samples he

dug out of the house's foundations," he said, instead. "He never knew what to look for, of course, so he never had the slightest idea what he was looking *at*. He wasn't coincidence-spotting. I never forgot you, you know—either of you. I've always followed your career."

"Didn't you follow the careers of all your ex-subjects?" I asked him. "Professional curiosity would demand no less, I would imagine."

"Not all of them," he said. "In fact, you could say that you were the only one."

He didn't mean that I was the only person; he meant that I was the only one who was no longer half of a pair. He hadn't entirely lost his talent to amuse.

"If you know," I said, "then you can explain to them that I won't give up."

"I've told them what I know," he told me. "They don't understand. Nor do I. I *think* I understand the significance of the tree, but it still doesn't make sense to me. I kept good records you know—even of the casual conversations we had. You were always under observation, Beth. We were interested in *everything*. I've still got the tape of my little lecture on the potential differentiation of clones—the one about the way that merely switching different genes on and off could make the difference between a whale and an ostrich."

"It was absolute balls, and you knew it," I said, resentfully. "If we'd been any older than twelve, you'd never have used such a lunatic oversimplification. I hadn't been in the cloning business for six months before I figured out the world of difference there was between growing tissue-cultures the size of houses and redesigning whole organisms."

"I was trying to make a point," he said, apologetically. "I was trying to tell you that you didn't *have* to regard yourselves as two parts of a single individual. I was trying to show you the way to free yourselves from everybody's expectations, including mine. Especially mine."

"Well, it wasn't necessary," I informed him, not making

the slightest attempt to shield my bitterness. "Some of us find freedom, others have freedom thrust upon us. At first, I thought that the *real* problem was the other way around—not how to make things more different but how to make them more the same. Your little homily about factors intruding on the switching process seemed to be identifying an enemy, then—a hurdle to be overcome. By the time the guys with the lucrative patents had figured out how to clone spare organs for transplantation and cosmetic rejuvenation, I'd already counted all the reasons why I couldn't clone myself a new twin a thousand times over. If I could have done it, I would have done it *properly*. If I could have produced another Kathy, I would have done *exactly* that, age-difference or no age-difference—but it's not as simple as that, is it?"

"No, it isn't," he conceded. "I can understand your wanting to do *that*. It's the rest I can't fathom."

"You should have played back a few more tapes, reviewed a few more of the things you'd already taught us. Two ways of coping, you'd always said. Two strategies. Some twins choose to be overlapping—and some choose to be complementary. Another oversimplification, of course, tailored to the shallow minds of seven-year-olds."

"Do you mean," he said, carefully, "that when you couldn't make an overlapping twin, you...."

The care with which he was choosing his words told me that he was as conscious of the gawkers as I was, and of all their zoom lenses and their focused mikes. He knew that it was all being recorded, however ineptly—and he was playing to the gallery. This must have taken him all the way back to the old days, when he was under observation along with all his subjects, his every word and gesture preserved for posterity. I didn't see why he should *still* get to write the script and direct the action, so I cut him off.

"It's not just a matter of switching things on and off, is it?" I snarled. "You can't turn a whale into an ostrich, no matter how young you catch her—and you can't *design* some other person out of your own cells. Maybe one day it *will* be possible to produce an embryo that really could develop into any of a dozen different functional forms—but we'll have to build the cells a hell of a lot more cleverly than natural selection built ours. At present, and for a while yet, all we can contrive are mosaics, and even they're not easy. Animal bodies are too complicated, and too delicately organized, to permit anything *really* adventurous. Plants are much more resilient—and they can also reproduce vegetatively. Even Humphrey Gerrard, the famous hairless judge, knows that. With plant-based mosaics, you don't need two identically-transformed individuals to found a dynasty. Not in *theory*, anyhow. But nothing's ever as simple as it seems, is it?"

"Is that why you introduced clones of your own cells into the xylem of the tree? You were trying to set up an immortal cell-line—one that could keep on reproducing itself asexually forever."

"Something like that," I agreed, stifling a sigh.

"Why didn't it work?"

"Because it's *not as simple* as that. It's that age-old fallacy about the identicality of clones. Every time you take a cutting from a tree, the new tree that grows is subtly different from the old. The resilience of plants is limited; making a stable mosaic of the parent doesn't guarantee that the cutting will carry forward the same stability. You have no idea, Doctor Burden, how difficult it was to produce this one viable tree—but I think you can understand well enough why it remains the only one."

He actually hesitated over the possibility of delivering a lecture, for the benefit of the amateur newshounds. I have no idea whether his decision to give it a miss was inspired by delicacy of feeling or an acute sensitivity to news-value.

"It's not *you*, Beth," said the man who had loved me, when I was part of something greater. "It might have some of your cells in it, but it's no more a part of you than a bandage into which you bled."

"No, she's not," I conceded. "Nor is she my sister, in any

intelligible sense of the word. She's just a tree." My voice sank to a stage-whisper then, in the hope that it would seem to all the eavesdroppers that I intended the clincher for him and him alone. "But what am I, Doctor Burden?" I added, in a voice like gently-rustling leaves. *"What am I?"*

The whole point, of course, was that the tree was just a tree— and a pretty lousy tree at that, as incapable of reproducing itself as I was. It was just a tree, but it was all I had: the only branch I had to sit on; the only flesh I had to defend.

The tree was innocent, but I wasn't. The tree had never done anything but follow the dictates of its own inbuilt nature, but I had no such excuse. I had been far more than that, once upon a time, and when I had become less than I had formerly been, I had tried to make more of myself, and had actually imagined that I could—but I had failed.

I was still failing. Thanks to the cherry-picker, I couldn't hold out long enough.

I had *tried*, over and over and over, to become something more than I was, but I had never contrived to make anything, or to be anything. more than I had become when I had slipped on that patch of invisible ice and broken the person that Kathy and I had been, so comprehensively that all the king's horses and all the king's men and all the wonders of twenty-first century biotechnology had not been able to put it together again.

Doctor Burden was still a clever man. He was even older than I was, with attitudes even harder than mine or Judge Humphrey Gerrard's. He looked at me, as I looked at myself, without being able to see someone who still had fifty or sixty years to live, someone who still had strength left in her. He looked at me, and saw someone *old*, someone *finished*, someone unnaturally attached to a perfectly useless and perfectly meaningless tree. I could see myself in his eyes, without even bothering to close my own.

"They won't do it, you know," the man on the cherry-picker said, as kindly as he could. "They won't shoot you—unless, of course you can bring yourself to shoot me. It'll have to be me, because no one else is stupid enough to come close enough, now that your neighbor's had his say. You won't shoot me, will you?"

He was pretty stupid himself, to say that while he was still within range—but he was right, for all the wrong reasons. I couldn't shoot him, and they wouldn't shoot me. That wasn't what I wanted.

Old Mister Manderley was right too, unfortunately; I couldn't stay awake forever, and the mines were no protection at all once they had the cherry-picker in place.

"You stupid idiot," I said, so softly this time that the mikes might not have been able to pick it up, although there was really no point in worrying about it. "Do you really think I'm trying to get myself killed? If that were all I wanted, all I'd need to do is put *this* gun to my head, or step down from the tree."

He looked genuinely surprised. Old attitudes die hardest among the old. He remembered me in my golden days, but all he saw now was a batty old woman. He still had his own wits about him, though. He was probably pushing ninety, but *he* knew what an opportunity this was to play to the gallery, to recover a tiny echo of his former fame, his erstwhile authority, and his long-lost lovability.

"Did you really think you could manufacture a nine-day wonder?" he said—and the uncertainty in his voice testified that he thought that perhaps I might have done so, if it hadn't been for the cherry-picker. The real question wasn't whether I could have attracted the eyes of the world, had I only got the story to run and run and run, but whether the eyes of the world were capable, even with all the help I could haven given them, of weeping for the fate of a tree.

* * * * * * *

In the end, they plucked me from my coign of vantage like an overripe cherry, quite unharmed. They blew up the mines, and then they killed the tree. From their point of view, it had all been for nothing—nothing but a waste of everybody's precious time.

Maybe I should have shot Doctor Burden, or Andrew Manderley—but what would have been the point? What would that have made of me that I'm not already? And what am I, now, but exactly what I've been for the last fifty-nine years?

It has always been my fate to be the one left behind, the diminished survivor.

It's certainly not for lack of trying to be something else, and it's certainly not because the Pope was right about Kathy and I having only one soul between the two of us, but the fact remains and always will: I'm not quite myself, and never shall be.

I often wish I were a tree, all questing roots and innocence—but I had my chance, and blew it. I'm only a branch of a broken and blasted family tree—but I'm not withered yet and I've fifty years of progress ahead of me, with which to become something more.

THE MILK OF
HUMAN KINDNESS

The argument was still going strong when the car pulled into the multi-storey behind the hypermarket. Gill could see the tension in Cliff's hands as they jiggled the wheel to steer the car neatly into the last slot on level five.

Her own fingers felt unusually fluttery as she tried to release the straps holding Jem in the baby-seat. She wished, not for the first time, that they had gone for the quick-release model, but Cliff wouldn't trust the manufacturer's guarantee that the mechanism couldn't possibly be triggered by the shock of a shunt or the pressure of a baby's wandering fingers. "That's just advertising," he'd said.

To Cliff, Gill knew, everything was "just advertising" except the things he wanted to believe.

As she loaded Jem into the push-chair, Gill wondered briefly whether it might have been better to delay raising the issue until the time actually came to take the cartons of milk off the shelf, but she dismissed the thought immediately. Whatever the result of the discussion, it would have been bad tactics. She could hardly have hoped that Cliff wouldn't notice which of the myriad brands she was picking up, even though he didn't really take a serious interest in her selections. From his point of view, doing "his share" in the food-shopping was just a weekly ritual, to demonstrate the kind of man he was: a *family* man. It would have been bad tactics because it would have looked as if she'd planned to buy the new product without consulting him, and that would have been breaking their agreement to take all the important decisions regarding Jem's upbringing *together*. Gill still wanted to be seen to be taking that agreement seriously, even though Cliff's idea of honoring it was to harass her with every argument he could think of, good or bad, whenever she put forward any proposition with which he didn't agree, until the sheer force of the torrent wore her down.

She could tell, as they walked towards the lift, that Cliff was preparing just such an onslaught, and she knew that it would be launched long before they reached their destination.

"It's not right," he said, as they paused behind another couple, whose two squabbling toddlers were obviously way past the bottle-feeding stage. "Extra amino acids is one thing, and plantigens are a sensible precaution, but this new thing is *behavioral engineering*. It's not right."

"All parenting is behavioral engineering," Gill pointed out, trying to keep Jem's push-chair well out of reach of the combative toddlers' flailing arms. "All education too."

"Parenting is *guidance*," Cliff told her, as the aluminum doors slid apart with a serpentine hiss and the toddlers fell over one another trying to be first across the threshold. "Education is education. Priming a kid's milk with hormonal regulators is *insidious*. If there'd been any advantage in packing that kind of punch into a newborn's milk, natural selection would have taken care to load *your* tits a hell of a lot better than it did."

That criticism had a double edge, and the unfair one was aimed at Gill rather than evolution. She had had problems breast-feeding from day one. Jem had been on rabbits' milk from the very start, and he'd made his preference abundantly clear before he was a week old. Gill had never been able to understand why Cliff had taken that personally, or why he thought it mattered, given that *everybody* knew that even the most basic pharmed milk was more nutritious than the natural product. It wasn't as if Cliff had been breast-fed when *he* was a baby. On one of the occasions when she wasn't playing the mother-in-law from Hell, Monica had told her that she'd had similar problems and knew exactly how Gill felt. Gill, on the other hand, hadn't been introduced to the commercial product until she was three months old. Not that such distant precedents had any relevance to the present case; in those days, bottle-milk had come from cows.

"Anyway," Cliff went on, as the lift moved smoothly downwards, "even if we were prepared to accept the principle of the thing, we'd still have to decide whether we wanted to afflict poor Jem with this kind of handicap. Let's face it, Gill, the only way the meek are ever going to inherit the Earth is if nobody else wants it. I'm all in favor of other people feeding this crap to their kids if they want to, but I want Jem to keep his competitive edge."

The doors opened to reveal the vast array of the check-out counters, every number lit and every till blinking furiously. The toddlers were as enthusiastic to exit the lift as they had been to get aboard, and they didn't care who was in their way. There didn't seem to be any danger that *they* would ever lose their competitive edge, given that they were already too old to benefit from the pharmers' latest triumph. Their mother muttered an apology as she hurried after them, but her partner was busy lifting his long-suffering eyes to Heaven. Jem whimpered a little as they walked towards the light, but fascination soon overrode fear. He'd been sleepy in the car but he was wide awake now. To him, Gill thought, the hypermarket must be a light-and-sound show, an American-style carnival complete with freaks.

Gill managed to get a few words in edgeways while Cliff was feeding a five-euro coin into the slot and jiggling the catch to spring the trolley from the rack. "All that stuff about a generation of milksops is just tabloid talk, Cliff. They always go for the cheap headline, even if they have to pull their puns from the graveyard of obsolete metaphors. It isn't so long ago that their pharming coverage was all crazy scare stories, and it's no saner now it's all rabbit jokes and milk jokes. This isn't about turning kids into wimps, it's about giving them adequate control over their feelings—and their lives."

"*That*'s just advertising," Cliff retorted, whirling the trolley around and taking aim at the WAY IN sign as if he were lining up the car to switch lanes before exiting the motorway. "There's many a true word spoken in jest, Gill, and the rabbit jokes are just a smokescreen that helps prevent us from thinking about what's really going on. If this is about control, it's about *government* control. Who gains from the elimination of stroppiness from the population? Whose interests does it serve to have an up-and-coming generation of well-behaved androids who'll always think at least twice before stepping out of line? You can see why the CEOs of the pharming companies and their tame MPs *love* the new formula—but why should we, hey? Why should we want *our boy* turned into an ideal consumer?"

Gill was busy by now because the fresh fruit and veg were just inside the entrance, and she always selected her own rather than picking up the pre-packed bags. That was the whole point of real-time shopping—at least, that was its rational basis. Cliff always said that virtual shopping was just a way of inviting the hypermarket to ship you all its shoddiest goods, and he wasn't *always* wrong. Why else would she have picked him to father *her child?*

She checked the bananas carefully, because new oral vaccines didn't attract the same intensity of press attention nowadays as new kinds of milk, but there was nothing in the bay that she and Cliff hadn't taken in adequate measure, and you had to be careful about eating too many of the plantigen-rich varieties once you'd actually formed the antibodies, just in case you got a reaction. When the time came for Jem to be weaned, of course, she'd be cramming mashed bananas into him at a rate of knots, but for now she could afford to concentrate on items modified for taste and nutrition.

The price of potatoes was up yet again, but tototomatoes were down and melons were on special offer. Even better, soft fruits were coming into season and strawberries were this week's loss leader. It was always worth selecting your own strawberries.

"I suppose you wouldn't make so much fuss," Gill said, softly, as she stocked the trolley with broccoli, stripey peppers, and narrow beans, "if Jem were a girl."

"Like hell I wouldn't," Cliff retorted, hotly. "This isn't just some atavistic sexist fit. Okay, so I said *our boy* instead of *our child*—but that doesn't make a damn of difference to the argument. If Jem were Jemima instead of Jeremy, that would be all the more reason to make sure that she didn't get turned into a good little girl who wouldn't say boo to a goose. I can't believe you'd stoop to a cheap shot like that. Don't I take my turns getting up in the night? Don't I stick my share of his smartnaps into the recycler? Don't I suffer just as much earache when he cries as you do? Don't you think I've wished that he could be a little bit less restless, a little more *controlled*? But he won't always be a baby, Gill. One day, he'll be a m—*person*."

The honest answer to at least two of Cliff's questions would have been no, but Gill knew that it would be too difficult to make the case, and it wasn't worth complaining about the belated reflex that had substituted "person" for "man," so she let them go while she picked out the most appealing items from the fresh pasta display and concentrated on the real heart of the dispute.

"I don't want to give him the new milk because I think it will make him easier to manage now," she said, soberly. "It's the long-term benefits I'm thinking about."

"But that's exactly what I'm trying to explain to you," Cliff said, lowering his voice slightly as they eased their way into the crush at the fish-counter. "It's *not* a benefit—not to him. They might advertise it as self-control, but control is control is control, and anything that'll make him more controllable will ultimately work to the advantage of others, not to him. Jesus, will you look at the size of those salmon steaks! Is that ten times natural, do you think, or fifteen?"

Gill had managed to thread the pushchair through the crowd without bumping a single ankle, but her good work was undone when Cliff skewered the trolley into the gap she'd made. Fortunately, the sharp glances were all directed at him. Jem whimpered again—surrounding crowds of adults were presumably even more intimidating than flashing lights—but he wasn't scared enough to amplify the whimper into a screech.

Part of Cliff's problem, Gill thought, was that he hadn't yet grown out of the habit of comparing the products of modern biotechnology to their "natural" counterparts. He hadn't seen a steak from a wild salmon since he was five years old, and probably never would again now that the Lords rump had finally rubber-stamped the law that would ban fishing. Cliff simply couldn't see that in today's world aquaculture *was* natural, just like rabbits' milk. He was stuck in the past, just like the genetic engineers who'd wasted so much time trying to produce transgenic sheep and cows whose milk contained all kinds of amplifications, simply because cows and sheep were what old-style farmers had always worked with. The trouble was that cows and sheep produced only one offspring at a time, at yearly intervals, and even when the engineers had been able to work on oocytes harvested from slaughterhouse with retroviral vectors, cloning the successful transformations, the whole process had been too slow. How much open-mindedness did it take to realize that although a doe rabbit couldn't produce anything like as much milk as a cow or a sheep, that disadvantage was more than offset by the fact that rabbits bred like proverbial rabbits? A pharmer could fill a facility for milking rabbits by the thousand in a fraction of the time that it took to fill a barn with transgenic cows, so nine out of every ten amplified milks now came from rabbit pharms, and all the stupid tabloid jokes in the world couldn't change that or make it any less reasonable than it was. Given that Monica was his mother, allowances had to be made for Cliff—but Gill was the woman in his life now, and it was time he adapted to that fact.

The zigzagged meat lane wasn't nearly as crowded as the fish counter, but that only meant that people whose trolley etiquette made Cliff look like a perfect saint felt free to indulge their worst habits. Cliff, of course, was more than willing to fight fire with fire if provoked, but the push-chair was a mere jeep among the tanks and Gill had to be content to be watchful while she compared the partridges to the quail and mentally weighed the venison against the sanglier. Sanglier was just pork, of course, and she knew that it really didn't make that much difference whether the animals were factoried or "free range," but Cliff always liked to think that the meat on his plate had once been running around enjoying life—and no matter how reluctant she was to believe crazy tabloid scare stories, she couldn't help but wonder what *was* happening to all those pigs engineered for xenotransplantation now that the organ glut had wiped out the NHS waiting lists.

Fortunately, she managed to steer the pushchair into wine-and-water without suffering any serious collisions, and Jem was still as good as gold. They didn't need to linger once she'd loaded up the extra-distilled.

"It's either distilled or it bloody isn't," Cliff observed, presumably forgetting that he'd said it a dozen times before. "How the hell can you *extra*-distil it?" Gill knew that Cliff still felt nostalgic for Evian, although only luck had spared him from more painful participation in the Great Pesticide Panic of 2015.

Visits to the bakery had been known to cause ructions in the past, but Cliff's mind wasn't on bread just now and they slid through smoothly enough.

Cliff was thinking ahead again. He knew that he hadn't yet unleashed a big enough broadside to blow the opposition out of the water. "Look, Gill," he said, "I don't pretend to understand all this crap about the sensitivity of the adrenal cortex, pituitary trigger-effects,and synergistic recoupling of the hormonal orchestra. Okay, so I know far more about fuse-boxes than homeoboxes, and maybe I still think of designer genes in terms of granddad's Calvin Kleins, but you can't pretend that you can figure out the metabolics any better than I can. Maybe the rabbit-pharmers mean exactly what they say when they rattle on about their new product making people less vulnerable to anger and aggression. Maybe it is about self-control, and not just another endogenous tranquilliser or built-in anti-depressant. Maybe. But you know full well that these things *always* have unforeseen side-effects. The cell and the body are jam-packed with feedback systems, so there's no way you can alter the level of any enzyme or hormone without setting off chain reactions. Society has its feedback systems too, so it's just as difficult to figure out the pattern of consequences that might spread from any change in people's personalities. *All* this is whistling in the dark, Gill. Do you really want our boy—our *child*—to be one more guinea-pig in the line? Why can't we leave him out of it, at least until we can see how this new thing is working out?"

Cliff always put on that kind of reasonable tone in order to plumb the ultimate depths of unreasonableness. He knew full well that if they kept Jem out of it now he wouldn't be able to opt back in at a later date. If he didn't get the supplement in his milk before he was a year old, there would be no way to fine tune the sensitivity of his adrenal cortex or adjust the synergistic complicity of his hormones. The child was father to the man, now as in any other era of history, and Gill knew that if you wanted to make the right sort of man you had to get the business of parenting as right as you possibly could. Would Jem ever forgive them if he grew up lacking self-control in a world where slaves to emotion were automatically relegated to the bottom of the social heap? Would he be prepared to accept the excuse that they were being cautious, that they didn't want to take a gamble even though the best calculations available put the odds ten to one in his favor?

"If not us, who?" Gill quoted, mildly. "If not now, when?"

"That revolution's over and done," Cliff informed her, scornfully. "This one's an entirely different kettle of giant salmon. *I won't stand for it, Gill.* You're not going to start feeding this stuff to Jem just because it's the new fashion. He has to keep his edge if he's going to get by. You might think that it isn't a dog-eat-dog world any more, but you work at home, in front of a screen. You don't know what it's like *out there*. You certainly don't know what it's going to take to get by when Jem reaches our age. We can only guess whether it'll be a world of fifteen billion people or a world wrecked by plague war—but either way, it won't be a world in which nice guys finish first. Even ours isn't that. no matter how hard you want to pretend. You have to let the kid hang on to his guts, Gill. You can't castrate him before his balls drop—okay, okay, bad sexist metaphor. You can't take away his *passion* before he's even had a chance to spend it. You have to listen to me, Gill. This stuff might be the biggest scam the people at the top have ever tried to put over on us. We have to say no—but that's all we have to do. It's as easy as that."

"It's not," Gill murmured, as she led the way through frozen foods towards their appointment with destiny in dairy produce. "Things are changing too fast. It's not enough any more just to say no to everything. You and I don't live in that kind of world, and Jem certainly won't." But she didn't say it loudly enough. She knew that Cliff couldn't hear her as he trudged in her wake with the three-quarters-laden trolley. He wasn't even trying to hear her—quite the reverse, in fact.

The battle was lost and Gill knew it. She marched forward in military style regardless. Where frozen items were concerned, it really did make more sense to order over the Internet—in fact, if you were the kind of person who was into frozen food, there was no point in coming to the market at all, but the market still kept the lanes open for all the people who were stuck in the past. At least Cliff wasn't stuck *that* far back. He and Gill were *serious* food-shoppers, and specialist food-shoppers too—although Gill figured that when Jem was a little bit older it would be a nice treat for him to take the occasional tour of the toy maze. Children didn't usually take to virtual play until they were seven or eight, sometimes older. The work that adults did in supplying visual images with tactile connotations had to be learned, and it had to be learned in the real world, so the toy maze was more than just a money-trap.

Cliff was very tense by the time they got to the first of the milk lanes, from which they could already see the crowd huddled around the new line. His fingers were blanched again—but he always had difficulty keeping up with the plot.

Gill observed the crowd with clinical detachment. People didn't usually talk to one another in the hypermarket—even if you bumped trolleys with somebody you recognized, convention demanded that you exchanged a hasty greeting and got on with business—but the milk lanes were governed by a subtly different set of norms. The milk lanes were always full of mothers anxious to be sure that they were doing right by their kids. If the market managers could bottle reassurance and stick it on the shelves at a suitably exorbitant price, the end-bays between milk lanes was where they'd put it.

"I mean it, Gill," said Cliff, in the low voice he always reserved for last ditch defenses. "I'm serious about this."

"I know," Gill said, bringing Jem to a halt six feet short of the debating society. "It's okay. If you feel that strongly about it, we'll stick to the usual formula. But when the day comes that Jem demands an explanation, you're the one who can deal with it. Any tantrums he throws once he turns twelve are *your* tantrums. okay? He wants to test his *competitive edge* on people, he tests it on *you*."

"Okay," Cliff said. "I can do that. No problem. Any time the kid wants to try his competitive edge, I'll be glad to take him on."

Gill knew that she'd had to put it like that if Cliff were to be convinced that she'd made a long-term commitment. She knew that she had to give in with an ill grace, or Cliff would never believe that she had really given in—but she wasn't angry, or petulant, or resentful, because she had no intention of losing the war. Losing the battle was good strategy, because it would allow Cliff to remember that the matter had been aired, and a decision made. He knew how seriously she took the matter of collective decision-making, so he would trust her to stick to it. But Jem was her child, and she had a strong enough sense of social responsibility to make sure that he would be her only child—unless, God forbid, Plague War One really did break out—and it was up to her to make sure that he got all the benefits of the biotech revolution as and when they became available.

It was as easy to arrange for back-door deliveries as it was to arrange for the front-door kind. All she had to do was pour the new milk into the usual cartons as she opened them, and make sure that Cliff never took stock of the amount of unmarked packaging that was going into the recycler along with all the smartnaps and babygros. All milk was creamy white and it all tasted sweet; nobody could tell any of the thousand kinds from any of the others by sight or taste.

Once the trolley was safely loaded with the kinds of milk that people who were only slightly stuck in the past preferred, Gill headed for the check-out, with Cliff trailing in her wake.

Jem was whimpering again, and this time Gill could tell that he wouldn't stop. He was getting hungry, and he was becoming resentful of the straps that confined him. This time, the whimper would grow and grow—but they would be back at the car soon enough, if only they could get through the check-out in good time.

If only.

If the meat lane's chicane was the severest test of customers' trolley etiquette, the check-out's queues were the severest test of their patience, and for every family man who couldn't meet the trolley challenge with adequate equanimity there were five who couldn't handle the pressure of merely waiting in line. Not that it was a sex-limited thing, of course—there were plenty of women, especially mothers, whose nerves were equally fraught.

They'd all be better off, Gill thought, if they could only take things a little easier. It wasn't really a matter of self-control, although that was part of it. It was mostly a matter of thinking ahead and taking other people into consideration.

It was a really matter of being just that little bit *kinder* to yourself and everybody else.

As Jem's whimpers turned to cries, so Cliff's muttering and shuffling increased. Gill looked along the line of tills, at thirty-some queues where exactly the same small rituals of impatience and stress were repeated in a potentially-infinite series of carbon copies—except, Gill had to remind herself, that carbon copies had long been extinct in a world of Xeroxes and backup discs. One more metaphor from the graveyard.

The simple fact was, she thought, as she bent down to tickle Jem's chin, that the world went right on changing, no matter how insistent people were on protecting their little foibles and failings. Progress went forward, gathering pace all the while, no matter how uncomfortable people felt about it. There was nothing to be gained by refusing to go with the flow, and nothing to be lost except that which couldn't be kept.

In the end, Gill had to leave it to Cliff to reload the trolley after the scanner had done its work, although she knew that he always made a pig's ear of the stacking. She couldn't help him because she had to pick Jem out of the push-chair and jolly him in her arms, shushing him as his cries became inexorably louder.

"It'll be all right," she told him, over and over again. "We'll soon be out of here, and you can have a bottle in the car while we're going home. Everything will be all right. Mummy will see to it. Just leave everything to Mummy, and it'll all be all right."

THE PIPES OF PAN

In her dream Wendy was a pretty little girl living wild in a magical wood where it never rained and never got cold. She lived on sweet berries of many colors, which always tasted wonderful, and all she wanted or needed was to be happy.

There were other girls living wild in the dream-wood but they all avoided one another, because they had no need of company. They had lived there, untroubled, for a long time—far longer than Wendy could remember.

Then, in the dream, the others came: the shadow-men with horns on their brows and shaggy legs. They played strange music on sets of pipes that looked as if they had been made from reeds—but Wendy knew, without knowing how she knew or what sense there was in it, that those pipes had been fashioned out of the blood and bones of something just like her, and that the music they played was the breath of her soul.

After the shadow-men came, the dream became steadily more nightmarish, and living wild ceased to be innocently joyful. After the shadow-men came, life was all hiding with a fearful, fluttering heart, knowing that if ever she were found she would have to run and run and run, without any hope of escape—but wherever she hid, she could always hear the music of the pipes.

When she woke up in a cold sweat, she wondered whether the dreams her parents had were as terrible, or as easy to understand. Somehow, she doubted it.

* * * * * * *

There was a sharp rat-a-tat on her bedroom door.

"Time to get up, Beauty." Mother didn't bother coming in to check that Wendy responded. Wendy always responded. She was a good girl.

She climbed out of bed, took off her night-dress, and went to sit at the dressing-table, to look at herself in the mirror. It had become part of her morning ritual, now that her awakenings were indeed awakenings. She blinked to clear the sleep from her eyes, shivering slightly as an image left over from the dream flashed briefly and threateningly in the depths of her emergent consciousness.

Wendy didn't know how long she had been dreaming. The dreams had begun before she developed the sense of time that would have allowed her to make the calculation. Perhaps she had always dreamed, just as she had always got up in the morning in response to the summoning rat-a-tat, but she had only recently come by the ability to remember her dreams. On the other hand, perhaps the beginning of her dreams had been the end of her innocence.

She often wondered how she had managed not to give herself away in the first few months, after she first began to remember her dreams but before she attained her present level of waking self-control, but any anomalies in her behavior must have been written off to the randomizing factor. Her parents were always telling her how lucky she was to be thirteen, and now she was in a position to agree with them. At thirteen, it was entirely appropriate to be a little bit inquisitive and more than a little bit odd. It was even possible to get away with being too clever by half, as long as she didn't overdo it.

It was difficult to be sure, because she didn't dare interrogate the house's systems too explicitly, but she had figured out that she must have been thirteen for about thirty years, in mind and body alike. She was thirteen in her blood and her bones, but not in the privacy of her head.

Inside, where it counted, she had now been unthirteen for at least four months.

If it would only stay inside, she thought, *I might keep it a secret forever. But it won't. It isn't. It's coming out. Every day that passes is one day closer to the moment of truth.*

She stared into the mirror, searching the lines of her face for signs of maturity. She was sure that her face looked thinner, her eyes more serious, her hair less blonde. All of that might be mostly imagination, she knew, but there was no doubt about the other things. She was half an inch taller, and her breasts were getting larger. It was only a matter of time before that sort of thing attracted attention, and as soon as it was noticed the truth would be manifest. Measurements couldn't lie. As soon as they were moved to measure her, her parents would know the horrid truth.

Their baby was growing up.

* * * * * * *

"Did you sleep well, dear?" Mother said, as Wendy took her seat at the breakfast-table. It wasn't a trick question; it was just part of the routine. It wasn't even a matter of pretending, although her parents certainly did their fair share of that. It was just a way of starting the day off. Such rituals were part and parcel of what they thought of as *everyday life*. Parents had their innate programming too.

"Yes, thank you," she replied, meekly.

"What flavor manna would you like today?"

"Coconut and strawberry please." Wendy smiled as she spoke, and Mother smiled back. Mother was smiling because Wendy was smiling. Wendy was supposed to be smiling because she was a smiley child, but in fact she was smiling because saying "strawberry and coconut" was an authentic and honest *choice*, an exercise of freedom that would pass for an expected manifestation of the randomizing factor.

"I'm afraid I can't take you out this morning, Lovely," Father said, while Mother punched out the order. "We have to wait in for the house-doctor. The waterworks still aren't right."

"If you ask me," Mother said, "the real problem's the water table. The taproots are doing their best but they're having to go down too far. The system's fine just so long as we get some good old-fashioned rain once in a while, but every time there's a dry spell the whole estate suffers. We ought to call a meeting and put some pressure on the landscape engineers. Fixing a water-table shouldn't be too much trouble in this day and age."

"There's nothing wrong with the water-table, dear," Father said, patiently. "It's just that the neighbors have the same indwelling systems that we have. There's a congenital weakness in the root-system; in dry weather the cell-terminal conduits in the phloem tend to get gummed up. It ought to be easy enough to fix—a little elementary somatic engineering, probably no more than a single-gene augment in the phloem—but you know what doctors are like; they never want to go for the cheap and cheerful cure if they can sell you something more complicated."

"What's phloem?" Wendy asked. She could ask as many questions as she liked, to a moderately high level of sophistication. That was a great blessing. She was glad she wasn't an eight-year-old, reliant on passive observation and a restricted vocabulary. At least a thirteen-year-old had the right equipment for thinking all set up.

"It's a kind of plant-tissue," Father informed her, ignoring the tight-lipped look Mother was giving him because he'd contradicted her. "It's sort of equivalent to your veins, except of course that plants have sap instead of blood."

Wendy nodded, but contrived to look as if she hadn't really understood the answer.

"I'll set the encyclopedia up on the system," Father said. "You can read all about it while I'm talking to the house-doctor."

"She doesn't want to spend the morning reading what the encyclopedia has to say about phloem," Mother said, peevishly. "She needs to get out into the fresh air." That wasn't mere ritual, like asking whether she had slept well, but it wasn't pretence either. When Mother started talking about Wendy's supposed wants and needs, she was usually talking about her own wants and supposed needs. Wendy had come to realize that talking that way was Mother's preferred method of criticizing Father; she was paying him back for disagreeing about the water-table.

Wendy was fully conscious of the irony of the fact that she really did want to study the encyclopedia. There was so much to learn and so little time. Maybe she didn't *need* to do it, given that it was unlikely to make any difference in the long run, but she wanted to understand as much as she could before all the pretence had to end and the nightmare of uncertainty had to begin.

"It's okay, Mummy," she said. "Honest." She smiled at them both, attempting to bring off the delicate trick of pleasing Father by taking his side while simultaneously pleasing Mother by pretending to be as heroically long-suffering as Mother liked to consider herself.

They both smiled back. All was well, for now. Even though they listened to the news every night, they didn't seem to have the least suspicion that it could all be happening in their own home, to their own daughter.

* * * * * * *

It only took a few minutes for Wendy to work out a plausible path of icon selection that got her away from translocation in plants and deep into the heart of child physiology. Father had set that up for her by comparing phloem to her own circulatory system. There was a certain danger in getting into recent reportage regarding childhood diseases, but she figured that she could explain it well enough if anyone took the trouble to consult the log to see what she'd been doing. She didn't think anyone was likely to, but she simply couldn't help being anxious about the possibility—there were, it seemed, a lot of things one simply couldn't help being anxious about, once it was possible to be anxious at all.

"I wondered if I could get sick like the house's roots," she would say, if asked. "I wanted to know whether my blood could get clogged up in dry weather." She figured that she would be okay as long as she pretended not to have understood what she'd read, and conscientiously avoided any mention of the word *progeria*. She already knew that progeria was what she'd got, and the last thing she wanted was to be taken to a child-engineer who'd be able to confirm the fact.

She called up a lot of innocuous stuff about blood, and spent the bulk of her time pretending to study elementary material of no real significance. Every time she got hold of a document she really wanted to look at she was careful to move on quickly, so it would seem as if she hadn't even bothered to look at it if anyone did consult the log to see what she'd been doing. She didn't dare call up any extensive current affairs information on the progress of the plague or the fierce medical and political arguments concerning the treatment of its victims.

It must be wonderful to be a parent, she thought, *and not have to worry about being found out—or about anything at all, really.*

At first, Wendy had thought that Mother and Father really did have worries, because they talked as if they did, but in the last few weeks she had begun to see through the sham. In a way, they *thought* that they did have worries, but it was all just a matter of habit, a kind of innate restlessness left over from the olden days. Adults must have had authentic anxieties at one time, back in the days when everybody could expect to die young and a lot of people never even reached seventy, and she presumed that they hadn't quite got used to the fact that they'd changed the world and changed themselves. They just hadn't managed to lose the habit. They probably would, in the fullness of time. Would they still need children then, she wondered, or would they learn to do without? Were children just another habit, another manifestation of innate restlessness? Had the great plague come just in time to seal off the redundant umbilical cord that connected mankind to its evolutionary past?

We're just betwixts and betweens, Wendy thought, as she rapidly scanned a second-hand summary of a paper in the latest issue of *Nature*, which dealt with the pathology of progeria. *There'll soon be no place for us, whether we grow older or not. They'll get rid of us all.*

The article that contained the summary claimed that the development of an immunoserum was just a matter of time, although it wasn't yet clear whether anything much might be done to reverse the aging process in children who'd already come down with it. She didn't dare access the paper itself, or even an abstract—that would have been a dead giveaway, like leaving a bloody thumbprint at the scene of a murder.

Wendy wished that she had a clearer idea of whether the latest news was good or bad, or whether the long-term prospects had any possible relevance to her now that she had started to show physical symptoms as well as mental ones. She didn't know what would happen to her once Mother and Father found out and notified the authorities; there was no clear pattern in the stories she glimpsed in the general news-broadcasts, but whether this meant that there was as yet no coherent social policy for dealing with the rapidly-escalating problem she wasn't sure.

For the thousandth time she wondered whether she ought simply to tell her parents what was happening, and for the thousandth time, she felt the terror growing within her at the thought that everything she had might be placed in jeopardy, that she might be sent back to the factory or handed over to the researchers or simply cut adrift to look after herself. There was no way of knowing, after all, what really lay behind the rituals that her parents used in dealing with her, no way of knowing what would happen when their thirteen-year-old daughter was no longer thirteen.

Not yet, her fear said. *Not yet. Hang on. Lie low...because once you can't hide, you'll have to run and run and run and there'll be nowhere to go. Nowhere at all.*

She left the workstation and went to watch the house-doctor messing about in the cellar. Father didn't seem very glad to see her, perhaps because he was trying to talk the house-doctor round to his way of thinking and didn't like the way the house-doctor immediately started talking to her instead of him, so she went away again, and played with her toys for a while. She still enjoyed playing with her toys—which was perhaps as well, all things considered.

* * * * * *

"We can go out for a while now," Father said, when the house-doctor had finally gone. "Would you like to play ball on the back lawn?"

"Yes please," she said.

Father liked playing ball, and Wendy didn't mind. It was better than the sedentary pursuits that Mother preferred. Father had more energy to spare than Mother, probably because Mother had a job that was more taxing physically. Father only played with software; his clever fingers did all his work. Mother actually had to get her hands inside her remote-gloves and her feet inside her big red boots and get things moving. "Being a ghost in a machine," she would often complain, when she thought Wendy couldn't hear, "can be bloody hard work." She never swore in front of Wendy, of course.

Out on the back lawn, Wendy and Father threw the ball back and forth for half an hour, making the catches more difficult as time went by, so that they could leap about and dive on the bone-dry carpet-grass and get thoroughly dusty.

To begin with, Wendy was distracted by the ceaseless stream of her insistent thoughts, but as she got more involved in the game she was able to let herself go a little. She couldn't quite get back to being thirteen, but she could get to a state of mind that wasn't quite so fearful. By the time her heart was pounding and she'd grazed both her knees and one of her elbows she was enjoying herself thoroughly, all the more so because Father was evidently having a good time. He was in a good mood anyhow, because the house-doctor had obligingly confirmed everything he'd said about the normality of the water-table, and had then backed down gracefully when he saw that he couldn't persuade Father that the house needed a whole new root-system.

"Those somatic transformations don't always take," the house-doctor had said, darkly but half-heartedly, as he left. "You might have trouble again, three months down the line."

"I'll take the chance," Father had replied, breezily. "Thanks for your time."

Given that the doctor was charging for his time, Wendy had thought, it should have been the doctor thanking father, but she hadn't said anything. She already understood that kind of thing well enough not to have to ask questions about it. She had other matters she wanted to raise once Father collapsed on the baked earth, felled by healthy exhaustion, and demanded that they take a rest.

"I'm not as young as you are," he told her, jokingly. "When you get past a hundred and fifty, you just can't take it the way you used to." He had no idea how it affected her to hear him say *you* in that careless fashion, when he really meant *we*: a *we* that didn't include her, and never would.

"I'm bleeding," she said, pointing to a slight scratch on her elbow.

"Oh dear," he said. "Does it hurt?"

"Not much," she said, truthfully. "If too much leaks out, will I need injections, like the house's roots?"

"It won't come to that," he assured her, lifting up her arm so that he could put on a show of inspecting the wound. "It's just a drop. I'll kiss it better." He put his lips to the wound for a few seconds, then said: "It'll be as good as new in the morning."

"Good," she said. "I expect it'd be very expensive to have to get a whole new girl."

He looked at her a little strangely, but it seemed to Wendy that he was in such a light mood that he was in no danger of taking it too seriously.

"Fearfully expensive," he agreed, cheerfully, as he lifted her up in his arms and carried her back to the house. "We'll just have to take very good care of you, won't we?"

"Or do a somatic whatever," she said, as innocently as she possibly could. "Is that what you'd have to do if you wanted a boy for a while?"

He laughed, and there appeared to be no more than the merest trace of unease in his laugh. "We love you just the way you are, Lovely," he assured her. "We wouldn't want you to be any other way."

She knew that it was true. That was the problem.

She had ham and cheese manna for lunch, with real greens home-grown in the warm cellar-annex under soft red lights. She would have eaten heartily had she not been so desperately anxious about her weight, but as things were she felt it better to peck and pretend, and she surreptitiously discarded the food she hadn't consumed as soon as Father's back was turned.

* * * * * * *

After lunch, judging it to be safe enough, she picked up the thread of the conversation again. "Why did you want a girl and not a boy?" she asked. "The Johnsons wanted a boy." The Johnsons had a ten-year-old named Peter. He was the only other child Wendy saw regularly, and he had not as yet exhibited the slightest sign of disease to her eager eye.

"We didn't want *a girl*," Father told her, tolerantly. "We wanted *you*."

"Why?" she asked, trying to look as if she were just fishing for compliments, but hoping to trigger something a trifle more revealing. This, after all, was *the* great mystery. Why her? Why anyone? Why did adults think they needed children?

"Because you're beautiful," Father said. "And because you're Wendy. Some people are Peter people, so they have Peters. Some people are Wendy people, so they have Wendys. Your Mummy and I are definitely Wendy people—probably the Wendiest people in the world. It's a matter of taste."

It was all baby-talk, all gobbledygook, but she felt that she had to keep trying. Some day, surely, one of them would let a little truth show through their empty explanations.

"But you have different kinds of manna for breakfast, lunch and dinner," Wendy said, "and sometimes you go right off one kind for weeks on end. Maybe some day you'll go off me, and want a different one."

"No we won't, darling," he answered, gently. "There are matters of taste and matters of taste. Manna is fuel for the body. Variety of taste just helps to make the routine of eating that little bit more interesting. Relationships are something else. It's a different kind of need. We love you, Beauty, more than anything else in the world. Nothing could ever replace you."

She thought about asking about what would happen if Father and Mother ever got divorced, but decided that it would be safer to leave the matter alone for now. Even though time was pressing, she had to be careful.

* * * * * * *

They watched TV for a while before Mother came home. Father had a particular fondness for archive film of extinct animals—not the ones that the engineers had re-created but smaller and odder ones: weirdly-shaped sea-dwelling creatures. He could never have seen such creatures even if they had still existed when he was young, not even in an aquarium; they had only ever been known to people as things on film. Even so, the whole tone of the tapes that documented their one-time existence was nostalgic, and Father seemed genuinely affected by a sense of personal loss at the thought of the sterilization of the seas during the last ecocatastrophe but one.

"Isn't it beautiful?" he said, of an excessively-tentacled sea anemone, which sheltered three vivid clown-fish while ungainly shrimps passed by. "Isn't it just *extraordinary?*"

"Yes," she said, dutifully, trying to inject an appropriate reverence into her tone. "It's lovely." The music on the soundtrack was plaintive; it was being played on some fluty wind-instrument, possibly by a human player. Wendy had never heard music like it except on TV sound-tracks; it was as if the sound were the breath of the long-lost world of nature, teeming with undesigned life.

"Next summer," Father said, "I want us to go out in one of those glass-bottomed boats that take sight-seers out to the new barrier reef. It's not the same as the original one, of course, and they're deliberately setting out to create something modern, something new, but they're stocking it with some truly weird and wonderful creatures."

"Mother wants to go up the Nile," Wendy said. "She wants to see the sphinx, and the tombs."

"We'll do that the year after," Father said. "They're just ruins. They can wait. Living things...." He stopped. "Look at those!" he said, pointing at the screen. She looked at a host of jellyfish swimming close to the silvery surface, their bodies pulsing like great translucent hearts.

It doesn't matter, Wendy thought. *I won't be there. I won't see the new barrier reef or the sphinx and the tombs. Even if they find a cure, and even if you both want me cured, I won't be there. Not the real me. The real me will have died, one way or another, and there'll be nothing left except a girl who'll be thirteen forever, and a randomizing factor that will make it seem that she has a lively mind.*

Father put his arm around her shoulder, and hugged her fondly.

Father must really love her very dearly, she thought. After all, he had loved her for thirty years, and might love her for thirty years more, if only she could stay the way she was...if only she could be returned to what she had been before....

* * * * * * *

The evening TV schedules advertised a documentary on progeria, scheduled for late at night, long after the nation's children had been put to bed. Wendy wondered if her parents would watch it, and whether she could sneak downstairs to listen to the sound-track through the closed door. In a way, she hoped that they wouldn't watch it. It might put ideas into their heads. It was better that they thought of the plague as a distant problem: something that could only affect other people; something with which they didn't need to concern themselves.

She stayed awake, just in case, and when the luminous dial of her bedside clock told her it was time she silently got up, and crept down the stairs until she could hear what was going on in the living-room. It was risky, because the randomizing factor wasn't really supposed to stretch to things like that, but she'd done it before without being found out.

It didn't take long to ascertain that the TV wasn't even on, and that the only sound to be heard was her parents' voices. She actually turned around to go back to bed before she suddenly realized what they were talking about.

"Are you *sure* she isn't affected mentally?" Mother was saying.

"Absolutely certain," Father replied. "I watched her all after-noon, and she's perfectly normal."

"Perhaps she hasn't got it at all," Mother said, hopefully.

"Maybe not the worst kind," Father said, in a voice that was curiously firm. "They're not sure that even the worst cases are manifesting authentic self-consciousness, and there's a strong contingent that argues that the vast majority of cases are rela-tively minor dislocations of programming. But there's no doubt about the physical symptoms. I picked her up to carry her indoors and she's a stone heavier. She's got hair growing in her armpits and she's got tangible tits. We'll have to be careful how we dress her when we take her to public places."

"Can we do anything about her food—reduce the calorific value of her manna or something?"

"Sure—but that'd be hard evidence if anyone audited the house records. Not that anyone's likely to, now that the doctor's been and gone, but you never know. I read an article that cites a paper in the latest *Nature* to demonstrate that a cure is just around the corner. If we can just hang on until then...she's a big girl anyhow, and she might not put on more than an inch or two. As long as she doesn't start behaving oddly, we might be able to keep it secret."

"If they do find out," said Mother, ominously, "there'll be hell to pay."

"I don't think so," Father assured her. "I've heard that the authorities are quite sympathetic in private, although they have to put on a sterner face for publicity purposes."

"I'm not talking about the bloody bureaucrats," Mother retorted, "I'm talking about the estate. If the neighbors find out we're sheltering a centre of infection...well, how would you feel if the Johnsons' Peter turned out to have the disease and hadn't warned us about the danger to Wendy?"

"They're not certain how it spreads," said Father, defensively, "They don't know what kind of vector's involved—until they find out there's no reason to think that Wendy's endangering Peter just by living next door.

"It's not as if they spend much time together. We can't lock her up—that'd be suspicious in itself. We have to pretend that things are absolutely normal, at least until we know how this thing is going to turn out. I'm not prepared to run the risk of their taking her away—not if there's the slightest chance of avoiding it. I don't care what they say on the newstapes—this thing is getting out of control and I really don't know how it's going to turn out. I'm not letting Wendy go anywhere, unless I'm absolutely forced. She might be getting heavier and hairier, but *inside* she's still Wendy, and *I'm not letting them take her away.*"

Wendy heard Father's voice getting louder as he came towards the door, and she scuttled back up the stairs as fast as she could go. Numb with shock, she climbed back into bed. Father's words echoed inside her head: "I watched her all afternoon and she's perfectly normal...*inside* she's still Wendy...."

They were putting on an act too, and she hadn't known. She hadn't been able to tell. She'd been watching them, and they'd seemed perfectly normal...but *inside*, where it counted....

It was a long time before she fell asleep, and when she finally did, she dreamed of shadow-men and shadow-music, which drew the very soul from her even as she fled through the infinite forest of green and gold.

* * * * * * *

The men from the Ministry of Health arrived next morning, while Wendy was finishing her honey and almond manna. She saw Father go pale as the man in the grey suit held up his identification card to the door-camera. She watched Father's lip trembling as he thought about telling the man in the grey suit that he couldn't come in, and then realized that it wouldn't do any good. As Father got up to go to the door, he exchanged a bitter glance with Mother, and murmured, "That bastard house-doctor."

Mother came to stand behind Wendy, and put both of her hands on Wendy's shoulders. "It's all right, darling," she said. Which meant, all too clearly, that things were badly wrong.

Father and the man in the grey suit were already arguing as they came through the door. There was another man behind them, dressed in less formal clothing. He was carrying a heavy black bag, like a rigid suitcase.

"I'm sorry," the man in the grey suit was saying. "I understand your feelings, but this is an epidemic—a national emergency. We have to check out all reports, and we have to move swiftly if we're to have any chance of containing the problem."

"If there'd been any cause for alarm," Father told him, hotly, "I'd have called you myself." But the man in the grey suit ignored him; from the moment he had entered the room his eyes had been fixed on Wendy. He was smiling. Even though Wendy had never seen him before and didn't know the first thing about him, she knew that the smile was dangerous.

"Hello Wendy," said the man in the grey suit, smoothly. "My name's Tom Cartwright. I'm from the Ministry of Health. This is Jimmy Li. I'm afraid we have to carry out some tests."

Wendy stared back at him as blankly as she could. In a situation like this, she figured, it was best to play dumb, at least to begin with.

"You can't do this," Mother said, gripping Wendy's shoulders just a little too hard. "You can't take her away."

"We can complete our initial investigation here and now," Cartwright answered, blandly. "Jimmy can plug into your kitchen systems, and I can do my part right here at the table. It'll be over in less than half an hour, and if all's well, we'll be gone in no time." The way he said it implied that he didn't really expect to be gone in no time.

Mother and Father blustered a little more, but it was only a gesture. They knew how futile it all was. While Mr. Li opened up his bag of tricks to reveal an awesome profusion of gadgets forged in metal and polished glass, Father came to stand beside Wendy, and like Mother he reached out to touch her.

They both assured her that the needle Mr. Li was preparing wouldn't hurt when he put it into her arm, and when it did hurt—bringing tears to her eyes in spite of her efforts to blink them away—they told her the pain would go away in a minute. It didn't, of course. Then they told her not to worry about the questions Mr. Cartwright was going to ask her, although it was as plain as the noses on their faces that they were terrified by the possibility that she would give the wrong answers.

In the end, though, Wendy's parents had to step back a little, and let her face up to the man from the Ministry on her own.

I mustn't play too dumb, Wendy thought. *That would be just as much of a giveaway as being too clever. I have to try to make my mind blank, let the answers come straight out without thinking at all. It ought to be easy. After all, I've been thirteen for thirty years, and unthirteen for a matter of months...it should be easy.*

She knew that she was lying to herself. She knew well enough that she had crossed a boundary that couldn't be re-crossed just by stepping backwards.

"How old are you, Wendy?" Cartwright asked, when Jimmy

Li had vanished into the kitchen to play with her blood.

"Thirteen," she said, trying to return his practiced smile without too much evident anxiety.

"Do you know *what* you are, Wendy?"

"I'm a girl," she answered, knowing that it wouldn't wash.

"Do you know what the difference between children and adults is, Wendy? Apart from the fact that they're smaller."

There was no point in denying it. At thirteen, a certain amount of self-knowledge was included in the package, and even thirteen-year-olds who never looked at an encyclopedia learned quite a lot about the world and its ways in the course of thirty years.

"Yes," she said, knowing full well that she wasn't going to be allowed to get away with minimal replies.

"Tell me what you know about the difference," he said.

"It's not such a big difference," she said, warily. "Children are made out of the same things adults are made of—but they're made so they stop growing at a certain age, and never get any older. Thirteen is the oldest—some stop at eight."

"Why are children made that way, Wendy?" Step by inexorable step he was leading her towards the deep water, and she didn't know how to swim. She knew that she wasn't clever enough—yet—to conceal her cleverness.

"Population control," she said.

"Can you give me a more detailed explanation, Wendy?"

"In the olden days," she said, "there were catastrophes. Lots of people died, because there were so many of them. They discovered how not to grow old, so that they could live for hundreds of years if they didn't get killed in bad accidents. They had to stop having so many children, or they wouldn't be able to feed everyone when the children kept growing up, but they didn't want to have a world with no children in it. Lots of people still wanted children, and couldn't stop wanting them—and in the end, after more catastrophes, those people who really wanted children a lot were able to have them...only the children weren't allowed to grow up and have more children of their own. There were lots of arguments about it, but in the end things calmed down."

"There's another difference between children and adults, isn't there?" said Cartwright, smoothly.

"Yes," Wendy said, knowing that she was supposed to have that information in her memory and that she couldn't refuse to voice it. "Children can't think very much. They have *limited self-consciousness*." She tried hard to say it as though it were a mere formula, devoid of any real meaning so far as she was concerned.

"Do you know why children are made with limited self-consciousness?"

"No." She was sure that *no* was the right answer to that one, although she'd recently begun to make guesses. It was so they wouldn't know what was happening if they were ever sent back, and so that they didn't *change* too much as they learned things, becoming un-childlike in spite of their appearance.

"Do you know what the word *progeria* means, Wendy?"

"Yes," she said. Children watched the news. Thirteen-year-olds were supposed to be able to hold intelligent conversations with their parents. "It's when children get older even though they shouldn't. It's a disease that children get. It's happening a lot."

"Is it happening to you, Wendy? Have *you* got progeria?"

For a second or two she hesitated between *no* and *I don't know*, and then realized how bad the hesitation must look. She kept her face straight as she finally said: "I don't think so."

"What would you think if you found out you *had* got progeria, Wendy?" Cartwright asked, smug in the knowledge that she must be way out of her depth by now, whatever the truth of the matter might be.

"You can't ask her that!" Father said. "She's thirteen! Are you trying to scare her half to death? Children can be scared, you know. They're not *robots*."

"No," said Cartwright, without taking his eyes off Wendy's

face. "They're not. Answer the question, Wendy."

"I wouldn't like it," Wendy said, in a low voice. "I don't want anything to happen to me. I want to be with Mummy and Daddy. I don't want anything to happen."

While she was speaking, Jimmy Li had come back into the room. He didn't say a word and his nod was almost imperceptible, but Tom Cartwright wasn't really in any doubt.

"I'm afraid it has, Wendy," he said, softly. "It *has* happened, as you know very well."

"*No she doesn't!*" said Mother, in a voice that was half way to a scream. "She doesn't know any such thing!"

"It's a very mild case," Father said. "We've been watching her like hawks. It's purely physical. Her behavior hasn't altered at all. She isn't showing any mental symptoms whatsoever."

"You can't take her away," Mother said, keeping her shrillness under a tight rein. "We'll keep her in quarantine. We'll join one of the drug-trials. You can monitor her *but you can't take her away*. She doesn't understand what's happening. She's just a little girl. It's only slight, only her body."

Tom Cartwright let the storm blow out. He was still looking at Wendy, and his eyes seemed kind, full of concern. He let a moment's silence endure before he spoke to her again.

"Tell them, Wendy," he said, softly. "Explain to them that it isn't slight at all."

She looked up at Mother, and then at Father, knowing how much it would hurt them to be told. "I'm still Wendy," she said, faintly. "I'm still your little girl. I...."

She wanted to say *I always will be*, but she couldn't. She had always been a good girl, and some lies were simply too difficult to voice.

I wish I was a randomizing factor, she thought, fiercely wishing that it could be true, that it might be true. *I wish I was....*

Absurdly, she found herself wondering whether it would have been more grammatical to have thought *I wish I were....*

It was so absurd that she began to laugh, and then she began to cry, helplessly. It was almost as if the flood of tears could wash away the burden of thought—almost, but not quite.

* * * * * * *

Mother took her back into her bedroom, and sat with her, holding her hand. By the time the shuddering sobs released her—long after she had run out of tears—Wendy felt a new sense of grievance. Mother kept looking at the door, wishing that she could be out there, adding her voice to the argument, because she didn't really trust Father to get it right. The sense of duty that kept her pinned to Wendy's side was a burden, a burning frustration. Wendy didn't like that. Oddly enough, though, she didn't feel any particular resentment at being put out of the way while Father and the Ministry of Health haggled over her future. She understood well enough that she had no voice in the matter, no matter how unlimited her self-conscious-ness had now become, no matter what progressive leaps and bounds she had accomplished as the existential fetters had shat-tered and fallen away.

She was still a little girl, for the moment.

She was still Wendy, for the moment.

When she could speak, she said to Mother: "Can we have some music?"

Mother looked suitably surprised. "What kind of music?" she countered.

"Anything," Wendy said. The music she was hearing in her head was soft and fluty music, which she heard as if from a vast distance, and which somehow seemed to be the oldest music in the world, but she didn't particularly want it duplicated and brought into the room. She just wanted something to fill the cracks of silence that broke up the muffled sound of arguing.

Mother called up something much more liquid, much more upbeat, much more modern. Wendy could see that Mother wanted to speak to her, wanted to deluge her with reassurances, but couldn't bear to make any promises she wouldn't be able to keep. In the end, Mother contented herself with hugging Wendy to her bosom, as fiercely and as tenderly as she could.

When the door opened it flew back with a bang. Father came in first.

"It's all right," he said, quickly. "They're not going to take her away. They'll quarantine the house instead."

Wendy felt the tension in Mother's arms. Father could work entirely from home much more easily than Mother, but there was no way Mother was going to start protesting on those grounds. While quarantine wasn't exactly *all right*, it was better than she could have expected.

"It's not generosity, I'm afraid," said Tom Cartwright. "It's necessity. The epidemic is spreading too quickly. We don't have the facilities to take tens of thousands of children into state care. Even the quarantine will probably be a short-term measure—to be perfectly frank, it's a panic measure. The simple truth is that the disease can't be contained no matter what we do."

"How could you let this happen?" Mother said, in a low tone bristling with hostility. "How could you let it get this far out of control? With all modern technology at your disposal, you surely should be able to put the brake on a simple virus."

"It's not so simple," Cartwright said, apologetically. "If it really had been a freak of nature—some stray strand of DNA that found a new ecological niche—we'd probably have been able to contain it easily. We don't believe that any more."

"It was *designed*," Father said, with the airy confidence of the well-informed—though even Wendy knew that this partic-ular item of wisdom must have been news to him five minutes ago. "Somebody cooked this thing up in a lab and let it loose *deliberately*. It was all planned, in the name of liberation...in the name of chaos, if you ask me."

Somebody did this to me! Wendy thought. *Somebody actu-ally set out to take away the limits, to turn the randomizing factor into...into what, exactly?*

While Wendy's mind was boggling, Mother was saying: "Who? How? Why?"

"You know how some people are," Cartwright said, with

a fatalistic shrug of his shoulders. "Can't see an apple-cart without wanting to upset it. You'd think the chance to live for a thousand years would confer a measure of maturity even on the meanest intellect, but it hasn't worked out that way. Maybe someday we'll get past all that, but in the meantime...."

Maybe someday, Wendy thought, *all the things left over from the infancy of the world will go. All the crazinesses, all the disagreements, all the diehard habits.* She hadn't known that she was capable of being quite so sharp, but she felt perversely proud of the fact that she didn't have to spell out—even to herself, in the brand new arena of her private thoughts—the fact that one of those symptoms of craziness, one of the focal points of those disagreements, and the most diehard of all those habits, was keeping children in a world where they no longer had any biological function—or, rather, keeping the *ghosts* of children, who weren't really children at all because they were *always* children.

"They call it liberation," Father was saying, "but it really is a disease, a terrible affliction. It's the destruction of *innocence*. It's a kind of mass murder." He was obviously pleased with his own eloquence, and with the righteousness of his wrath. He came over to the bed and plucked Wendy out of Mother's arms. "It's all right, Beauty," he said. "We're all in this together. We'll face it together. You're absolutely right. You're still our little girl. You're still Wendy. Nothing terrible is going to happen."

It was far better, in a way, than what she'd imagined—or had been too scared to imagine. There was a kind of relief in not having to pretend any more, in not having to keep the secret. That boundary had been crossed, and now there was no choice but to go forward.

Why didn't I tell them before? Wendy wondered. *Why didn't I just tell them, and trust them to see that everything would be all right?* But even as she thought it, even as she clutched at the straw, just as Mother and Father were clutching, she realized how hollow the thought was, and how meaningless Father's reassurances were. It was all just sentiment, and habit, and pretence. Everything couldn't and wouldn't be "all right," and never would be again, unless....

Turning to Tom Cartwright, warily and uneasily, she said: "Will I be an adult now? Will I live for a thousand years, and have my own house, my own job, my own...?"

She trailed off as she saw the expression in his eyes, realizing that she was still a little girl, and that there were a thousand questions adults couldn't and didn't want to hear, let alone try to answer.

* * * * * * *

It was late at night before Mother and Father got themselves into the right frame of mind for the kind of serious talk that the situation warranted, and by that time Wendy knew perfectly well that the honest answer to almost all the questions she wanted to ask was: "Nobody knows."

She asked the questions anyway. Mother and Father varied their answers in the hope of appearing a little wiser than they were, but it all came down to the same thing in the end. It all came down to desperate pretence.

"We have to take it as it comes," Father told her. "It's an unprecedented situation. The government has to respond to the changes on a day-by-day basis. We can't tell how it will all turn out. It's a mess, but the world has been in a mess before—in fact, it's hardly ever been out of a mess for more than a few years at a time. We'll cope as best we can. *Everybody* will cope as best they can. With luck, it might not come to violence—to war, to slaughter, to ecocatastrophe. We're entitled to hope that we really are past all that now, that we really are capable of handling things *sensibly* this time."

"Yes," Wendy said, conscientiously keeping as much of the irony out of her voice as she could. "I understand. Maybe we won't just be sent back to the factories to be scrapped...and maybe if they find a cure, they'll ask us whether we want to be cured before they use it." *With luck*, she added, silently, *maybe we can all be* adult *about the situation.*

They both looked at her uneasily, not sure how to react. From now on, they would no longer be able to grin and shake their heads at the wondrous inventiveness of the randomizing factor in her programming. From now on, they would actually have to try to figure out what she *meant*, and what unspoken thoughts might lie behind the calculated wit and hypocrisy of her every statement. She had every sympathy for them; she had only recently learned for herself what a difficult, frustrating and thankless task that could be.

This happened to their ancestors once, she thought. *But not as quickly. Their ancestors didn't have the kind of head-start you can get by being thirteen for thirty years. It must have been hard, to be a thinking ape among unthinkers. Hard, but...well, they didn't ever want to give it up, did they?*

"Whatever happens, Beauty," Father said, "we love you. Whatever happens, you're our little girl. When you're grown up, we'll still love you the way we always have. We always will."

He actually believes it, Wendy thought. *He actually believes that the world can still be the same, in spite of everything. He can't let go of the hope that even though everything's changing, it will all be the same underneath. But it won't. Even if there isn't a resource crisis—after all, grown-up children can't eat much more than un-grown-up ones—the world can never be the same. This is the time in which the adults of the world have to get used to the fact that there can't be any more families, because from now on children will have to be rare and precious and strange. This is the time when the* old people *will have to recognize that the day of their silly stopgap solutions to imaginary problems is over. This is the time when we* all *have to grow up. If the old people can't do that by themselves, then the new generation will simply have to show them the way.*

"I love you too," she answered, earnestly. She left it at that. There wasn't any point in adding: "I always have," or "I can mean it now," or any of the other things that would have underlined rather than assuaging the doubts they must be feeling.

"And we'll be all right," Mother said. "As long as we love one another, and as long as we face this thing together, we'll be all right."

What a wonderful thing true innocence is, Wendy thought, rejoicing in her ability to think such a thing freely, without shame or reservation. *I wonder if I'd be able to cultivate it, if I ever wanted to.*

* * * * * * *

That night, bedtime was abolished. She was allowed to stay up as late as she wanted to. When she finally did go to bed, she was so exhausted that she quickly drifted off into a deep and peaceful sleep—but she didn't remain there indefinitely. Eventually, she began to dream.

In her dream Wendy was living wild in a magical wood where it never rained. She lived on sweet berries of many colors. There were other girls living wild in the dream-wood but they all avoided one another. They had lived there for a long time but now the others had come: the shadow-men with horns on their brows and shaggy legs who played strange music, which was the breath of souls.

Wendy hid from the shadow-men, but the fearful fluttering of her heart gave her away, and one of the shadow-men found her. He stared down at her with huge baleful eyes, wiping spittle from his pipes on to his fleecy rump.

"Who are you?" she asked, trying to keep the tremor of fear out of her voice.

"I'm the Devil," he said.

"There's no such thing," she informed him, sourly.

He shrugged his massive shoulders. "So I'm the Great God Pan," he said. "What difference does it make? And how come you're so smart all of a sudden?"

"I'm not thirteen any more," she told him, proudly. "I've been thirteen for thirty years, but now I'm growing up. The whole world's growing up—for the first and last time."

"Not me," said the Great God Pan. "I'm a million years old and I'll *never* grow up. Let's get on with it, shall we? I'll count to ninety-nine. You start running."

Dream-Wendy scrambled to her feet, and ran away. She ran and she ran and she ran, without any hope of escape. Behind her, the music of the reed-pipes kept getting louder and louder, and she knew that whatever happened, her world would never fall silent.

* * * * * * *

When Wendy woke up, she found that the nightmare hadn't really ended. The meaningful part of it was still going on. But things weren't as bad as all that, even though she couldn't bring herself to pretend that it was all just a dream that might go away.

She knew that she had to take life one day at a time, and look after her parents as best she could. She knew that she had to try to ease the pain of the passing of their way of life, to which they had clung a little too hard and a little too long. She knew that she had to hope, and to trust, that a cunning combination of intelligence and love would be enough to see her and the rest of the world through—at least until the next catastrophe came along.

She wasn't absolutely sure that she could do it, but she was determined to give it a bloody good try.

And whatever happens in the end, she thought, *to live will be an awfully big adventure.*

ABOUT THE AUTHOR

Brian Stableford was born in Yorkshire in 1948. He taught at the University of Reading for several years, but is now a full-time writer. He has written many science-fiction and fantasy novels, including *The Empire of Fear, The Werewolves of London, Year Zero, The Curse of the Coral Bride, The Stones of Camelot*, and *Prelude to Eternity*. Collections of his short stories include a long series of *Tales of the Biotech Revolution*, and such idiosyncratic items as *Sheena and Other Gothic Tales* and *The Innsmouth Heritage and Other Sequels*. He has written numerous nonfiction books, including *Scientific Romance in Britain, 1890-1950*; *Glorious Perversity: The Decline and Fall of Literary Decadence*; *Science Fact and Science Fiction: An Encyclopedia*; and *The Devil's Party: A Brief History of Satanic Abuse*. He has contributed hundreds of biographical and critical articles to reference books, and has also translated numerous novels from the French language, including books by Paul Féval, Albert Robida, Maurice Renard, and J. H. Rosny the Elder.